BARRY MAITLAND grew up in London and went
to work as an architect and urban designer in the UK. In
1984 he moved to Australia as Professor of Architecture at
the University of Newcastle. *The Marx Sisters*, the first in his
London-based Brock and Kolla crime novels, was published
in 1994 and twelve more have followed. In addition he has
published four crime novels set in Australia. Barry's novels
have been published throughout the English-speaking world
and in translation in a number of other countries.

PRAISE FOR BARRY MAITLAND'S BROCK AND KOLLA SERIES

'Riveting, intelligent crime writing from one of Australia's best.' —*The Weekend West*

'No one drops so many wonderful threads to a story or ties them so satisfyingly together at the end.'—*The Australian*

'Maitland crafts a suspenseful whodunit with enough twists and turns to keep even the sharpest readers on their toes.' —*Publishers Weekly*, USA

'This Australian crime writer's popular Brock and Kolla series continues to do what it does best—intrigue and entertain. Verdict: tight suspense.' —*Herald Sun*

'There is no doubt about it, if you are a serious lover of crime fiction, ensure Maitland's Brock and Kolla series takes pride of place in your collection.'—*The Weekend Australian*

'Barry Maitland is one of Australia's finest crime writers.'—*Sunday Tasmanian*

'Comparable to the psychological crime novelists, such as Ruth Rendell ... tight plots, great dialogue, very atmospheric.'—*The Sydney Morning Herald*

'Maitland is a consummate plotter, steadily complicating an already complex narrative while artfully managing the relationships of his characters.'—*The Age*

'Perfect for a night at home severing red herrings from clues, sorting outright lies from half-truths and separating suspicious felons from felonious suspects.'—*Herald Sun*

'A leading practitioner of the detective writers' craft.'—*The Canberra Times*

'Maitland is right up there with Ruth Rendell in my book.'—*Australian Book Review*

'Forget the stamps, start collecting Maitlands now.'—*Morning Star*

'Maitland gets better and better, and Brock and Kolla are an impressive team who deserve to become household names.'—*Publishing News*

'Maitland stacks his characters in interesting piles, and lets his mystery burn busily and bright.'—*The Courier-Mail*

BARRY MAITLAND
THE RUSSIAN WIFE

ALLEN&UNWIN
SYDNEY · MELBOURNE · AUCKLAND · LONDON

First published in 2021

Allen & Unwin
83 Alexander Street
Crows Nest NSW 2065
Australia
Phone: (61 2) 8425 0100
Email: info@allenandunwin.com
Web: www.allenandunwin.com

A catalogue record for this book is available from the National Library of Australia

NATIONAL LIBRARY OF AUSTRALIA

ISBN 978 1 76087 964 8

Set in 13/17 pt Bembo by Midland Typesetters, Australia
Printed and bound in Australia by Griffin Press, part of Ovato

10 9 8 7 6 5 4 3 2 1

To Margaret

With many thanks to all those who made this book possible, especially my wife and first reader, Margaret, my agent, Lyn Tranter, and the brilliant team at Allen & Unwin, in particular Annette Barlow, Angela Handley, Ali Lavau and Clara Finlay. Among the sources of inspiration I am particularly indebted to Gwendolen Webster of the Kurt Schwitters Society.

1

'It's like finding yourself dropped on another planet.'

Brock was out of sorts, uncharacteristically grumpy, Kathy thought. They were three old colleagues, all of them detective chief inspectors in the Met—David Brock, Bren Gurney and herself, Kathy Kolla—veterans of Brock's former homicide squad. Though they now worked in different Scotland Yard departments, they tried to lunch together at least once a month, if their schedules allowed, which was why they were now sitting in the Two Chairmen pub in Westminster on a Monday in November eating pot pies.

'They don't interview suspects,' Brock continued. 'They never see them! They just sit at their screens all day, following money trails around the globe. I asked one of them, *But where are they? Where are the crooks?* And he just pointed out the window at the towers of the City and Canary Wharf, then turned back to his computer.'

Bren laughed, but Kathy could see that Brock was genuinely disconcerted. His hair and beard, silvery white now and cropped short, looked a bit shaggy and neglected. A big steady figure in her life, it was unsettling to see him like this. After the debacle of his arrest during the Hampstead murders, the Met had reluctantly agreed to let him come back from retirement and take up his old rank, but not in Homicide. There were no vacancies in the twenty-four murder investigation teams, they told him, and posted him to Fraud, where he was clearly a fish out of water. It made Kathy feel sad, especially because the Hampstead murders had been the making of her in her new role as head of one of those teams. Since then she'd had a series of successes, all cleared up in rapid time. Her team was working well and she had been featured in an article in one of the Sunday supplements about the new breed of women detectives in the Metropolitan Police. Even her boss, Commander Torrens, head of Homicide and Serious Crime Command, had given her a rare pat on the back, expressing his satisfaction with her performance since she had 'stepped out of the shadow of the old guard'. He'd meant Brock, of course, for whom she'd worked all those years, and her pleasure at the compliment was tinged with regret as she saw him struggling now.

'What's so embarrassing is that I'm about fifty years older and outrank them all,' Brock was saying. 'I'm sitting there like a useless appendage, a waste of space, with nothing to contribute.'

Bren, trying to be supportive, said, 'But they must be able to use your experience, Brock. Remember that bloke with the Ponzi scheme who started to murder his victims? What was his name? There must be villains like that in the City.'

'No, Bren. Fraud is abstract, digital and bloodless. You've no idea. It's another world.' He sighed, then roused himself. 'Anyway, enough of that. What about you, Kathy? What have you been up to?'

'Well . . . I've got a locked-room mystery.'

'Ah! That's more like it. Go on.'

So she told them the story of Ahmed Majeed.

~

A month ago, Kathy had been called to a house in Titmus Street, Clapham. Her car pulled up outside a row of three identical brick houses, very plain and dull compared to the more elaborate Victorian terrace houses that made up the rest of the street. Maybe a bomb had dropped there during the war, Kathy thought, and these were a 1950s gap-filler. There were half-a-dozen emergency vehicles parked outside, and people were making their way between the plastic wheelie bins that cluttered the pavement. Kathy approached two men in white crime-scene overalls who were standing at the front door of number thirty-three, conferring over a clipboard. One of them was DI Peter Sidonis from her team, and he took her inside.

'A bloody mess,' he warned her, and when they reached the top of the narrow staircase she realised that he'd meant it literally. Looking through the open bathroom door to the scene inside she saw blood everywhere, sprayed over the walls and puddled and smeared across the tiled floor. Stretched out on the floor lay a naked male of around forty, jet-black hair, a gaping wound across his throat.

'Ahmed Majeed,' Sidonis said. 'Resident here. He returned early this morning from his night shift at Clapham Junction and came upstairs to have a bath while his wife Haniya cooked him a meal in the kitchen below. She heard a shout and a crash and ran upstairs. She thought she heard someone moving about inside the bathroom, but her husband didn't respond to her knocking on the locked door. She got it into her head that someone must have broken into the house through the bathroom window and attacked him, so she rang triple nine. A patrol car in the area responded. One officer went round to check the back garden while the other, PC Ashley Osborn, came in the front. She went up the stairs and broke open the bathroom door. As she burst in, she slipped on the blood and went down.' Sidonis pointed to a smear on the tiles. 'She's in the dining room downstairs now, recovering. The ambos checked her out, say she's twisted her ankle. She's covered in blood and in a bit of a state. So's the wife. She's in the living room with another woman PC.

'Ahmed's throat was cut presumably with what looks like a kitchen knife lying on the floor beside the body. He'd have died very quickly. The bathroom window was locked from the inside and has no bloodstains or signs of tampering. The door was secured with a sliding bolt which couldn't be opened from the outside. You can see the damage where Osborn forced her way in, ripping it out of the frame.'

~

'Suicide,' Bren said.

'That's what it looked like,' Kathy agreed, 'and that's how it stands. But there were some strange anomalies. Ahmed gave

4

no indication to anyone that he was depressed or contemplating suicide. In fact, he'd only just made arrangements to spend time with friends the following weekend. And he would have been dead seconds after he cut his throat and dropped the knife, so what were the sounds Haniya heard from inside the bathroom when she ran upstairs? Then the crime scene analyst insists that the blood spatter pattern is consistent with someone else being in the room. And, finally, the pathologist says the throat was cut from left to right, suggesting he held the knife in his right hand—but Ahmed was left-handed. Yet there's no way anyone could have got out of that room without leaving either the window or the door unlocked.'

'Good one, Kathy,' Bren said. 'Nothing like a good locked-room mystery. But it's quite common for intending suicides to give no prior warning. Witnesses' memories of the sequence of noises and events are often confused. Blood spatter is notoriously hard to interpret if the victim was moving at the time of injury. And a left-handed person can slit their own throat from left to right if they hold the knife like this . . .' Bren demonstrated with his steak knife.

'Very good, Bren. That's what we reckon. How about you, Brock?'

'PC Osborn did it,' he growled, and Kathy and Bren's laughter was interrupted by their phones ringing simultaneously, calling them back to duty. They went reluctantly, leaving Brock to poke forlornly at the remains of his pie.

~

When he got back to his office, the senior DI, Matt Stone, was waiting for him.

'Brock. Job for you.'

'For me?' Brock looked at him, astonished.

'Yes, sir. From Assistant Commissioner Cameron, no less.'

No one so elevated as an assistant commissioner would allocate jobs to floor ten, and Stone looked both perplexed and impressed.

'Well, fire away.'

'The wife of the assistant commissioner's cousin received a disturbing email this morning, and they would like us to investigate it.'

'Oh dear.'

Stone was keeping a straight face, but Brock sensed his hidden amusement. He rather liked Stone, and appreciated his deadpan approach with the more difficult members of his team. A couple were prima donnas and several seemed to find non-digital interpersonal communication impossible, but Matt Stone never lost patience with them. Brock suspected that he had a sense of humour, but he didn't have much opportunity to reveal it in this place. Now he presented Brock with a printout of the email.

From: Marylyn Smart marylsom239@inbox.ru

Subject: Nadyababington86—887321

Date: 12 November 2018 at 8:21:16 am GMT

To: nadyababington86@btinternet.com

Reply-To: Marylyn Smart <marylsom239@inbox.ru>

Hey there

I am the hacker who cracked your email address and device.

Here's your password from nadyababington86@btinternet.com upon time of compromise: 887321.

Obviously you can will change it or perhaps already changed it.

Still it won't change anything, my own malware modified it each and every time.

Do not really consider to contact me personally or even find me.

Via your own email I uploaded malicious code to your Operation System.

I saved all your emails, addresses of contacts and visits to the internet, even those now deleted.

Additionally I installed a Trojan on your system.

I am shocked to discover what you have been up to, and I am sure all your family and friends will be too.

BUT I am certain you do not want that.

Thus, I expect to have payment from you for my silence.

I believe £10,000 is an satisfactory cost for this!

Pay with bitcoin.

My bitcoin wallet address is 6NahgenKtqTcKpmP6LSbVVSnn 5QAXly8paqrzfM

If you do not know how to do this—enter in to Google 'how to transfer money to a bitcoin wallet'. It is not difficult.

Following payment of the given amount all your data will be destroyed automatically. My computer virus will additionally clear away itself out of your operating system.

My computer virus possess auto alert, so I know when this email is read.

I give you 2 days (48 hours) in order to make payment.

If this does not happen you will be exposed.

Do not end up being silly!

Authorities or pals won't aid you for certain . . .

I expect for your wisdom.

Hasta la vista.

'I see,' Brock said, although he didn't really.

'It's rubbish, of course,' Stone said. 'These things fly around the internet all the time, but the Babingtons are alarmed. They rang the assistant commissioner, who promised a swift response from Fraud. Here are the Babingtons' contact details. Best get on to it straight away.'

'Well, I'll need a bit more information about this scam. It is a scam, I take it?'

Stone gave him what Brock's mother would have called 'an old-fashioned look', then launched into a rapid briefing while Brock took notes.

'Just sound confident,' Stone concluded. 'Absolutely no need for concern.'

'But there's nothing we can do?'

'Nothing short of getting on to MI6.' He laughed. 'It's a Russian email address. Take Charlie Wardle with you for the technical stuff.'

Brock went and introduced himself to DS Wardle, a short, rumpled man who listened without comment to what Brock had to say, then groped around beneath his desk for a piece of equipment and stuffed it into a backpack. 'Okay, boss, lead the way.'

While Wardle drove, Brock did a quick search on his phone. Julian Babington was a corporate lawyer in the firm of Babington and Smythe with offices in the City and in New York. But the most remarkable thing about him seemed to be his collection of twentieth-century paintings, acquired by his father and grandfather, and considered to be one of the most important private art collections in the UK. His wife Nadya was described as 'glamorous'.

'Here we are, boss.'

Brock looked up as the car slowed outside a neat Georgian brick terrace house on the east side of Montagu Square, a couple of blocks north of Marble Arch in London's moneyed West End. Brock's ring was answered by a man in a beauti-fully tailored black suit, gleaming white shirt and a collegiate tie that added a stripe of colour. The deep lines on his face confirmed the age of sixty-three that Brock had garnered from his web search, though the boyish quiff of blond hair that flopped across the forehead suggested someone who believed he was younger.

Brock introduced himself and Wardle, and Julian Babington shook their hands and said, 'I hope we're not wasting your time with this, but my wife's very concerned about it and I have to fly to the US tomorrow, so I'd like to reassure her before I leave.'

He showed them into a sitting room, where Brock was immediately struck by the art on the wall facing him—two spectacular large abstract expressionist paintings on either side of a marble fireplace, with a portrait on the chimney breast between them which, despite its small size, held its own against their clamour.

Babington murmured, 'Let me introduce you to my wife, Nadya. Darling, these are experts from the Fraud Squad, Detective Chief Inspector Brock and Detective Sergeant Wardle.'

She must have been at least twenty years younger than him, Brock thought as he turned to the woman standing against the light from the tall windows facing the square. Strikingly beautiful, with hair as black as her husband's suit, her complexion was very pale, and the hand that Brock shook was cold.

Babington indicated seats around a coffee table on which sat an open laptop computer. 'This is Nadya's laptop. She asked me to check it for messages this morning while she was getting dressed, and I found this. You've seen it? What do you make of it?'

So Brock launched into the explanation that Stone had given him—commonplace scam, nothing to worry about, don't respond to it, change your password and think no more about it.

'There, Nadya,' Julian said, 'that's what I told you, wasn't it? Nothing to get upset about.'

'But they know my password!' Nadya cried. Brock caught an accent—Eastern European? She was clearly very upset, and was having trouble containing her agitation. 'How could they do that?'

Brock answered, trying to sound confident. 'They've probably hacked into some online retailer that you've used and stolen the email addresses and passwords of their customers. They'll have sent out thousands of these messages in the hope that someone with something to hide will react and give them money. They're just fishing blindly.'

'Exactly,' Julian said. 'What could they possibly find on your laptop to damage us?'

Seeing the panic in Nadya's eyes, Brock was wondering the same thing.

'Perhaps information about your meetings, your business,' she protested. 'There's a list of all my other passwords. They could get information about our bank accounts, steal our money.'

'But, darling, if they could do that then they'd have done it already, surely, without bothering to try to blackmail us,' Julian reasoned patiently.

'But Julian, their email address—they're Russian!'

'Ah ... that's what's worrying you.' Babington turned to Brock. 'Nadya is Russian, Chief Inspector. She married young to a very unsavoury character in St Petersburg and finally, seventeen years ago, ran away from him and came to London with her young son to stay with her uncle who lives here. Subsequently she divorced her husband and we met and married. So you're worried Sergei may be behind this, darling?'

'Yes, yes, Sergei.' To Brock she said, 'Please, you must stop them. Shut them down. Arrest them.'

How appropriate that she's Russian, Brock thought, with that look of a tragic heroine—Anna Karenina, perhaps, or *Dr Zhivago*'s Lara. Both of whom, he reminded himself, had been having affairs. 'If they're in Russia, I'm afraid there's not a lot we can do, Mrs Babington. Charlie, do you have any thoughts?'

Wardle grunted and pulled the device out of his backpack. 'Yes. If I may have your laptop for a moment, ma'am ...'

'What for?'

'When I connect it to this piece of equipment, it'll show me exactly what's in your hard drive. I'll be able to see if there's anything that shouldn't be there.'

Nadya's eyes widened. She stared at him for a moment, biting her lip, then reached for the laptop and snapped it shut. 'No. That is not necessary.' She snatched it up, clutching it to her chest, and stared at Brock. 'Please! I appeal to you. Stop him!' She got abruptly to her feet and hurried out of the room.

Babington sighed. 'I'm sorry,' he said. 'Nadya's first husband was an absolute thug. She still has nightmares about him. She is a very strong and resilient woman normally, but this stupid email has unnerved her.'

'I understand,' Brock said. 'It must have taken a lot of courage for her to escape here to London.'

'Exactly, yes. Her husband's name was Sergei Semenov. Maybe you could check the name? Make sure he hasn't come into the UK?'

'What can you tell me about him?' Brock scribbled in his notebook as Babington told him what little he knew— they had lived in St Petersburg; Semenov was physically large; probably now in his mid-fifties; not sure what he did for a living. 'Hang on, I believe Nadya has a photograph.' He rose and hurried after his wife.

There was a murmur of voices and he returned, handing Brock a picture of a heavily built man in swimming trunks standing in front of a lake. His hands were on his hips, leaning forward at the camera with a grin on his bearded face.

'It was taken almost twenty years ago, I'm afraid. Best we can do. Well'—Babington checked his watch—'unfortunately I have to dash to a meeting, but I hope we've reassured her.'

They made their way out to the hall. There Brock noticed a small artwork on the wall, a collage of scraps of paper.

'You have some amazing art here, Mr Babington,' he said. 'Could that be a Kurt Schwitters?'

'Indeed it is!' Babington sounded surprised. 'You know Schwitters?'

'Oh yes. As a matter of fact, I own one.'

'Really? But—' He was interrupted by his phone ringing. 'Excuse me ...'

He turned away, and Brock looked at the little work. Its composition was very similar to his own. He took out his phone and snapped a quick picture.

'I'm sorry,' Babington said. 'I have to rush. I'll see you out, if you don't mind.'

He had offices in both London and New York, Brock mused as he took the steps down into the square. What did Nadya get up to when he was away? What had she been doing on her computer?

When he returned to his office he spoke to Matt Stone, saying he'd like to do a quick check on Sergei Semenov.

'Sure, then fire off a report to the assistant commissioner.'

There was no Sergei Semenov in police records. Google, LinkedIn and Facebook had several—a software engineer, an orienteer, a mixed martial arts fighter—but none resembled Semenov's picture. Brock contacted UK Border Force and asked for an alert to be sent to him should Semenov enter the country. They already had four Sergei Semenovs on record, though none was in the UK at present. Brock asked for photos and details and wrote his report.

~

It was raining when he caught the train home and walked through the archway off the High Street, across the courtyard, beneath the old chestnut tree and into Warren Lane. As he put his key in the front door, he had to dodge the water streaming down from the broken gutter overhead. He picked up the envelopes on the mat and made his way upstairs to the living room. When he'd shaken off his dripping coat, he switched on the gas fire, poured himself a Scotch and sat down and opened the mail. The only thing of interest was a quotation from a builder he'd asked to look at repairing the roof and gutters. He stared in shock at the bottom line, wondering if the typist had made a mistake with the zeros.

On that gloomy note, he sat back and thought about the Babingtons: wealthy, cultured and troubled by something lurking beneath the surface of their civilised lives. He reached for his laptop and looked for images. There they were together at a function to celebrate the opening of the Royal Academy's 250th Summer Exhibition at Burlington House in June, and again, an elegant couple at the BAFTA awards night. Nadya's face was calm and even more beautiful in those pictures, but Brock's memory of her was more compelling—pale, haunted, a deer caught in the headlights. Why was she so frightened? Did the sight of a Russian email address really terrify her after seventeen years away?

He looked at his little Schwitters on the opposite wall and wondered if it was worth much. It was a memento of his first murder case, the death of Emily Crab, and he vividly remembered seeing it hanging above the fireplace in the house in Stepney as he struggled to stem the flow of blood from her slashed throat. It was a weird thing to see in such a place—an abstract composition of scraps of paper, a bus ticket, a newspaper headline glued together—and later he had asked Emily's husband Walter about it. He explained that his mother, Lily Crab, had taken in a refugee from Nazi Germany during the war, a penniless artist who had given it to her in lieu of a month's rent. Her friends had laughed and told her it was rubbish, and Brock was the first person to admire it. Later Walter confessed to Brock that he had murdered Emily, and some time after he was sentenced Brock received a parcel in the post containing the Schwitters and a letter from Walter gifting it to him as compensation for his ruined suit. On the back of the picture Brock found the signature *K. Schwitters*, and the title, *Merz 598a, London, 1943*.

It was soon afterwards that he had bought this house in Warren Lane, a bit of a wreck at the time, and worked on it until it fitted him like a comfortable set of old clothes, with his books lining the winding staircase up to the main living room, and the oriel window with its seat overlooking the lane and, beyond it, the railway cutting and the trains on the Sevenoaks line. The house and the Schwitters had been with him for so long that they felt like a part of him, permanent fixtures in his life. But perhaps, he told himself, he was wrong to think like that. Perhaps they were just obsolete relics from which he should shake himself free. Maybe it was time to sell them both and start afresh.

2

Kathy had caught a cab back to her office after the lunch
with Brock and Bren, checking her phone for messages on
the way. As usual there were plenty and she worked through
them until she looked up and saw the familiar outline of the
glass tower they called the Box, which was the West London
home of her team. She went up to the open-plan office with
its views out over the city, checked the desks and computers
to see who was in, then settled down at her own place in the
corner and got to work. After a while she heard a quiet cough
and looked up to see Phil standing there.

'Ma'am.'

Phil, the action manager, was the oldest member of Kathy's
unit and the only one now who addressed her as 'ma'am',
the rest preferring 'boss' or 'chief'. She thought of him as a

benevolent old uncle to the team and he would occasionally warn her about some problem or point of friction she should know about.

'Hello, Phil. What can I do for you?'

'It's about the venue for our Christmas party.'

'Christmas party? But it's only the twelfth of November. Can't it wait?'

'Oh good heavens, no; most venues are already booked. But I know someone who can get us the top deck of a Thames party boat for the evening of Friday the twenty-first. Someone's just cancelled and it's a great opportunity, so I wanted to check it with you.'

'A party boat? Have you discussed it with the others?'

'Of course. They're all very keen.'

'I see. Well, go for it. I'll have to let you know nearer the time if I can come.'

As he walked away Kathy had a sudden uncomfortable sense of her team having a shared social life of which she knew little. Now she came to think about it, she had been invited to several other group events in the past, but had never been able to make it because of clashes with work commitments she couldn't avoid. She decided she'd better make this one a priority.

She turned to the next thing on her pile, the final draft of their report to the coroner's office on the Ahmed Majeed case. She read it through again. Both the pathologist and the forensic blood spatter analyst had conceded that their initial reservations about suicide could be set aside. There really was no other conclusion. She thought about Brock's comment that PC Osborn did it and smiled to herself—typical Brock, thinking the unthinkable.

The day after Majeed's death she'd interviewed Ashley Osborn and been impressed by the constable's quiet dignity and good sense. Her inspector at Clapham had confirmed Kathy's opinion, saying that Ashley was the sort of steady and dedicated police officer everyone respected and liked, and he assumed that the only reason she hadn't been promoted to sergeant was that she'd moved about a bit. Kathy checked her service record and saw that it was true: she'd been in the force for sixteen years and in that time worked in Nottingham, Leicester, Derby and Luton, transferring from there to Clapham just five months ago.

They hadn't found anyone with a good word to say about Ahmed Majeed, on the other hand. His workmates regarded him as a troublemaker and tried to avoid him. His neighbours spoke of often hearing his angry shouts and violent bangs, and pitied his cowed wife. Though he had no criminal convictions, he'd had a warning after a complaint about suspected domestic violence. That wasn't in Clapham, though ... Kathy thumbed through the document to check. No, it was in Luton. That was a coincidence. Both PC Osborn and the Majeeds had lived in Luton before coming to Clapham. Kathy checked the timing. The Majeeds moved there in April, Ashley Osborn in June.

Kathy sat back and thought about it. She could almost hear Brock's chuckle. She shook her head. No. Luton was a big place. How many people—quarter of a million?

Thinking of Ashley Osborn, a model officer, she wanted to stop right there, but she couldn't. Whereabouts in Luton had she and the Majeeds lived?

It didn't take her long to find out. Bury Park, just a few streets apart.

Kathy checked the file again. In Luton, the domestic violence complaint against Ahmed Majeed had been made by a colleague of Haniya's at Bury Park Library. Ashley Osborn hadn't been involved in the case. Kathy looked up the number of the library and spoke to the librarian on duty. Yes, Ashley Osborn had a reader's ticket there. She remembered her, a nice woman, but the librarian didn't think she'd been in recently. She checked the computer. Ashley had been a regular borrower, every week for two years, but had stopped in April. She didn't know why.

Kathy did. Haniya had moved to Clapham.

She picked up the phone and called DI Peter Sidonis, her 2IC. 'Peter, I'm going to hold on to the Majeed report a bit longer. There are a couple more things we need to check.' Then she went over to Judy Birch's desk. Detective Sergeant Judy Birch, dressed in a tracksuit and trainers, radiated health and confidence, still on fire from her success at the London taekwondo championships. An energetic woman in her early thirties, she made Kathy feel old.

Kathy checked what she was doing, then asked her to set up interviews with Haniya Majeed and Ashley Osborn for the following day.

~

They went to Titmus Street to speak to Haniya. Kathy noticed how immaculate the little house was as soon as they entered the living room, everything neat and back in place after the terrible events of the previous month. The central heating was on high and smells of Indian cooking came from the kitchen. Kathy commented on how good it smelled, and Haniya gave a modest little bow and thanked her for the compliment.

'It helps me to keep busy,' she whispered. 'I have prepared something for you. Please sit down.' She went into the kitchen and returned with a tray. As Judy got up to help her, Kathy noticed that Haniya was walking with a slight limp and asked if she had hurt her leg.

'I broke it long ago,' Haniya said. 'It's nothing.' She poured tea and offered them slices of cake, still warm from the oven.

'That's delicious,' Kathy said when she'd had a bite. 'Haniya, we just wanted to make sure that you're getting all the help you need. I suppose, not having been in Clapham long, you might not know many people yet?'

'Mrs Woodley next door has been very kind.'

'That's good. And do you have a GP?'

'Yes, we . . . I've registered at the group practice.'

'You've been to see them?'

'No, not yet.'

'Perhaps you should go and get them to check your leg, and maybe give you something to help you sleep.'

'I don't need drugs to sleep.'

'Good. I noticed from the file that you worked as a librarian in Luton. Are you planning to do that here?'

'I've applied to all the libraries in South London, but there are no vacancies at present. I hope something will turn up soon.'

'I hope so too.' There was silence for a moment, and then Kathy said, 'I don't want to take you back through the events of that morning again, Haniya, but I just wanted to check that you were entirely satisfied with our response.'

Haniya looked puzzled. 'Your response?'

'Yes—PC Osborn's response in particular. Were you happy with her response to the problem that morning?'

'Oh!' Haniya's face cleared. 'Oh yes! She was brilliant. I could never have coped without her.'

'Had you ever met her before?'

'Met her?'

'Yes. This is her patrol area; I just wondered if you'd ever seen her around here.'

'Oh, I see ... no, never.' She smiled. 'Can I top up your tea?' She reached for the teapot.

'How about in Luton?'

Haniya hesitated for a moment, then concentrated on pouring the tea. 'Why Luton?'

'Well, you both lived in Bury Park.'

Haniya focused on the teapot. 'Did we?'

'Yes. I spoke to Ms'—Kathy checked her notes—'Ms Specklefield, at the library where you worked. She said Ashley Osborn was a regular there. Surely you must have come across her?'

'Did PC Osborn say we met there?'

'It's a remarkable coincidence, isn't it?'

'Yes, it is, isn't it? But no, I don't remember ever meeting her before.'

'Oh well, I thought I'd ask. We'll leave you in peace, Haniya. You've got our office number, haven't you? Give me or Judy a ring anytime.'

As they left the house, Kathy looked back and saw the net curtain twitch in the window of the terrace next door. 'Let's have a word with Mrs Woodley.'

Mrs Woodley was only too pleased to have a word. 'That poor woman. What she had to put up with. I used to hear him yelling at her, and worse.'

'Worse?'

'I couldn't say for sure—the sounds were muffled through the wall—but it sounded like he was giving her a hiding, thumps and bumps.'

'Did she ever confide in you?'

'Never. Always loyal she was. I tried to get her to talk about him, but she wouldn't be drawn.'

'Bruises?'

'Well, it's hard to tell with that brown skin, isn't it? But she had a puffy face one time, and lately she's had a limp.'

'Did you ever report it?'

'Their only party wall is with me, isn't it? He'd have known straight away who reported him, and I didn't want him having a go at me, great brute.'

'Okay, thank you, Mrs Woodley. Get in touch if anything specific comes to mind. He can't bother you now.'

They returned to their car and Kathy turned to Judy. 'What do you think?'

'Haniya was lying.'

'Yes, that's what I thought.'

~

They spoke to Ashley Osborn that afternoon in an interview room at Lavender Hill police station. She looked cheerful and confident, her jet-black hair drawn back in a ponytail, and again Kathy was struck by the impression she gave of humane competence, ideal in a police officer.

Kathy introduced her to Judy, and asked how her ankle was.

'Fine, almost back to normal, thanks.'

'I want to finalise our report to the coroner on Ahmed Majeed's death, Ashley, and there's something I need to clear up with you. You were driving the patrol car that morning, weren't you?'

'Yes, it's in my report.'

'And you were just two streets away from Titmus Street when you got the call. Is that right?'

'Yes.'

'You were nearly at the end of your shift, I believe. Where else had you been that night?'

'Stockwell, Brixton.'

'So wasn't Clapham a bit out of your way?'

'No. I regularly drive through that area.'

'Were you familiar with thirty-three Titmus Street?'

Osborn frowned. 'Familiar?'

'Had you been there before?'

'The street, yes. I've been patrolling that area for several months.'

'Had you been inside number thirty-three before?'

'No, certainly not.'

'What about Ahmed and Haniya Majeed? Had you met or heard of them before?'

'No.'

'The neighbours tell us that they thought he was abusing his wife. Were you aware of that?'

'No. The call we got didn't mention that; it just said an intruder was suspected.'

'And was it yours or your partner's decision that he should go round the back and you go in the front of the house?'

'Mine. Gregory's new to the job and he expects me to take the lead. He's a big bloke and I wanted him to block anyone skipping out the back while I went in the front.'

'Quite. So, just to be absolutely clear, you're saying you'd never seen Haniya Majeed before.' Kathy slid a photograph of Haniya across the table.

'That's right.'

Kathy was silent, looking at PC Osborn, and thought she saw something subtle change in the other woman's expression as she looked back, unblinking.

'You moved to Clapham earlier this year, didn't you, Ashley?'

'Yes.'

'When exactly?'

'Five months ago. June first.'

Kathy consulted her file. 'From Luton . . . Bury Park?'

'That's right.'

'Why did you move?'

Ashley shrugged, quite relaxed. 'I don't like getting stuck in one place for too long, so I've moved around a bit. But I've always wanted to end up in the Met—in Homicide, actually. Just like you.' She smiled.

'The reason I'm asking is that Ahmed and Haniya Majeed also lived in Bury Park, and moved here to Clapham just two months before you did, in April.'

'Is that right?'

'Yes. That's quite a remarkable coincidence, isn't it?'

'It certainly is! I'm amazed.'

'So I have to ask you again: had you ever met or communicated with Ahmed or Haniya Majeed before you attended the scene on the twelfth of October?'

'No, never ... at least not to my knowledge. When I attended that scene in Titmus Street I didn't recognise either Haniya or Ahmed Majeed.'

Kathy looked at her for a long moment, then closed her file. 'All right, Ashley, that's all I wanted to know. We'll let you go.'

'Thank you.' Ashley got smartly to her feet, nodded to them both—'Chief Inspector, Sergeant'—and left the room.

When she'd gone, Kathy turned to Judy. 'You're working on the road-rage killing with Andy, aren't you? Can he cope on his own for a few days?'

'I reckon so. We're pretty sure we know exactly what happened and we're just waiting for the crash analysts to finish their report. It could take them another week or more.'

'Okay. First, I want you to get hold of Haniya's and Ashley's private phone records. Find out if they had any contact, and in particular whether Haniya contacted Ashley after we left her this morning.'

'Yes, Ashley seemed very calm, didn't she? As if she knew what was coming.'

Kathy nodded. 'That's what I thought. And then I want you to see what you can find out about Ashley's past history. What areas of work was she involved in? Why did she keep moving around? Be discreet. Don't suggest to anyone that she's in trouble. Just say you're getting background for a case she's working on. And let's keep this just between the two of us here. I don't want any whispers getting back to Clapham.'

'Okay, boss. How long have I got?'

'Till Friday morning. Okay?'

'Okay.'

3

Tuesday, 13 November, the morning after he'd met the Babingtons, Brock received an email from the assistant commissioner thanking him very nicely for reassuring them. Then on Thursday morning, just as he was thinking about a coffee break, Matt Stone brought him the news that Nadya Babington had been found dead.

Stone seemed lost for words, but this was Fraud after all, not Homicide, where death was an everyday occurrence, and Brock had to prompt him to get the story. Earlier that morning a birdwatcher in the Kentish marshlands on the southern side of the Thames Estuary had come across an abandoned vehicle on a dirt track beside a large pond. Then he'd noticed what looked like some clothing in the water and called the police. A woman's body had been recovered from the pond, her driving licence identifying her as Nadya Babington, and a police computer check had found her recent contact with the Met.

'I'd better get down there,' Brock said.

'I'm not sure you should, Brock,' Stone said. 'We might be better staying out of it.'

'Nonsense.' Brock was pulling on his coat. 'Who's handling it?'

He got the details, made a call to the Kent police and ran down to his car, where he checked his satnav. He was to meet a Detective Sergeant Will Holt outside the church of St Mary Hoo on the Hoo Peninsula. A largely blank area on the map, the long bulge of land east of Gravesend lay between the estuaries of the Thames and Medway rivers. He wondered how it was he'd never heard of the Hoo Peninsula, apparently so close to London and yet so empty. And he wondered what on earth had taken Nadya Babington there.

He drove south across the Thames and then turned eastwards onto the A2 through Kent. Past Gravesend he left the highway and headed north-east into the flat country of the Hoo Peninsula. The roads became narrower, the settlements more scattered and the fields broader beneath a brooding dark November sky. Eventually he caught sight of a police 4x4 standing at the roadside in front of a rugged old stone church. He got out and introduced himself.

'Best travel with us, sir,' Sergeant Holt said. 'It gets a bit boggy.'

They left the metalled road and bounced and splashed along an increasingly uneven and muddy track. On either side the hedgerows and cultivated fields fell away, replaced by bottle-green marshland with meandering waterways and black pools. He knew that on the far side of the Thames lay the London Gateway container port, but over here the marshes felt utterly remote from civilisation.

Finally, they rounded a bend and came to a broad gravel area that marked the end of the track. Here was an ambulance, another police vehicle and a truck, on the back of which was secured a dark green Range Rover streaked with mud.

The sergeant led Brock to the ambulance, where a white body bag lay on a stretcher. The ambulance officer unzipped it and Brock confirmed that it was Nadya Babington. His heart was struck by that lovely pale face, framed by wet black hair. She had the preoccupied look of the dead, as if dealing with some new and unimaginable reality. Her face was free of make-up, and she was wearing jeans and a quilted jacket.

'There are no signs of violence or of anyone else being involved,' the sergeant said. 'Looks like she just came to the end of the path, switched off the engine, left the keys in the ignition, then walked into the pond and drowned herself. We'll take her back to Gravesend for the post-mortem.'

They walked over to the black pool which lay beyond the gravel, and Brock stared at the grass and mud at its edge chewed up by the footprints of the rescuers.

'So there's no indication of another vehicle having been here?' Brock asked.

'No.'

'Any idea of timing?'

'The doctor reckons eighteen to twenty-four hours, so sometime during daylight yesterday. The birdwatcher reported it at two minutes past nine this morning.'

Brock stared at the marks on the ground for a while, thinking about the timing. The threatening email had been dated Monday morning and gave Nadya forty-eight hours to pay, which would correspond with the estimated time of her death yesterday, Wednesday morning. He said, 'Okay, where's the birdwatcher?'

'Over there.'

The sergeant led him to the other police car and opened the rear door. An elderly bearded man wearing an anorak and rubber boots got out and shook hands with Brock. A pair of binoculars and a camera hung around his neck.

'What were you doing out here?' Brock asked.

'There's a pair of peregrine falcons I've been studying.'

He handed Brock a notebook in which he'd been record-ing his daily observations. The previous day, while Brock had been laboriously working through a pile of tedious old case files, this man had been out here alone in the fresh autumn air gazing at wigeons and redshanks and little ringed plovers. Brock envied him.

'Haven't seen them today yet. Not likely to with all this activity. But when we're done I'll go back to the nest site and see if I can catch them there.'

Brock looked around at the treeless landscape. 'Where the hell do they nest?'

'In the church tower.'

'At St Mary Hoo?'

'No, no. St Chad-on-the-Marsh. Over there. You can just see the top of the tower.'

Brock looked where he was pointing and managed to make out a dark bump on the horizon.

'That's the nearest building?'

'Yes. There's a couple of farms over there as well.'

'Have you ever seen the Range Rover around here before?'

'I've never seen any car around here before, but I've only been in these parts for a couple of weeks—since I got news of the falcons.'

'Okay, thanks.'

Brock turned to the sergeant and they walked over to Nadya's car. 'What did you find inside?' he asked.

'A handbag, a box of tissues. Only manuals in the glove box. The car's just six months old. Nothing in the back.'

'No computer? Laptop?'

'No, nor a phone, either in the car or on her person. I wondered about that. Could be at the bottom of the pond, I suppose. I'll see if we can get a fix on it.'

'Map?'

'No, but she had the GPS, of course.'

'I'd like a report on the GPS. I'm interested in the places she's been to since she had the car, especially around here. Can you do that for me?'

'Right.' He regarded Brock for a moment, then his eyes lit up and he said, '*Brock*. Sorry, sir, I should have recognised the name. Homicide, right? I've heard about some of your murder investigations. Is that what we're looking at here? A possible homicide?'

'I'm on secondment to Fraud at the moment,' Brock said airily, as if this was just a temporary aberration, 'and we've been advising Mrs Babington. She may have been the victim of a financial scam. So if anything odd turns up, let me know directly, will you?' He gave the sergeant his card.

'I'll make sure forensics do a thorough job on the car and I'll send you a copy of the pathologist's report as soon as we get it. I'll let you know what he says about time and cause of death as soon as I hear.'

'That would be appreciated. Many thanks. Has anybody contacted her husband? I think he may be overseas.'

'Yes. When he didn't answer his home phone we contacted his office, and they told us he's in New York. I spoke to him there at ten-thirty this morning.'

Brock took a picture of Nadya's driving licence photograph and walked around the gravel area while the truck and ambulance drove away, and then was taken back to his car at St Mary Hoo. He got in and sat there for a while looking around at the bleak landscape. 'Why here?' he said to himself. 'Why the hell did you come here, Nadya?' He felt unsettled, reluctant to return to the city, and instead set the GPS to *St Chad, Hoo Peninsula* and drove off across the marshes.

Though he was forced to go slowly on the narrow winding lane, it wasn't long before he made out the dark stump of St Chad's tower against the lowering sky. The church was a squat structure of rubble stone, surrounded by a churchyard of tilted gravestones. The bleak landscape and graveyard reminded him of a novel. What was it? Then he remembered— in *Great Expectations* the boy Pip was grabbed in just such an isolated Kentish graveyard by Abel Magwitch, a convict who had escaped from one of the prison hulks moored nearby in the Thames Estuary. This was Dickens country after all; he'd lived in Rochester, not far away.

As Brock walked around the church he saw scaffolding against the far side, and two figures crouching on a platform at the top. He called hello and one of them, dressed entirely in black, straightened and waved. He turned and said a few words to the other man, who was wearing a hard hat and day-glo builder's jacket, then began to slowly descend the ladder. He was elderly with ruddy pink cheeks and a halo of white hair, and as they met on the gravel path Brock saw that he was wearing a vicar's white dog collar.

'Sorry to disturb you,' Brock said.

'Not at all, not at all. Time for a tea break; I'm getting stiff. Come and join me.'

As the vicar led the way towards the door of the church, Brock said, 'You should be careful on that scaffolding, you know.'

The vicar chuckled and said, 'Yes, yes, I know, old men on ladders, a fatal combination. But the work is almost finished now, and I have faith that the good Lord will let me see it completed.'

Inside the church door was a small vestibule, rather dark, beneath the tower, and beyond it an arched entrance into the barn-like nave.

'Oh.' Brock stepped into the body of the church and looked around at the great oak beams spanning the roof, the rough stone walls, as bare and primitive inside as they were out, with no decoration except for a simple full-sized wooden cross mounted on the far wall above a plain stone altar.

The vicar smiled. 'You're impressed?'

'I am. I've never seen anything like it. Very ... archaic. How old is it? Norman?'

'No, no, much older. Saxon, four hundred years before the Normans arrived. It's one of the oldest churches in

England—possibly the very oldest. Like its namesake on the other side of the estuary, it was founded by Chad and his brother Cedd, the evangelist monks from Northumbria who came south to convert the East Saxons. Alas, even such a simple building as this requires constant upkeep. When I came here it had fallen into a ruinous state.'

'I suppose the Church is keen to help you maintain such an important relic.'

'Ha! The Church has forgotten we exist! They have so many other old parish churches to attend to. We fend pretty much for ourselves.'

They returned to the vestibule and went into a room to one side, the vestry, where the vicar bent to fiddle with a kettle and a small gas camping stove, muttering about making tea to warm them up.

Brock looked around at the bookshelves laden with worn copies of religious texts, an image of Christ on the wall like a Russian icon, and an ancient manual typewriter on the desk.

The vicar got the stove going at last and offered his hand. 'Alwyn Bramley-Scott.'

Brock introduced himself and the vicar frowned. 'A police officer? And what brings you here, sir?'

'Earlier today the body of a woman was found in one of the ponds out there in the marshes.'

'Oh no, how very sad. Have you been able to identify her?'

'Her name is Nadya Babington.' He saw the vicar's startled expression. 'You know her?' Brock took out his phone and showed him her picture.

The vicar blinked at it and nodded. 'Yes, yes indeed. Oh, this is dreadful.'

'How do you know her?'

For a moment the man seemed unable to answer; then, 'Nadya is . . . was . . . a very good friend to this church.'

His face had turned pale and Brock, afraid that he might pass out, told him to sit down and poured him a glass of water from a jug on the desk. The vicar sipped, then murmured, 'Oh, poor Callum.'

'Who's Callum, Vicar?'

'Callum McAdam—the young man who . . . Ah!'

Brock turned to see the builder, a wiry man of about thirty, standing in the doorway. He frowned at the vicar. 'You all right, Alwyn?' A broad Scottish accent.

'Callum, my dear boy, the most dreadful news. Dreadful! This is a police officer . . .'.

Brock showed his ID and said, 'I'm sorry to have to tell you that we've found the body of a woman, Nadya Babington, drowned in a pool near here.'

Again the same reaction, as if an invisible hand had slapped the colour from the man's face. He whispered, 'Nadya?'

'I'm afraid so.'

'An accident?'

'It seems more likely that she took her own life.'

The young man stared at Brock in disbelief, then he seemed to crumple. Covering his face with his hands, he cried, 'No . . . *No!*'

The vicar got unsteadily to his feet and reached out to take the man's arm, but Callum turned abruptly and stumbled away. Bramley-Scott stared after him, shaking his head. 'Oh dear, oh dear.' To Brock he said, 'He's best left to himself for now. I'll talk to him later.' He sighed. 'Please, sit down.'

They sat and the vicar reached into a drawer in his desk and produced two small glasses and a bottle of sherry. 'Will you keep me company, Chief Inspector?'

Brock nodded and the vicar filled the glasses. He took a sip from his own and stared up at the ceiling. 'A sad business. And her husband . . . a London lawyer, I believe?'

'Yes. How did she find this place?'

'Because of Callum, who lives close by, at the Smithy. They've known each other for a number of years. He was at art school with her son Miki, you see, and she had been an art student once too, in Russia, and she told me that mixing with the art students was a relief from the London social scene of her husband's friends. Then, when Callum moved out here, they both became involved in our campaign to save and restore St Chad's. Nadya was a frequent visitor. Perhaps, in retrospect, too frequent . . .' He sighed.

'You mean they were lovers?'

The vicar winced. 'One assumes so, yes.'

'Did she ever bring her husband out here?'

'Oh no, I don't think so. Not to my knowledge.'

'And do you have any idea why she might have wanted to end her life now?'

The vicar hesitated, gazing at the amber fluid in his glass. 'I have been aware of a certain tension in their relationship recently, but I don't know what it was about. You really would have to ask Callum.'

'I'll do that.' Brock thanked the vicar and gave him his card.

He saw no sign of Callum outside the church and got back into his car and drove further down the lane until he came to farm buildings—a large shed and an old barn with a sign, *The Smithy*—but all seemed deserted. There were no lights on and, when he went to the door, no one responded to his knock.

~

Brock drove back through the dark empty spaces of the Hoo until he came to the flowing river of traffic on the A2 and turned towards the city. As he drove, he reflected that Nadya's affair seemed to explain well enough her reaction to the scam email she'd received, with its key sentence: *I am shocked to discover what you have been up to, and I am sure all your family and friends will be too.* No wonder she didn't want Charlie Wardle to check her computer. He wondered if her son Miki knew of her affair with his friend and, if so, did she suspect that he had been in touch with his father in Russia, who had then devised that email?

When he got back to his office, Matt Stone looked up from the report he was reading. 'Oh, you're back. What's the story?'

Brock gave him a quick briefing, but decided not to mention Nadya's affair with Callum McAdam.

Stone nodded gloomily. 'Well, it's out of our hands. The husband is on his way back from New York. He's sent a blistering message to the AC. We're in deep shit apparently. Off the case. No further contact. Disciplinary review.'

'You've got details of his flight?'

Stone consulted a note. 'BA one-seven-eight to Heathrow. Gets in later tonight.'

'Right.' Brock went to his desk and opened the file on insurance fraud that he was supposed to be studying, but his mind soon returned to Nadya Babington and the look of fear on her face when he'd met her. He checked when BA178 was due in.

~

That evening, Brock said goodnight to Stone, who was still working on his computer, and made his way down to his car in the basement. Instead of driving south across the river to home, however, he headed west towards Heathrow and at 10.15 pm was standing waiting in the arrivals hall at Terminal 3 when Julian Babington came through the gate pulling a bright red suitcase, a satchel slung over one shoulder. He looked exhausted and gazed around as if expecting to be met. Brock hurried forward. Babington glanced at him but didn't seem to recognise him, and his attention flicked away.

'Mr Babington—David Brock.'

Then it clicked and Babington frowned. 'What the hell are you doing here?'

'I'll give you a lift.'

'I'm being picked up.' He brushed past Brock and marched on through the exit doors, looking left and right. It was cold, the rain streaming down, headlights shimmering on the wet tarmac, people everywhere struggling with luggage. Babington stopped and pulled out his phone. Behind him, Brock heard his words above the hubbub of voices and slamming of car doors.

'Miki? Where are you? ... I'm at Heathrow, for God's sake! ... No, no. You said ... Oh never mind, I'll get a cab.' He rang off, stuffing the phone back into his pocket angrily.

'My ride's right here,' Brock said, pointing to the car with the police emergency sign on the dash. 'There are things we should discuss.'

Babington turned on him, furious. 'Your incompetence caused this tragedy. I'll make my own way, thank you.'

'I'm very sorry for what's happened, Mr Babington, but I'm not responsible for your wife's death. Without access to her computer, there was nothing we could have done. But I'd like to help you now.'

Babington glared at him for a moment, then his anger seemed to leak away. 'Oh ... very well.'

Brock opened the car door for him and carried his suitcase to the boot.

As he eased out into the heavy stream of traffic moving slowly towards the exits, Babington said, 'Where is she now?'

'Gravesend.'

'Dear God,' Babington whispered. 'What kind of sick joke is that? I'd like to see her.'

'You look all in. Why not leave it till tomorrow?'

Babington didn't reply, and they came to a junction. Brock pointed at the sign. 'Left for Gravesend, right for Central London. What do you say?'

'Don't I have to identify her?'

'I did that. She looks very peaceful. She'll be there for you in the morning.'

Babington sighed. 'Yes, all right. I'll be in a better frame of mind tomorrow. Right now I'm just trying to take it in.

They told me . . . They said she just walked into a lake. Is that right?'

'Yes.'

'Just like that? Walked into a lake and out of my life, out of her life? How did she get out there?'

'In your Range Rover.'

'Did she . . . did she leave a note?'

'Not at the scene, no, nothing.'

'Has anyone been to the house?'

'Not as far as I know.'

'Miki—her son—may have gone there. I phoned and told him the news from New York. He was supposed to pick me up.'

'He'd be very upset.'

Babington didn't reply at first, staring out through the rain-streaked window. 'They were close. So . . . what can you tell me?'

Brock described his visit to the Hoo Peninsula and discussions with the Kent police, without mentioning St Chad's and the possibility of an affair. 'When were you last in touch with her?'

'I had to catch a six am flight to New York on Tuesday, so I didn't disturb her when I left. Then I was in meetings all day, but I tried to phone her at about five in the afternoon, New York time. That would have been ten in the evening in London. I couldn't get through so I sent her a text.'

'So the last time you actually saw or spoke to her was when?'

'Monday night, bedtime, about ten-thirty. We have separate rooms. When . . . when do you think she did it?'

'We think yesterday morning.'

Babington groaned. 'So if I hadn't left I might have been able to prevent this happening.'

~

The journey into London was relatively quick, Babington silent as he digested what Brock had told him. The rain had eased to a light drizzle by the time they reached Montagu Square and Brock drove slowly along the east side, looking for a space. As they came to Babington's house the front door opened and a man stepped out, carrying a suitcase.

'Stop!' Babington cried, and Brock pulled to a halt. Babington got out of the car and Brock followed.

'Miki?'

The man on the front steps hesitated. 'Julian ... hi.'

'That's Nadya's suitcase,' Babington said. 'What are you doing?'

'Oh, just, um ... picking up a few things—souvenirs, you know.' Miki swayed unsteadily.

'Souvenirs?' Babington looked at his stepson as if he were mad. Brock thought it more likely he was high.

'Yeah. Stuff of mine. How are you doing, Julian? Isn't it awful? I mean, Jesus ...'

'Yes, it is. Dreadful. Come inside and we'll talk.'

'Not now, mate.' Miki waved, the rain glistening on his hair, black as his mother's. 'Gotta go.'

He blundered past Babington and got into a parked car. Brock saw the face of a young man at the wheel.

'Wait,' Babington cried, but the car pulled out and swept away. While he stood, exasperated, looking after it, Brock found a parking space further along the street and returned with Babington's suitcase.

Babington stared at his front door. 'I don't want to go in there; I'm scared of what I'll find.'

Brock followed him up the front steps. Babington fumbled his key in the door, switched on the hall light and tapped a keypad. 'At least he remembered to reset the alarm,' he muttered. The house was silent, the central heating warm. He began to go from room to room. After a while he called to Brock from the back of the house. Brock found him in a room lined with shelves on which were arranged books, magazines and box files. Two tall windows looked out to a darkened garden.

'This is her office,' Babington said. 'She was a freelance interior designer. That's her work table. Her laptop's gone, see?'

The table was neat and orderly, everything in its place— filing trays, pens, a stapler, a magnifying glass. There were a mouse and a power cable trailing across the surface, but no computer.

'Could she have taken it in the car?'

'No,' Brock said, 'it wasn't in the car.' Unless, he thought, she carried it with her into the pond.

They moved back out to the hall and Julian went upstairs to continue his search. Brock waited in the hallway, wondering what Miki had taken from the house in such a hurry; his mother's computer?

Babington appeared at the head of the stairs. 'No note or computer, but her phone's here. She must have forgotten to take it with her.' He stood there looking lost, then took out his phone and made a call. 'Miki,' he said, 'did you see

a note? . . . In the house—a note, a letter from your mother . . .
What about her computer, have you got it? . . . Your mother's
laptop . . . You're quite sure?'

Brock heard a squawk of protest from the phone, and
Julian rang off, shaking his head. He looked at Brock. 'I'd offer
you a drink, but I'm bushed.'

'I'll pick you up tomorrow morning and take you to
Gravesend,' Brock offered, but Julian said, 'No, I'd rather do it
alone. Will you text me the details of where to go?'

'Of course. I'll phone the Gravesend station first thing in
the morning and make sure they're ready for you.'

'Thanks. I'm sorry I reacted badly at Heathrow.'

Brock looked at the man, sagging with weariness, and
felt sorry for him, thinking of the unwelcome discoveries he
might be about to make of his life with Nadya.

'Only natural,' he said. 'Try to get some rest.'

4

On Friday morning, Kathy sipped her third coffee of the day and looked up from her computer. 'Hi, Judy. Take a seat.'

'Thanks, boss.' The DS opened her laptop on Kathy's desk and scrolled down. 'Well, Ashley Osborn. *Very* interesting.'

'Yes?'

'Born in Nottingham. Her parents died when she was young, brought up by her sister Gillian, nine years older and very attractive. When Ashley was eleven, Gillian married a rugby union footballer, Ryan Turton, second row forward for Nottingham RFC. Over the next four years there were persistent rumours of domestic violence, including two visits to hospital for broken bones. In the fifth year of the marriage, Gillian was found by Ashley at the foot of the staircase with a broken neck. At the funeral, Ashley, now sixteen, stood up and accused Ryan of murder. Police investigated but didn't lay charges. Ryan moved to Leicester. Ashley joined the police, served in Nottingham for five years, then asked for a transfer to Leicester. Two years later, Ryan Turton was stabbed to death in a backstreet near the city centre. Drugs were involved apparently—a packet of heroin was found under his body. Case unsolved. Four months later, Ashley applied for a transfer to Derby.'

Judy took a deep breath and glanced at Kathy, who said nothing.

'In Derby, Ashley joined the domestic violence unit and was a popular visitor at schools, where she gave talks on the subject. She was also assigned to the protection of women's refuges. She had a reputation for being very calm and firm and compassionate. While she was there, she was involved in several extreme cases. One was Mervyn Byrne, who was suspected of pouring petrol on his estranged wife in a super- market car park and setting fire to her. The case against Byrne was strong, but there were no reliable witnesses to place him at the scene, and he was provided with an alibi by a man called Upshot, who also had a record of domestic violence. After three months, the case against Byrne was dropped by the DPP. Two months later, Byrne and Upshot died in a fire in Upshot's caravan on the coast. The cause of the fire was ruled suspicious, but no suspects were identified.

'Ashley moved on to Luton, and while she was there she arrested a man called Izad Patel for the vicious rape of an under- age girl. The girl's mother took her to hospital, where the girl made a full statement to police, accusing Patel and another, unknown man. But three weeks later she withdrew the accusation and Patel was released. Two months after that, Patel's body was found in a wood at Beech Hill, outside Luton. He'd apparently hanged himself. Patel was the cousin of Ahmed Majeed, who moved with his wife Haniya to Clapham not long after.'

Kathy looked up from the pad where she'd been taking notes. 'That's it?'

'That's it.'

'So, the sister's husband in Leicester, Byrne and Upshot in Derby, Patel in Luton and finally Majeed in Clapham. Five sudden deaths of men accused of violence against women.'

'Yes, and Ashley Osborn connected one way or another with all of them.'

Kathy said, 'Did you speak to anyone about the previous cases?'

'Yes, I contacted Osborn's sergeant at Luton to confirm what happened there to Patel. I pointed out the coincidence of the two cousins both committing suicide, and when I mentioned Osborn's name he became very cautious. He wanted to know the details of the Clapham case and asked why Homicide were interested. I told him there was an initial suspicion that a third party might have been involved, but we'd now discounted that and were treating it as a suicide. Then he asked if Osborn was under suspicion, and I told him no, we just had to prepare a report for the coroner. He told me she was a first-class copper, respected by everyone she worked with and he could vouch for her completely.'

'So what's your feeling, Judy?'

'If she was involved in the deaths of those bastards, then personally I'd give her a medal. But we're Homicide, aren't we?'

'Yes, we are.' Kathy thought for a moment, trying to come to terms with what Judy had just told her. The idea of an officer like Ashley Osborn as some kind of vigilante serial killer was so bizarre that her instinct was to dismiss it out of hand, but she had to reason it through. 'The other cases are all suggestive, but entirely circumstantial. They were all different from each other, with no common MO. We'd have a lot of trouble reopening them without new evidence. Even if she was somehow involved, Osborn's a cop, and she'd know how to cover her tracks.'

Judy nodded. 'I also got the strong impression that she's established an excellent reputation along the way. Her file is full of positive reports and commendations. Everybody thinks she's a model officer working in a difficult but crucial area.'

'So that leaves Clapham, the only case where she was directly involved in the crime scene. I think we can only focus on that, and so far we don't have anything concrete to raise suspicions. What about her personal life?'

'I couldn't find a thing. No lovers or close friends. The really weird thing is that she doesn't appear to have any social media accounts. Not on Facebook, Twitter, Instagram— nothing. Can you believe that? Always rented accommodation, the perfect tenant. She belongs to a gym, and she runs. She seems to live a very private life.'

They were silent, thinking about this, then Kathy said, 'No, I think we have to put all that background to one side. We'll stick to the Majeed case. I'm not satisfied we've got to the bottom of that. Did you get the phone records?'

'Yes—again, nothing. If Haniya and Ashley were in touch, they weren't using the phones we know about.'

'Well, I think it's quite possible that they did know each other; that Ashley was keeping an eye on Haniya, and when something got out of control that morning she stepped in and fixed the crime scene to keep Haniya out of the picture. I need to put that to her, see if she wants to change her story.'

Judy hesitated, then said, 'Maybe I'm the wrong person for this job, boss.'

'What do you mean?'

'My parents' marriage broke down when I was fifteen. The divorce was bitter, and on the rebound, in a kind of panic, my mum hitched up with this macho guy who owned a gym. Pretty soon I realised he was bashing her. I tried to persuade her to leave him, but she said she couldn't. In the end, when he started coming on to me, I left. I still feel guilty about it all. Maybe you should get one of the blokes to do this one.'

Kathy thought. Maybe Judy was right, but the fact was that all her male detectives were tied up with higher-priority cases at present. She said, 'If you want to step down, Judy, that's fine with me. I can swap you with Wiss on the Murdoch case. But maybe it's time you came to terms with what happened to you and your mum. No matter what, we have to put our own histories behind us and deal with each case on *its* merits, not ours. You've done well so far, and I think it would be good for you to see this one through.'

Judy straightened in her seat. 'Yes, boss. You're right. I'll do it.'

'Good. Well, let's set up another interview with Ashley on Monday. You have a good weekend.'

When the DS had gone, Kathy wondered if she'd made a mistake. Maybe this wasn't the right case for Judy. But what she'd said was true—Judy had acquitted herself well thus far—so she dismissed the thought and moved on to the next problem at hand.

~

At the end of the day, she filled up a bag of groceries at the local Sainsbury's and caught a bus home. The traffic slowed crossing Vauxhall Bridge, and she looked out at the lights of her apartment block on the far side of the river. She noticed someone standing at the rail of the bridge apparently doing the same thing: a woman, dressed for a run in tracksuit and trainers, bare head, ponytail. As the bus went past, Kathy caught a brief glimpse of her face, and thought how much she looked like Ashley Osborn. She thought again of the scenario that had presented itself to them, of the serial-killer cop, and turned away with a feeling of deep unease. She couldn't ignore it, yet the notion seemed so outlandish and absurd. Whatever the truth, she'd better get it right. She thought again of Brock's original comment: *PC Osborn did it.* At the time it had seemed like a bizarre joke, but now she wondered what had been in his mind. For a moment she thought of contacting him and talking it over, getting his opinion, but then decided against it. This was her case, her call.

5

That Friday afternoon Brock had been reading a report that Will Holt had sent him on the Nadya Babington drowning. A post-mortem examination had been completed, with the pathologist favouring an earlier time of death, possibly as early as Tuesday morning, forty-eight hours before the discovery of the body. DS Holt had provided the transcript of an interview with the husband, Julian Babington, who had last seen his wife on Monday at 10.30 pm, before leaving their house in Montagu Square at approximately 5.15 am on Tuesday to catch his 8.20 am Delta flight to New York. He had been unable to reach her by phone later on Tuesday and had not heard from her again before receiving DS Holt's phone call from the Hoo site at 5.30 am New York time notifying him of Nadya's death.

Brock read on through the details of the pathology examination and the forensic inspection of her vehicle and the site,
and it was only when he glanced again at the times that he
noticed the discrepancy: Babington had told Holt that he was
on the Delta 8.20 am flight to New York on Tuesday, whereas
when Brock picked him up at Heathrow he'd said that
his flight left at six. But Babington had been exhausted
when Brock met him and had presumably made a simple
mistake. Brock checked the flights on his computer and found
that the only Heathrow to New York flight between 6 and
7 am on the Tuesday morning was a Virgin flight that departed
at 6.12 am. He got on the phone and, after a couple of calls,
established that Babington had in fact been booked on the
Virgin flight, but had cancelled and switched to the later
Delta flight instead. So it was understandable that he might
have confused the two times when he spoke to Brock. All
the same, Brock was curious, and checked when Babington
had made the switch. The answer was 1.28 am on Tuesday.
Brock sat back and thought about it. At one-thirty in the
morning Babington was still awake and busy, changing his
flights to give himself an extra two hours in London before
he left for the States. Why? There might be a dozen reasons.
Might one of them have been to give him time to kill his
unfaithful wife?

Brock was scribbling timeline diagrams when a young
woman approached his desk and said hello. 'We haven't met.
I'm Molly Fitzherbert, Art and Antiques—or what's left of it
around here. And you're Brock, ex-Homicide, right?'

Brock pulled over a chair for her and she unfolded that
day's copy of *The Guardian*. 'Seen this?' She pointed to an

article: *Death of art collector's wife.* There was an accompanying photo of Julian and Nadya Babington, beaming at the camera.

'No,' Brock said, 'I haven't.' He scanned the article, some of which covered the mysterious drowning in the Hoo, but the focus was mostly on the famous Babington art collection.

'So, what do you reckon?' Molly said.

'Kent Police say it's suicide.'

'Weird place to do it. What do the Metropolitan Police say?'

'Seems we're not allowed to say anything.'

'Aha, I detect a note of frustration. Good. Well, it's obviously all about the art.'

'Is it?'

'Come on! Nadya Babington studied art in St Petersburg and married the owner of London's most important private art collection. Her son Miki also studied art and now works for a dodgy art-dealing company. What else could it be about?'

Brock smiled. 'You've been doing a bit of detective work.'

Molly shrugged. 'It's all in the public domain. But the sources are a bit vague as to what exactly is in the fabulous Babington Collection. Did you get into his house in Montagu Square, by any chance?'

Just then Matt Stone appeared, talking on his phone, and Molly lowered her voice and said, 'Let's go to my office.'

Brock got to his feet. 'You have your own office?' he asked, surprised. The Fraud floor was determinedly open plan and as far as he knew no one had a room of their own. He followed Molly between the desks to an area he had never visited on the far side of the lift lobby; in the furthest corner they came to a barrier of filing cabinets and stacked chairs that looked as if it was a storage area for surplus furniture. Weaving her way through them, Molly led him into a snug little den completely walled in by bookshelves and storage boxes. Here was a computer desk and a table piled high with files, art books and copies of the *British Art Journal*, as well as a coffee pot and crockery.

Brock looked around. 'This is your hideout, is it?'

'I hate open-plan offices. I like to work in a small space where I can focus. Take a seat. So, did you get into Babington's house?'

'A couple of times, but very briefly.'

'You must have seen something. What about the Joan Mitchells? They say he's got a classic pair of hers.'

'Who's Joan Mitchell?'

'A very fine American abstract expressionist of the New York school.'

'I'm afraid I don't know her work.'

Molly turned to her computer and tapped away, bringing up some images.

Brock nodded. 'Ah yes, he's got two big paintings like that on each side of his fireplace. Would they be valuable?'

She turned back to her computer. 'How big are they?'

'They must each be about eight feet by six.'

She searched and then her eyes lit up. 'Eight years ago, Sotheby's in New York sold one of that size, painted in 1960, for nine million dollars. They'll be worth more now. What else has he got?'

'Well, I particularly remember a Schwitters collage in the hallway, because it looked a bit like mine.'

'Yours? Are you kidding?'

'No, I really do have one.' He showed her the images on his phone and told her about *Merz 598a* and Walter Crab.

'What a marvellous story! A real Merz.'

'Merz is the German word for "collage", is it?'

'No, no; Schwitters just invented it. He made a collage including the letters MERZ cut out of a newspaper advertisement for Commerz Bank, and adopted the term for all his collages. Have you had yours authenticated?'

'No, I haven't. How does that work?'

Molly listed the three things that were necessary for an artwork to be recognised as authentic: an expert scholar of that artist's work would have to agree that it looked right; forensic tests would have to confirm that the age and character of the work's materials were appropriate; and there should be documentation connecting the present owner back to the artist in order to establish provenance.

'Usually all three of these have to be satisfied for the body that's responsible for maintaining the official record of that artist's work—the catalogue raisonné—to accept it as genuine, although in practice provenance can sometimes be hard to prove. History is so messy.'

Brock was taking notes. 'It all sounds very onerous.'

'It has to be. The world is awash with forgeries and fakes. It's said that in his lifetime Picasso created twenty-four thousand original works, of which sixty thousand are in American collections. One highly respected authority has suggested that forty per cent of the art in museums is fake. So, what documentation do you have for your Schwitters?'

'Nothing really. There's just the signature and title written on the back, and the date, 1943.'

'In Stepney, you said?'

'Yes.' He watched as Molly worked her computer for a while, then she straightened with a frown.

'Schwitters fled from Germany to Norway in 1937, when the Gestapo declared his work "degenerate" and he heard they wanted to interview him. Then, when they invaded Norway in 1940, he managed to get on the last boat to Scotland. He was interned on the Isle of Man until forty-one, when he went to London, and in forty-five moved up north to Ambleside in Cumbria. What you should do is get hold of any documents you can find to back up your story, and then take them and the Merz over to Hanover, to the Sprengel Museum, where they have the archive and official catalogue raisonné. Maybe they've got a record of it. You never know.'

Brock checked his watch. 'I'm going to have to go now, Molly, but thanks for your advice.'

'Lovely to meet you, Brock. Come and see me any time you feel the need to escape from the robots out there. And I mean it about the Babingtons. If Nadya Babington's death is a sign of some crisis within the family, then you can bet that the art collection is involved somehow. Keep me posted, and if you get another chance to see inside the house, try to remember as much as you can about the paintings—or, better still, take some pictures.'

Brock returned to his desk. He had just picked up his bag and was preparing to head off for the weekend, when Matt Stone came over.

'Ah, there you are, Brock. Glad I caught you. There's a two-day workshop coming up next week and we need someone to represent us—you're the perfect man. Insurance fraud, ideal for you.' He handed Brock a printout.

Brock looked in horror at the workshop's title—*The Role of Data and Analytics in Insurance Fraud*—then at the date. 'Next Monday and Tuesday? Oh, I'm afraid I can't manage that, Matt. I've got to tie up the Babington suicide case.'

'No, no. That's finished. The super in charge at Kent called me to say that the case was closed as far as they were concerned and I agreed to terminate our involvement. This'—he tapped the printout—'is much more relevant to us, and no one else is available. You can give the team a one-hour summary briefing on Wednesday morning to bring us all up to date.'

~

Brock left the office feeling despondent and made his way to Charing Cross station, where he bought a bunch of roses and caught a train down to Sussex to spend the weekend with Suzanne. They'd been together for thirty years now, but they had never married and they lived forty miles apart. On the whole, the arrangement had worked for them both, although from time to time they had considered a change. The main problem had been Suzanne's two grandchildren, Stewart and Miranda, who had been in Suzanne's care for most of their lives after their mother had abandoned them. Intensely insecure, they had felt threatened by Suzanne's relationship with Brock and had occasionally tried to derail it. But now they were gone, with Stewart just starting his first year up north at Durham University studying business and management, and his younger sister Miranda on a school exchange, staying with a family in Bremen. Thinking about this as he stared out of the train window, Brock tried to convince himself that all life was change, and even when that change seemed to lead to a dead end, as with his current posting in Fraud, it also offered opportunities. He resolved to think positively and keep his gloomy thoughts to himself.

He got off the train at Battle, the last stop before Hastings on the coast, and made his way to Chambers Antiques on the High Street. He let himself in by the street door to the flat above the shop and went upstairs to find Suzanne in the kitchen preparing a Malaysian curry. He kissed her and gave her the flowers, and they talked about their respective weeks. It had been a quiet one for Suzanne, with few customers in the shop; Brock, for his part, told her about the death of Nadya Babington.

'I heard it on the news,' she said. 'All alone in the marshes. How very sad.'

He poured them each a glass of wine and sat at the kitchen table, watching Suzanne making roti. How competent and at ease she looked, secure in her abilities and her place in the world, whereas he was feeling the opposite. Despite his resolution on the train to say nothing, he began, 'I was wondering . . .'

'Mm?'

She was brushing the dough portions with melted butter, then deftly folding and twisting them before rolling them flat.

'I was wondering if I should sell the house in Warren Lane.'

'What?' She stopped and looked at him. 'But you love that house. Do you want somewhere smaller?'

'I thought about moving in here. If you'd have me.'

She said nothing for a moment, then, 'What's brought this on, David?'

He examined his fingers, thick and clumsy in comparison to hers. 'Oh ... the house needs money spent on it. I got a horror estimate from the builder to redo the roof.'

Suzanne wiped her hands and sat down facing him. 'It's not just that, though, is it?'

'Well ... no. I think it may have been a mistake to go back to the Met.'

'Why?'

He shrugged. 'I'm just a waste of space in Fraud, a drain on resources that'd be better spent on someone younger and more up to date.'

'Oh dear. Is it that poor woman's death that's unsettled you?'

'Maybe. It reminded me of what I used to do ... what I should be doing. In my mind, I began trying to make it into something it isn't—a murder mystery, perhaps, something to justify my existence, when really it's just another sad case of a pointless suicide.'

'Did your instinct tell you it was more than that?'

'Yes, but maybe my instinct is past its use-by date. Like me.'

Suzanne reached forward and gripped his hand. 'David, you'll always have a home here, but in all the years I've known you I've never heard you talk like this. Maybe you should see someone, a counsellor. But I think you'll feel really bad if you give up work now, thinking you're a failure.'

'Maybe.'

'Tell me more about this Hoo place.'

So he told her about the bleak marshes and the bird-watcher and the ancient church.

'So that's why you're unsettled. You finally get the scent of a good mystery and then you're told to drop it. Did you get a chance to see inside Babington's house, his artworks?'

'You know about his collection?'

'Of course, it's famous. Now, if the wife's death was linked to that, well, that'd be the crime story of the year.'

Brock laughed. 'Yes, that's what our art fraud expert told me. I mentioned to her that I'd seen a Schwitters like mine at Babington's house, and she told me I need to take mine to the experts at Hanover to have it authenticated.'

Suzanne's face brightened. 'Bremen's not far from Hanover. Miranda says the family she's staying with are wonderful and they'd love to meet us. We could make a long weekend of it.'

Brock thought about it. The idea of escaping from Fraud for a few days certainly was attractive. 'But it's probably pointless going to Hanover. I'm sure the Schwitters can't be worth much.'

'Well, find out. Google it.'

So while Suzanne finished the roti, Brock turned to the computer. After a while he sat back in his chair, looking stunned. 'Bloody hell.'

Suzanne looked up. 'Well?'

'Christie's sold one just like mine recently. How much do you reckon?'

'A thousand? Two?'

'A quarter of a million.'

'Really? Worth a trip to Hanover then.'

They agreed that Suzanne should make the travel arrangements, and she returned to preparing the curry while Brock settled down to study some of her books on twentieth-century art.

6

Kathy spent Saturday at home catching up on paperwork for the cases her team was working on, and
by the evening felt myopic and stale. She walked over to
the Vauxhall Leisure Centre, did an hour in the gym then ten
laps in the twenty-five-metre pool and felt better. On the
way home she stopped for a meal at the Dirty Burger
in the arches beneath the railway viaduct of Vauxhall station,
then continued through the dark towards the riverfront by
her apartment block. A few people were running along the
riverside walk, their breath steaming in the cold air, and it
was a moment before Kathy made out one stationary figure,
almost invisible in a black tracksuit, with black hair, staring
up at the tall buildings. As Kathy focused on her the woman
turned and began to jog away, ponytail bobbing. *The girl on*

the bridge, Kathy thought, *watching my apartment.* Or not—she really couldn't be sure.

~

On Sunday she headed for Hampshire to meet up with her old friend Nicole Palmer, who was now a senior manager in criminal records—ACRO—which had moved out of London to Fareham, near Portsmouth. Kathy set off on the two-hour journey soon after eight. The dark skies of the past few days had cleared and she felt a sense of freedom and release on getting out of London.

She hadn't seen Nicole in over a year, and was pleased to find her looking so bright and well. After a coffee in her new flat, Nicole drove them into Portsmouth, which Kathy hadn't visited since she was a small girl. She wondered if it would bring back memories of that distant, innocent past, when she was safely part of what she believed to be a solid, respectable family, before her father's disgrace and suicide. But she recognised nothing, the historic old buildings looking immaculate among sparkling new developments, as if her memories were as fraudulent as her father's air of respectability.

After a walk through the harbourside area, they found a table on Gunwharf Quays, below the steel pinnacle of Spinnaker Tower, and ordered wine.

'Cheers!' Nicole said. She was wearing large, stylish sunglasses and looked remarkably relaxed and content, not really like the old Nicole at all.

'I must say, you're looking terrific, Nic,' Kathy observed. 'Life down here must really suit you. Or am I missing something?'

'What do you mean?'

'Is there a new man?'

Nicole grinned. 'Detective Kolla on the case! Is it that obvious? I was trying not to show it.'

His name was Bradley, and they'd met in the corniest of circumstances—they'd collided in a crowded bar and he spilled his red wine on her new dress. 'He was mortified, made such a fuss, and I just knew, straight away.'

The way she said it, with her face lit up, made Kathy smile. 'I'm so glad for you, Nic.'

'Yeah. It's been a long time. Remember how I tried to get you to go onto *Partners Perfect* with me?'

They both laughed. For years Nicole had been in a relationship with Lloyd, a cop in the Met, but they had never married, and after they broke up no one had taken his place. Bradley, on the other hand, was an osteopath.

'Such a relief! Nothing to do with the police or the law. We can talk about other things—books, movies, holidays . . . my back.' She laughed. 'He really wanted to meet you, but his mother in Manchester had a fall and he had to go up. What about you? You had all that wonderful publicity. What are you doing these days?'

'Work. This is the first day off I've had in ages. There's so much to do. But I enjoy it.'

Nicole was shaking her head. 'Oh, Kathy, that's no good, they'll burn you out. You've lost weight, haven't you? And you look tired. You need to have a balance. We've got to find you someone, preferably not a cop. What happened with Brock's son in Canada?'

'Too hard—me here, him there and neither of us wanting to move. Anyway, I'm past it. I've been living alone for too long.

I couldn't share my space with anyone else now. I'm fulfilled, Nic, really.'

Nicole smiled sadly. 'It's never too late, Kathy. Well, let's order lunch.'

When she got home that evening, Kathy tried to shrug off a feeling of loss she'd had since leaving Nicole, as if sensing that their friendship was fading away. She returned to her notes on Ashley Osborn in preparation for the following day.

~

On Monday morning Kathy got into the office early for the team briefing, then went down with Judy Birch to the interview room on the first floor, where Ashley was waiting for them. On the way she was conscious of Judy biting her lip, seeming preoccupied, and hoped that she'd done the right thing in urging her to continue with the case.

'Good morning, Ashley. Thanks for coming in.' Kathy tried not to stare at the younger woman's black hair, the ponytail. 'I'm going to make this a formal recorded interview, and I want to begin by asking you to describe in detail the events surrounding the death of Ahmed Majeed at thirty-three Titmus Street, Clapham, on the morning of Friday the twelfth of October of this year.'

Ashley frowned. 'I've already done that, ma'am, several times.'

'Yes, but I have to tell you that forensic services have brought to our attention several features of the scene that are not consistent with your previous statements. I'm therefore giving you the opportunity—'

'What features?'

'—I'm therefore giving you the opportunity to reconsider your account. If you'd like time to think about it before you make your statement, we will withdraw for fifteen minutes.'

'No, I don't need time, and I don't need to make a new statement. I stand by what I've already told you.'

Kathy said nothing for a long moment, then, 'Very well. When you received the message to answer Haniya Majeed's triple-nine call, you were in a parked patrol car in Charter Street, less than one hundred yards from thirty-three Titmus Street. Why did you stop there?'

'To get a Polo mint out of my pocket. I offered one to Gregory. Maybe he's forgotten.'

Kathy went step by step through Osborn's account of the following hour in Titmus Street, then she abruptly changed tack.

'You have a very distinguished record of service in the area of domestic violence, Ashley. You joined the domestic violence unit in Derby and were assigned to the protection of women's refuges, and you were involved in a number of serious cases. Same again when you transferred to Luton. In fact, for the past nine years you have been immersed in that area of police work, and must have dealt with . . . how many? Dozens—hundreds, even—of cases of domestic abuse, primarily abuse against women. That's right, isn't it?'

Ashley listened to this in silence, eyes fixed on Kathy, jaw set. She gave a brief nod.

'Aloud, please, Ashley, for the record.'

'Yes.'

'And you have a personal reason, too, for your interest in this area, don't you? The violent death of your sister Gillian, when you were just sixteen. You were very angry about that, weren't you? So much so that at her funeral you publicly accused her husband of murdering her. Yes?'

Silence, then Ashley spoke in a whisper. 'What are you getting at?'

'What I'm getting at is that with all that background, all that experience, you must be able to spot a domestic violence victim a mile off. The limp, the bruises, the cowed air. Am I right?'

Ashley didn't reply and Kathy repeated, more insistently, 'Am I right, Ashley?'

'Sometimes I can. Not always.'

'So now let's consider Haniya Majeed, an obvious case if ever I saw one. Wouldn't you agree?'

'I didn't get a chance to judge. I only saw her for a few minutes and she was in a state of panic.'

'No, you knew her better than that. Not only did you both live for years in the same area of Luton, just a few streets apart in Bury Park, but she also worked at the local library, which you visited regularly, every week.' Kathy checked her notes. 'Nonfiction mainly—history, explorers, science. I suppose, with your background, romance would have been a bit hard to stomach. You went there every week, Ashley, and every week there was Haniya behind the counter, so helpful, covering up her bruises. You knew her, didn't you?'

'No.'

'Oh yes you did. And the reason I know that is because when she moved to Clapham you immediately stopped going to the library. And then you applied for a transfer to the Met, to Clapham. So what I'm getting at, Ashley, is that you knew Haniya, and you knew she was in trouble. In fact, you didn't just know her, you knew the whole family, didn't you? In Luton you arrested Ahmed Majeed's cousin Izad Patel for rape. So when Haniya moved to Clapham, you decided to come and keep an eye on her. That's what you were doing in Charter Street on the morning of the twelfth of October, wasn't it?'

Ashley shook her head. 'No.'

'And now you're protecting her. You arrived at Titmus Street and saw immediately that Haniya's story made no sense, so you reconstructed the scene, slid on the floor to hide the pattern of footprints, and told Haniya what to say.'

'No.'

'I admire you, Ashley, I really do. You've been doing great work in a vitally important area. But if you persist in covering up for Haniya, you'll be putting all that at risk. Think about it—there are just too many coincidences, too many lies. Come clean now while you still can. Tell us the truth before it's too late.'

She looked expectantly at Ashley, who calmly returned her gaze and said, 'I told you the truth.'

Kathy shrugged and closed her notepad. 'I'll give you twenty-four hours. See us again tomorrow morning at eleven. Maybe you should think about bringing a solicitor.' She got to her feet and, gesturing to DS Birch to follow, left the room.

Judy Birch fell into step with her outside. 'What now, boss?'

'If she doesn't change her tune tomorrow, we'll charge her with conspiracy and incitement under the *Criminal Law Act 1977*. We have no other choice.'

'Oh . . . that's terrible.'

'It may only be the beginning, Judy. Remember the other deaths—Byrne and Upshot, Patel, and Osborn's brother-in-law, Ryan Turton. I've got another meeting now. I'll see you later.'

She got into the lift, leaving Judy to escort Ashley out of the building.

~

The following day, Ashley didn't appear at the appointed time. After waiting ten minutes, Kathy called her mobile, which went straight to messages. She rang Clapham Police and the duty inspector informed her that Ashley had reported with a doctor's certificate and was likely to be on sick leave for a week with severe gastroenteritis.

7

At ten o'clock on Wednesday morning, as arranged, Brock made his presentation to the Fraud team on the workshop he'd attended on the previous two days. Despite knowing that the presentation itself was a fraud, Brock carried it off with sufficient confidence and use of arcane phrases to satisfy his audience. He had assiduously collected information and summary sheets and diagrams from the conference and duplicated them for everyone, and based his talk on one of the few presentations he had understood. Question time threatened to be a problem, when a prickly character called Kerwin challenged him on some obscure point, but someone else in the audience saved the day by immediately contradicting Kerwin's premise and Brock stood back while an argument developed between them. At the end, as the group broke up, Stone came over and, with some astonishment, congratulated him on an excellent presentation. Brock took the opportunity to say that he planned to take the following day as leave.

During the breaks between workshop sessions, he'd been checking news sites for any further information on the Babington case, and had come across a reference to a memorial service for Nadya Babington to be held at St Mary's in Marylebone at noon on that Thursday. Although he wasn't aware of any new developments in her case, he hadn't been able to stop thinking about it and resolved to go to the service, and to spend the hours before it reacquainting himself with the stretch of London's West End that contained so many of its prestigious art establishments and private galleries. When he was a young copper based at West End Central he'd often explored those places in his lunch hour, fascinated by the diversity of what they had to offer, from the rich dark tones of old masters to the exuberance of the latest action painters or the uncanny facility of photorealists, and it was there that he'd first come across the work of Kurt Schwitters. Some-where at home he had a stack of the catalogues he'd gathered from those exhibitions, along with a number of second-hand art books he'd acquired along the way.

~

On Thursday morning he started in the St James' area in the south, visiting the Institute of Contemporary Arts, Christie's sales rooms and the White Cube gallery, and then continued north across Piccadilly to the Royal Academy, where he took in an exhibition of Lucian Freud's portraits, which closely resembled the portrait he remembered over the fireplace in Babington's living room. From there he moved on to the narrow streets beyond—Dover, Albemarle, Bond and Cork streets—with their private art dealerships, and up to Sotheby's in the north.

After an early sandwich lunch, he crossed Oxford Street into Marylebone, and so to St Mary's Church, just a couple of blocks away from the Babingtons' house in Montagu Square. Designed by Robert Smirke, the nineteenth-century architect of the British Museum, St Mary's had a very grand tall stone tower facing down the long axis from Marble Arch. Brock slipped in through the great entrance portico between clusters of mourners and went into the church, moving into a corner from where he could quietly observe the gathering. He studied a pamphlet explaining that St Mary's was now a charismatic Christian church which aimed to connect people with God in a religion-free way. The building had been reconfigured so that it could be used for a variety of functions, including conferences, fashion shows and concerts, as well as religious services. Brock looked around, taking in Smirke's galleried nave with its vaulted ceiling, and the loose arrangements of furniture and fittings for the different uses that now took place within it. The sense of history adjusting to dynamic change made him think of the very different circumstances of St Chad's at Hoo, the rugged relic of an ancient church clinging to life in its marshy wilderness. He wondered if Nadya might have been attracted to the contrast between it and her gilded life here in the West End.

He studied the people coming in, prosperous and confident, most dressed in sober dark clothes, but some garnished with an artistic flourish of colour or hairstyle. He wondered if the assistant commissioner, Julian's cousin, was here. He had met her before and thought she would probably recognise him, and he would prefer to keep out of her way.

As the seating filled up, music came from loudspeakers around the hall, a male chorus, singing in Russian. After a time, the music died away and a young man wearing a black T-shirt and jeans stepped forward to a microphone on the low dais at the front, next to a table bearing flowers and a large photograph of Nadya.

'Good day to you all. My name is Wayne, I'm head of our worship team here at St Mary's, and I'd like to welcome you to this wonderful building in which Nadya felt so much at home.

'The music you've just been listening to was the Slavyanka Men's Chorus singing Otche Nash, the Lord's Prayer, by Nikolay Kedrov, in Russian. You can find it on YouTube. It was one of Nadya's favourites. It reminded her of her early life in St Petersburg, where she was born forty-two years ago. There she studied at the St Petersburg Art and Industry Academy, and developed her great love of art, which she continued to pursue when she came here to London to stay with her uncle Egor.' He gestured to a man seated in the front row next to Babington. 'Soon she met Julian, and together they took inspiration from art and shared their passion with Nadya's son Miki, who also belongs to that world—a world to which I know many of you are similarly connected.

'So we are here today to celebrate Nadya's love of beauty with her many friends. Here is more of the Otche Nash, while we contemplate Nadya's gift of beauty to the world.'

He pressed a remote and the music filled the hall again.

When it finally faded away an elderly man made his way to the microphone. He introduced himself as an old friend of Nadya and Julian, and a former president of the Royal Academy of Arts nearby in Burlington House. He spoke of the Babingtons' generous support for the Academy and for the Royal Academy Schools, the oldest art school in Britain.

'Some of you will know that earlier this year, the year of the two hundred and fiftieth birthday of the Academy, Julian and Nadya announced that they would donate their marvellous collection of modern art to us. We are currently in the process of converting one of our gallery spaces to provide a fit home for it. The Babington Gallery will stand as a permanent celebration of their lives' work together.'

Applause broke out, and he waited till it died down before he resumed speaking, his voice filled with emotion as he related stories of Nadya's infectious enthusiasm, her Russian passion and her incorrigible sense of humour. Brock caught sight of people wiping tears from their eyes.

When he stepped down from the dais, helped by Wayne, Miki bounded up and grabbed the microphone with the confidence of a rock star.

'Hi, I'm Miki—Nadya's son, if you don't know me. I spoke to Mum last night.'

He paused to let that sink in, and Brock sensed the stillness in the room, people exchanging looks with raised eyebrows.

'And she wanted me to tell you that she is at peace. All the hassles and shit that she had to put up with in her life are over.' He raised a fist in the air. 'She wants us all to make up our differences and love each other. She is at peace, and she is on high!'

And so are you, Brock thought.

'That's all I've got to say.'

Wayne managed to grab the mic from him as he strode away. 'Thank you, Miki. It's a very emotional time for all of us. Would anyone else like to speak?'

Nobody moved, and Wayne went on, 'I'm sure you all have many memories of Nadya's life that you want to share with each other. Her family has provided refreshments for us at the other end of the hall, and you're more than welcome to stay as long as you wish. God bless you all.'

He stepped down and went to Julian, who got to his feet along with others from the front row, and together they walked towards the back of the hall. As people began moving, whispering as they went, Brock thought about the old friend's description of Nadya. He himself had only gained a very partial impression of her, and he thought of the preoccupied and frightened woman he had met that day in Montagu Square and was filled with a sense of guilt at having somehow failed her. He wondered how many other people there were experiencing the same feeling; the usual reaction to a suicide, he supposed, the dreadful thought, *If only I had . . .* And then there was that outburst of Miki's, his reference to the 'hassles and shit' she'd had to put up with. What was that all about? To an outsider she appeared to have lived a privileged life with Julian.

And yet it seemed she had nursed a poisonous secret—a secret that had killed her.

There were tables laid out at the other end of the nave, with waiters dispensing champagne and caviar blinis. Brock took one of each and mixed with the mourners, about a hundred of them, wondering if he might see Callum McAdam, but there was no sign of him. He caught snatches of conversation. 'But *why*? . . . What exactly *happened* to Nadya? . . . She was always very impulsive, wasn't she? . . . Did she actually *worship* here? . . . Julian's a rock. My sister's looking for a new partner. I suppose he'll have them lining up . . . Oh God, Miki! At least he kept it short . . .'

He looked around to see where Miki was now, and saw him talking intently to a short, stocky man with a pugnacious red face whom he recognised as the man that Wayne had indicated as Nadya's uncle Egor. He eased his way through the throng towards them, and picked up the growl of the man's voice, thick with what sounded like a Russian accent. Before he could reach them, Miki turned abruptly and hurried away towards the doors. Brock approached the other man.

'Hello, you're Egor, am I right?'

The man stared at him with a frown. 'And you?'

'My name's David Brock. I was one of the police officers who attended the scene. I'm very sorry for the loss of your niece.'

'What the hell are you doing here, eh? Are you still investigating?'

'No, no. I'm just here to pay my respects.'

'The police must have a lot of time on their hands these days,' he barked angrily. 'Can't you leave the family in peace?' And with that he turned and marched away after Miki.

'Brock?'

He turned and saw Julian Babington looking at him with a puzzled frown. Then his face cleared. 'How good of you to come.' He shook his hand.

'I'm not here officially, but I thought I should pay my respects. I hope that's all right.'

'Of course, of course. I do appreciate it.'

'I'm afraid Egor seemed upset by my being here.'

'Oh, take no notice of Egor. It's a difficult time for him. He was very attached to Nadya. What did he say?'

'He asked if we were still investigating the matter.'

'And are you?'

'No, although of course the coroner will have the last word. Nothing new at your end?'

Babington sighed. 'No, nothing.'

Brock sipped at his drink. 'Ever heard of a church called St Chad's?'

Babington blinked. 'Sorry?'

'St Chad's. Mean anything to you?'

'I don't think so. Why?'

They were interrupted by a small elderly woman with sharp, pointed features, wearing a black outfit dominated by a large scarlet silk bow at her throat. 'Julian!' she cried. 'Oh, my poor boy. How are you coping? I only flew back last night. I hadn't heard the news! It's too awful, too awful.'

'Hello, Rosa. I'm so glad you could make it.' Babington bent to give her a hug, and this seemed to take all of the momentum out of her, so that when they separated she looked limp and there were tears in her eyes.

'Rosa, let me introduce you to David Brock. David, this is

74

the wonderful Rosa Lipmann, the queen of the London art market.'

Rosa sniffed and wiped her eyes with a small handkerchief she produced from her cuff.

'Rosa owns the Lipmann Gallery in Cork Street. David is a collector, Rosa. He has a Schwitters.'

'Has he indeed!' She focused on Brock for the first time. 'Have we met?'

'I don't believe so, but I have visited your gallery, of course.'

'Well, come and visit again soon. Give me a call before-hand and I'll make sure I'm there.' She gave Brock her card. 'Did you buy the Schwitters from me? Surely I would have met you if you did.'

'No, it was a gift from the son of Schwitters' landlady, when he lived in Stepney.'

'Really! You knew him? How fascinating . . .'

They were interrupted by another mourner who knew both Rosa and Babington. As Brock began to move away, Babington touched his arm and said, 'I'd like to have a private word before you go, if that's all right. Can you wait?'

Brock agreed, but it was another hour before the gather-ing began to disperse, by which time he had had several glasses of champagne but not much caviar. Babington shook hands with one of the last to leave, then came over. He too seemed to have taken comfort in the Bollinger. 'Thanks for waiting, Brock. Are you all right for time?'

'I've taken a day's leave, so I'm all yours.'

'Good, excellent. As you know, I live just a couple of blocks away. Let's go back there.'

They walked in silence, the overcast November sky bringing on the lights in the buildings even in the early afternoon, Brock relishing the cold air that cleared his head. He hoped for something tangible, some insight or clue to put an end to this story, some words from Babington to reassure him that Nadya's suicide was as it seemed.

When they reached Montagu Square, they stood on the steps of Babington's house while he took out his keys. As he fumbled with them he was seized suddenly by a coughing fit. Reaching quickly for an inhaler from his pocket, he stood for a moment, taking deep breaths as the attack subsided. 'Sorry,' he said, and opened the front door. Inside he tapped his code into the alarm. It seemed to Brock a rather flimsy protection for such a valuable art collection and he said so.

'Oh, don't worry, every artwork in here is protected by a separate system. Each has a hidden magnetic device that immediately sounds an alarm if it's touched or moved. Only Nadya and I know the release code. But it is a concern . . .'

He led the way through to the living room, Brock noting the artworks they passed so that he could describe them to Molly.

'I can't stand the thought of hiding all these beautiful things away, but there's always that doubt. Will someone be able to bypass the system one day? And then there's the cost of insurance. Prohibitive. That's why we decided to give the collection to the RA. Also, we wanted to make it available to everyone to enjoy. As it is, most of the stuff is in a strongroom in the basement, and we rotate the works here on the walls and lend individual pieces out for exhibitions. Scotch?'

As Babington poured two glasses from a decanter, Brock went over to examine a watercolour, a view of Venice. He remembered a similar work in one of Suzanne's books. 'I do like this,' he said. 'Sargent?'

Babington came and stood by his side. 'Yes indeed, John Singer Sargent, *Santa Maria della Salute*, 1904. Not by any means the most valuable, but of all the works in the collection one of my favourites. You like him?'

'I do. I remember seeing an exhibition of his water-colours many years ago. I'd spent the day questioning a suspected child molester and felt dirty. Seeing the Sargents was like a fresh shower, a promise that the world could also be beautiful.'

Babington handed a glass to Brock and showed him to a plump armchair. 'I know what you mean. Sometimes I wish I could look at these paintings like that again, instead of as an onerous duty. So, you mentioned a church . . .?'

'St Chad's—a very old church near where Nadya died. The vicar there recognised her photo, said she'd visited and contributed to their restoration fund.'

'Oh yes, that sounds like her. She loved lame ducks. Chad, you say? Unusual name. Yes, I believe I do remember us discussing it. She was always wanting us to donate to worthy causes, the more obscure the better.'

Brock sipped. 'No sign of her computer?'

'No. I've searched everywhere. I've gone through all her business files and can't find anything out of the ordinary.'

'Interior design, you said. Did she have many jobs on at the moment?'

'No, it was a small operation, just a few favourite clients, word of mouth. She had a real talent and loved doing it, but she hasn't had anyone on the books for a couple of months.

She was talking about going to a show in Salzburg next March, then flying on to Singapore Design Week.' He shrugged. 'Now this. Do you think there could be anything in the Russian email? That seemed to spook her.'

'We checked with Border Force, but no Sergei Semenov has entered the country this year. Apart from the Russian email domain, has there been anything to suggest he might be involved?'

'Absolutely nothing. Miki says he hasn't heard from his father in years. I wondered ...' He hesitated, pursing his lips as if tasting something sour. 'She had this exaggerated idea of being indebted to me for rescuing her from Semenov and a life of drudgery back in Russia. I told her that was nonsense. I fell in love with her and she owed me nothing. But I think she always had this sense of insecurity, of dread that the dream might suddenly end.'

He sat brooding on the thought. The light was dying outside the windows and the room was growing dark.

Brock drained his whisky and made to move, but Julian lunged forward and took his glass, pressed the switch on a table lamp, and took up the decanter.

'The thing is,' he said harshly, filling their glasses, 'if there was no Semenov, then all I can think is that I was responsible for her death.'

'How so?'

Babington sighed. 'When my father was alive he sent me to New York to establish a branch of the firm over there. It did quite well, and took up more and more of my time. It was one of the reasons my first marriage broke down—I was away so much. When Nadya and I got together I resolved not to make the same mistake again. But while the London practice was sluggish, particularly after the financial crisis in 2008, New York thrived and demanded my attention, and I've had to keep shuttling back and forth between the two. Nadya hated my absences. She was easily bored and didn't really relate to my London friends. Her moods became more volatile. I begged her to get help, counselling, but she never did.' He sighed heavily. 'I should have done things differently, spent more time with her, given her more attention.'

They sat in silence for a moment, then Brock said, 'What about Miki?'

'Oh, Miki. He was only ten when Nadya and I first met and she doted on him. They were very close throughout his adolescence, but then of course he became more independent and she saw less and less of him.'

'Mm,' Brock said. 'He's a bit of a wild card, isn't he?'

'Wild card? Dear God, yes. Well, you saw him at the funeral. He'd *spoken* to his dead mother, no less! He was stoned, obviously. The man's a menace.'

'In what way?'

'Oh . . . Nadya would hate me saying this—she idolised him and forgave him everything. When I first met him, sixteen years ago, I thought he was a charming little boy, supportive of his mother and polite to me. He still had a strong Russian accent that made him sound rather quaint and old-fashioned. Any reservations I had about taking on someone else's child faded. Divorced two years, with no children of my own, and deeply in love with his mother, I began to see him as a rather fine bonus. I agreed that he should change his surname to Babington. But after we were married I discovered that Miki was charming only as long as he got what he wanted. If he didn't, there would be tantrums and rages until Nadya gave in. As he moved into his teenage years things got worse. I tried to intervene, but he was uncontrollable, and increasingly violent. I managed to get him a place at my old boarding school, but that didn't work out. He stole from other boys, got mixed up in drugs and assaulted one of the masters. He was lucky not to be prosecuted. Anyway ... I won't go on. On his eighteenth birthday he announced that he would be an artist, and with a bit of help from me he managed to get into Camberwell College of Arts.'

Julian contemplated his empty glass, then reached for the decanter again and topped them both up.

'He stayed about eighteen months, then dropped out and did little except get into trouble before finally disappearing off to the Continent. Every now and then we'd get demands for money, but otherwise it was a great relief to have him out of our lives. He returned to London three or four years ago, and I was pleased to see that he seemed to have grown up. He was dressed reasonably smartly and was civil. Nadya was overjoyed, but I didn't believe he'd really changed, and it soon became apparent that he was still involved with drugs. But, amazingly, he had a job ... Anyway, enough of Miki. Tell me about yourself, Brock. Married?'

'No. I have a partner, though.'

'Ah. And an art collection.'

Brock smiled. 'I'm afraid my art collection consists of just one work—the Schwitters.' And he told the story of Walter Crab.

Julian chuckled. 'Your first murderer! What a wonderful tale. And an English Merz! But have you registered it? Had it authenticated?'

'No, I'm afraid not.'

'Oh, my dear chap, of course you must. Provenance is everything. Look, I'll show you.'

He lurched to his feet and Brock did the same but more slowly, feeling the effects of the whisky. He followed Julian over to a small drawing hanging near the door.

'Most of the works in the collection were acquired by my father, Derek. He was a lawyer too.' Julian pointed back at the oil portrait hanging above the fireplace, an elderly man glowering at the viewer. 'That's him. He helped Lucian Freud out over a family matter and then got him to paint a portrait in lieu of a fee. Anyway, one day in 1956 he was passing Sotheby's on the day of a sale. On a whim he went inside and bought this pen-and-ink sketch for thirty pounds.'

'It looks a bit like a Van Gogh,' Brock suggested.

'Yes, it does, doesn't it? But there's no signature. There's a title—*Jardin Public à Arles*—scribbled in pencil on the back, but in a hand that clearly wasn't Vincent's, so Sotheby's had played safe and described it as "in the style of Van Gogh". But my father got in touch with the seller, an elderly American collector, who told him the name of the dealer in Paris whom he'd bought it from back in the 1920s. So Dad went to Paris. The dealer's gallery was still there, and he went through their records and found the receipt for their purchase of the sketch from Vincent Willem van Gogh, who had inherited it from his father, Theo, Vincent's brother and dealer. Dad had authenticated copies made of all the records he found, and eventually the sketch was recognised in the catalogue raisonné as an authentic Van Gogh drawing.' Julian drew a breath. 'Three years ago, Sotheby's sold an almost identical sketch by Vincent, the same size, five and a quarter by six and a half inches, for one-point-five million US.'

Brock stared at the little piece of paper, the scribbled brown ink strokes. 'How long do you think it took him to do it? Ten minutes?'

'About that.'

'Over a million pounds. That's obscene.'

Julian laughed, nodding his head in agreement. 'Yes, obscene. All that useful cash tied up in a useless scrap of paper. But it's a useless scrap of paper with *provenance*! Provenance is the difference between a piece of rubbish and a holy relic of immeasurable value.'

Brock thought he sounded a bit like the vicar talking about St Chad's. He said, 'I think it's time I went, Julian.'

'Before you go, I'll show you something really special, something even more obscene. Come, come.' He set off, swaying a little, and Brock followed him out to the hallway. They stopped at the Schwitters and Babington stared at it for a moment and said, 'Yes, that fellow really knew what he was doing. I'm very attached to this one.'

They continued to a door which Babington unlocked with a key from a bunch in his pocket. 'This way to the treasure house.'

He switched on a light and they descended a flight of steps into the basement. There was another door down there, protected by another keypad. Babington entered the code and pulled the door open. 'The fireproof treasure house.

The building could burn down around it, but this room would survive intact.'

He turned on lights and Brock saw a low-ceilinged room lined with racks of paintings and drawings. Babington led the way in. 'This is the bulk of the works collected by my father, together with their provenance documents in that cabinet over there. But among them is the thing that inspired my father's obsession and which now outshines them all. During the First World War, his father, my grandfather, was an officer in the British army on the Western Front in France, and in 1917 he visited Paris while on leave. There he passed the window of an art dealer in which was displayed a painting that struck his fancy. He went in and bought it for five hundred francs, about twenty-five British pounds. Here it is ...'

Babington reached to a box in the rack and laid it on the table in the centre of the room. Opening it, he drew out a painting in a frame and held it up for Brock to see.

Brock stared at it, astonished. 'But I've seen this before. It's in the National Gallery in Trafalgar Square—Van Gogh's *Sunflowers*.'

'Quite right! It was painted by Van Gogh in Arles in August 1888. He painted several versions of the same subject in that month, and this, like the one in the National Gallery, is one of them.'

Brock looked more closely at it, the golden sunflowers glowing against a turquoise background, the bold paint strokes. 'It's fabulous. How much is it worth?'

'Ha!' Babington laughed. 'Yes, that's the question, isn't it? The most precious work in the collection. The last major Van Gogh to go on the market, *Portrait of Dr Gachet*, was auctioned back in 1990 for eighty-two million dollars, but this would be worth many times that now. Over two hundred and fifty million, certainly.'

'Really?'

'Yes. So this is the cross I've had to bear, Brock, the family curse: keeping all this safe. It's an inheritance I could really have done without. It will be a great relief when I finally hand it over to the Academy. In fact, I've arranged for them to pick up the *Sunflowers* tomorrow, in advance of the rest.'

He looked suddenly very tired as he put the painting back in its box.

Brock said, 'Thank you for showing me. It's been a long day for you. I'd better be on my way.'

They climbed the stair back up to the hall, where Brock took out his phone and called for a cab. Julian opened the front door and they stood together in silence, breathing in the cold air, until the cab appeared. As he got in, Brock looked back and saw the stricken expression on Babington's face as he stood there in the hallway, surrounded by his treasures. Brock turned away, feeling dissatisfied. There had been plenty to interest him, but not the enlightenment about Nadya's death that he had been hoping for.

8

The following day, Friday, Brock sat at his computer studying Miki Babington's police record—three separate convictions for drug possession and supply, two as a juvenile. He'd been lucky to avoid jail time. He heard a soft cough and looked up to see Matt Stone standing there, a serious look on his face. 'Brock, I just had a note from the assistant commissioner about a member of the Fraud Squad going to Nadya Babington's memorial service.'

'Really? I didn't think she saw me.'

'Oh, she saw you all right.' Stone smiled suddenly. 'She said it was very thoughtful of us to send a representative.'

'Good.'

Stone continued, 'But that's the end of it, okay? You did a good job with your presentation on Wednesday.

Clearly you've got a flair for insurance fraud. Just stick to that, okay?'

'I wonder if that's wise, Matt.'

'How do you mean?'

'Well, the reason I went to the memorial service was that Molly Fitzherbert spoke to me. She'd seen the press reports of Nadya's death and she was concerned that it might be more than a simple case of suicide. Given the significance of the Babington art collection, she felt we shouldn't ignore the possibility of an art fraud dimension. And I thought we'd look pretty silly if it turned out she was right, and we in Fraud hadn't considered it.'

Stone frowned. 'Ye-es, I see your point. What kind of art fraud are we talking about?'

'I'm not sure yet, but I thought it would be worth me working on it with Molly for a few days, just to cover our backs.'

'Okay, but tactfully, eh? We don't want to cause needless alarm.'

'Of course.'

Stone had only just gone when Brock got a call from Molly, who said she had something for him. He made his way over to her den.

'Brock, come in, have a seat. Take a look at this.'

She handed him an email from a body called KSUK, the Kurt Schwitters Society UK.

Dear Molly,

How good to hear from you, and what a fascinating question.

At the Kurt Schwitters Society we regularly have to deal with queries from people who claim they have a genuine Schwitters, but as we are not authorised to determine such matters, we pass inquiries on to the Schwitters Archive at the Sprengel Museum in Hanover, as they are now the only people entitled to judge whether such works are forgeries. I would, then, urge you to contact the archive director, Dr Helena Stark, who is the ultimate arbiter of such cases. It is a thorny business for her, I might add, as this sort of thing takes up a lot of her valuable time and can prove dreadfully irritating.

Although we at KSUK are therefore not the professionals, I can nonetheless regale you with a few stories from my own stock of anecdotes, just to be going on with. There used to be a couple on the Portobello Road in London—for all I know they're still there—who manufactured on average one Schwitters forgery a week to sell on their stall. If I remember, their collages were known as the postage stamp forgeries, as they always featured an old postage stamp. Another rather more dramatic case from decades ago occurred during a Schwitters exhibition in America. On the day before it opened, Schwitters' son turned up and declared that one of the collages on show was not his father's work. Panic among the curators. In those days the Schwitters guru was the eminent Professor Werner Schmalenbach, who lived in Düsseldorf. They immediately rang him—it was the middle of the night in Germany—and Schmalenbach, practically still in his pyjamas, was flown across the Atlantic right away. They asked him to enter the exhibition and identify any picture that didn't look authentic, and without saying a word he made straight for the collage that Schwitters' son had already pronounced a forgery. The show was going on to a gallery in London, which had already printed its own catalogue with the now disgraced collage adorning the front cover. All the catalogues had to be pulped (I managed to get hold of one nonetheless) and a new version printed. Some years later, I attended the opening of a Schwitters exhibition in the Netherlands, and as I was studying a large assemblage displayed at the entrance, guess who walked in right after me? Werner Schmalenbach. He marched up to the picture and said, 'Get that out of this exhibition *now*. It's a fake.' A trembling curator took it down immediately, such was Schmalenbach's clout, so from then on visitors were confronted by a strangely blank wall when they entered.

What is really enlightening is to look at a Schwitters collage with the experts at the Sprengel Museum and get them to point out the subtleties—forgers seldom have any idea of Schwitters' masterly technique and grasp of composition, which are formidably difficult to imitate. The Kurt Schwitters catalogue raisonné contains several items that have not been conclusively identified as genuine, but these are few and far between.

If you have a collage you think might be a Schwitters, it's not so easy to get the experts even to look at it. Provenance is the keyword, and if you don't have that, you're lost. Someone once approached me with an early landscape that I could have sworn was an original Schwitters, but as he had bought it on eBay, with no provenance, that was the end of the story. Then an American sent me a photo of his small framed Schwitters collage, with a clear-cut provenance—his father had bought it from a famous gallery after the war. I notified the staff at the Schwitters Archive, who went to see it. It was a fine work, and they already knew of its existence, if not its whereabouts. As it turned out, the gallery had purchased it from Schwitters himself, and what's more, it was an early collage, so really valuable. The owner revealed to me that he'd just been burgled, and the thief had made off with a bulky and very unwieldy booty of expensive electronic equipment, at the same time knocking the collage off the wall. It had been left on the floor, luckily undamaged. If the thief had known it was worth a million or so, he needn't have bothered with the rest of his haul . . .

Anyway, I'm really grateful to you for drawing my attention to this topic, and if I can aid you any further, please let me know.

Very best wishes, and please keep in touch,

Gwendolen Webster

President, Kurt Schwitters Society

'So there you are,' Molly said. 'You've got to gather all the information you can on your Merz and take it to Hanover to show Dr Stark. I did discover one problem you may have though. I've been looking at Schwitters' time in London, and found his addresses in Paddington and Barnes, but I can't find any record of his having lived in Stepney.'

'Are you sure? I can recall the house so clearly, and the Merz hanging over the fireplace.'

'Well, that's why it's important you go to the Sprengel Museum. They'll know for sure.'

'I'm supposed to be going to Germany at the end of next week. To Bremen, not far away. Do you think Dr Stark would agree to see me?'

'We can try. I've met her once or twice; shall I see if I can get you an appointment?'

She picked up her phone, and after a series of calls looked up at Brock and said, 'Monday, December third, eleven o'clock. Okay?'

'Perfect. Thanks, Molly. And as it happens, I was about to come and see you when you rang.' He told her about his conversation with Stone and added, 'You were the one who said that Nadya's death must be linked to the art collection in some way, so how do we investigate that?'

'Well, to my mind Miki Babington is the weak link. If anyone in that family was involved in fraud, I'd have thought he would be it.'

'You mentioned that he was working for a dodgy art business.'

'Yes,' Molly said, 'DPF—the Dufort-Poirier Foundation. Sounds impressive, doesn't it? If you look at their website you get the impression that they're a philanthropic group devoted to sponsoring art students, education and research, but really they're a smooth vehicle for selling so-called artworks to gullible people with a bit of surplus income to spend. We investigated them a couple of years ago for suspected fraud. They sell artworks online and through respectable-looking premises in London, Paris, Tokyo and New York. They also hold auctions on board cruise ships. You know how it is—you've had a few drinks over lunch and you go along to the art auction for a bit of amusement, and after a high-powered sales pitch about the amazing escalating investment value of art, you find yourself signing a contract for five or ten thousand quid for a genuine signed Picasso pastel sketch, which is almost certain to double in value every five years and is delivered to your door a few weeks later in a smashing gold frame. Only it wasn't made by Picasso, but by one of several hundred very skilful Chinese art students working out of an industrial estate in Shanghai.

And when you come to examine the documentation, you find that DPF didn't actually say that it was a Picasso, only that it had been authenticated as a Picasso by a company called Lotus Art Analytical, whose certificate was provided with the artwork. Though it has a nominal office address in Paris, Lotus Art Analytical is curiously hard to pin down, but again seems to be based in Shanghai.

'Julian Babington would never deal with an outfit like that,' Molly continued, 'but that doesn't mean Miki hasn't got them involved without his stepfather's knowledge. Suppose it involved compromising the Babington Collection in some way? Something so terrible that when Nadya found out about it, she couldn't face the consequences? Though why she chose such a strange place to die is beyond me.'

'I think I know the answer to that,' Brock said, 'and it does involve Miki. When he was in his teens, Miki Babington decided that he wanted to be an artist and managed to enrol at Camberwell. He struck up a friendship with another student there, a young Scot called Callum McAdam. Nadya Babington took a close interest in Miki's progress and went to all the student shows and exhibitions, and met McAdam. After Miki dropped out, it seems Nadya continued her friendship with McAdam, which developed into an affair. McAdam lives not far from the pool where Nadya drowned.'

'Ah, another artist. Have you spoken to him?'

'Only very briefly. I'd like to ask him a few questions, though. I think it's time I paid him a visit.'

~

Later that afternoon Brock was on the Hoo Peninsula, and parked at the turn-off onto the track that led to Nadya's pool. He pulled on a pair of boots and set off along the muddy path, turning up his coat collar against the North Sea wind. He studied the muddy surface that had been so thoroughly churned up by the police and rescue vehicles and came at last to the dark pond. For a moment he was overcome by a feeling of sadness at the bleakness of the place and the memory of the beautiful pale face in the ambulance.

He turned back, a bleary winter sun in the west showing up the confusion of vehicle tracks in a raking light. Will Holt had been satisfied that no other car tracks had been present when they arrived, so Brock focused on the margins, looking for the possibility of footprints. And then, approaching the junction with the road, he spotted something different: a thin line of marks half hidden by the grass at the edge. He stooped down to look more closely, then took some pictures on his phone. A bicycle track, surely.

Brock drove on past St Chad's to the cluster of farm buildings. As before, there seemed to be no one around, and when he stopped at the Smithy there was no response to his knock on the front door.

He walked around the end of the building to a court-yard at the rear, where a light showed through a window next to the back door. There was a bicycle leaning against the wall nearby, Brock noted, and as he got closer he could hear the faint sound of music coming from inside. He went over and knocked on the door. Again there was no response, and he peered in through the grimy cobwebbed glass of the window. It took him a moment to make out the dark shape of a figure hanging by a rope from one of the roof trusses.

He tried the door, a solid timber thing that didn't yield, then took out his phone and called the number Will Holt had given him and told him what he'd found.

The Kent detective arrived in a patrol car twenty minutes later with a couple of other officers, big men, one of whom took a battering ram from the boot and slammed it into the lock of the door. It flew open and Holt stepped carefully inside, Brock at his shoulder, sniffing the fetid air.

Callum McAdam's face was grotesquely distorted, his tongue hanging from the corner of his mouth. He was wearing paint-stained overalls, his arms hanging limply by his sides with a piece of brightly coloured fabric tied around his left wrist. Below his dangling feet an old wooden chair lay on its side in a puddle of stinking fluid from which a fly rose buzzing into the air.

While Holt spoke into his phone, Brock looked around at what was clearly a workroom, with tools on racks around the walls. In places he noticed streaks of paint on the old worn benches.

Holt said, 'What's that tied around his wrist?'

'Looks like a woman's silk scarf,' Brock replied. He was remembering the look of shock on Callum's face that day in the vestry of St Chad's when Brock had told him of Nadya's death. 'I'd be interested to know if it belonged to Nadya Babington.'

'Eh?' Holt looked at him in surprise.

'I called in at the church, St Chad's, after I left you at the pond that day we found Nadya Babington. I wanted to find out if anyone had seen her around here before. This bloke—his name's Callum McAdam—was there with the vicar, helping with the building work. The vicar said she had often visited the church and had donated money to their restoration fund. I gathered that she and McAdam were close friends. That's why I came back here today, to have another chat to him.'

'I see.' Holt frowned, thinking. 'So the scarf ... You think McAdam and Babington were lovers?'

'It's possible.'

'That would fit, wouldn't it? The timing, a double suicide.'

'Yes ...' He was suddenly reminded of Kathy's case, the dead man in the locked bathroom. 'All the same, I'd like to be sure, Will. Let's treat this as a potential homicide scene, order a full forensic examination, just in case.'

Holt shook his head. 'My super won't like that. We're in the second phase of another cost-cutting round. He'd need to have strong grounds for suspicion. I'll do what I can.'

'And we need to check the keys.'

'Keys?'

'That back door is secured with an old mortice lock. If someone else did this, they'd have to have taken Callum's key with them so as to lock the door on their way out. Maybe they threw it away somewhere when they left. A locked-room mystery, Will. The best kind.'

Holt gave a rueful smile. 'The only mysteries our super's interested in these days are the financial kind.'

~

Brock returned to his car and drove back along the winding lane until he saw the tower of St Chad's up ahead, a dark shape against the glow of the setting sun in the west. He noticed a car parked by the front door and stopped beside it.

He found the Reverend Alwyn Bramley-Scott sitting in the tiny vestry, polishing a silver chalice. He turned at the sound of Brock's footsteps and smiled vaguely. There was the bottle of sherry and an empty glass standing beside the metal polish.

'Hello, hello. Do come in.' He sounded preoccupied and didn't seem to recognise Brock.

'Good evening, Vicar. My name's David Brock. I spoke to you last week following the discovery of Nadya Babington's body in the marshes. I'm a police officer.'

'Oh ... yes, of course, of course.' His eyes seemed to focus suddenly and he rose to his feet.

'Have you spoken to Callum McAdam in the past few days?'

'Callum? Of course. He often drops in.'

'When was the last time, exactly?'

'Um, let's see. Today is ...?'

'Friday.'

'Ah, well, about two days ago. Wednesday? Or was it Tuesday?'

'How did he seem?'

'Seem? Well ... he's been very low since we heard about poor Nadya, very low. I've tried to comfort him, but he's heartbroken. Why?'

'I'm afraid we've found his body at the Smithy.'

The vicar blinked as if having difficulty digesting this, then he groaned. 'Oh no ... Was it ... Did he ...?'

'I'm afraid so. It seems he hanged himself.'

'I must go to him ...' The vicar began to struggle to his feet, but Brock put a hand on his arm.

'The police are there now. You won't be able to go in. Tell me, when did Callum first come here to the Hoo?'

'Let me see ... He moved into the Smithy five or six years ago. It was about the time we decided, what with the state of the roof, that it was no longer safe to hold services in the church, and I began to use the barn at Ingall's farm instead. One Sunday morning I noticed Callum in the congregation and I spoke to him afterwards. He seemed a very sincere young man, lonely and a little lost. Later he told me he'd had a breakdown of some kind, was estranged from his family in Glasgow and was an artist. As I got to know him, I thought of Van Gogh—so intense and dedicated to his work—and I had a word with someone I knew in Rochester who owns a small gallery. She tried to sell his paintings, but they were not popular. Well, neither were Van Gogh's, were they? He only sold one work in his lifetime, and look at them now. And now, like Van Gogh, Callum is tragically dead. I always feared it might happen and I tried so hard to help him.'

'You suspected he might be suicidal?'

'He was of a rather gloomy disposition, his paintings didn't sell and he had no friends except Nadya and the other young man, Miki.'

'And you said you've never met Nadya's husband Julian?'

'No, I knew next to nothing about her life, except that she lived in the city and mixed with society people. She was a very private person.'

'Did Callum ever have any other visitors?'

'Not that I'm aware of. I have no idea who his family are

to contact them. Please let me know, if you can. I would like to send my commiserations. He was such a fine young man.'

~

Brock left him and returned to the Smithy, its lane now crowded with vehicles. Will told him that he'd called in scene-of-crime specialists without consulting his super. The people at Ingall's farm had returned and said that Callum kept pretty much to himself. They hadn't seen him for several days and couldn't recall anyone having visited him in over a week. Forensics had cleared the rest of the Smithy, and Brock went through to the big barn facing the road. It was scattered with pots and tubes of paint, jars of brushes, canvases, boards, a couple of paint-stained easels and all the other clutter of an artist's studio. Propped against the walls were half-a-dozen large canvases, big brooding abstracts, almost entirely black.

Holt came to his side and stared at them. 'Blimey, you wouldn't want one of them in your living room, would you?' He showed Brock an image on his phone of the scarf they'd removed from Callum's wrist, and sent a copy to Brock's phone. 'They're putting the time of death at around noon today,' he said.

Brock returned to his car and put a call through to Babington, saying that he'd like to speak to him in person concerning a new development.

~

Babington was waiting for him when he arrived at Montagu Square almost exactly an hour later, opening the door as soon as Brock came up the front steps.

'Come in, come in. Tell me what's happened.'

They went through to the living room and Brock asked Julian if he'd heard of a man called Callum McAdam.

'I don't believe so. Why?'

'It appears he hanged himself earlier today, in his home not far from where Nadya died.'

'Another suicide in the Hoo? Good grief. Who was he?'

'A young man, early thirties, an artist apparently, rather unsuccessful.'

'An artist?' Babington shook his head. 'This is bizarre.'

Brock took out his phone and showed him the photo of the scarf. 'Ever seen this before?'

Babington stared hard at it, and his voice dropped to a whisper. 'I like to bring Nadya little gifts when I come back from New York. This ... this looks very like a scarf I bought her at Saks earlier this year. Where did you find it?'

'It was tied around his wrist.'

'Oh God.' Babington closed his eyes, took a deep breath. 'Well,' he said wearily. 'That's it then, isn't it? That's what this was all about. Jesus.'

Brock waited a moment, then said, 'I'm sorry to bring you this news, Julian. Are you sure you've never heard of Callum McAdam? The reason I ask is that it seems he may have been a student at Camberwell College of Arts at the same time as Miki. Did Miki ever mention him?'

'Not that I recall, but I didn't get involved with his activities there, whereas Nadya went to all their exhibitions and open days. Maybe she met this fellow then, years ago. I'll have to speak to Miki.'

Brock hesitated, then said, 'It's not for me to say, Julian, but you might want to keep a low profile. If there's an inquest and the press get hold of this . . .'

'Yes, yes, I see what you mean, a juicy scandal. And the presentation to the Royal Academy coming up . . . But thank you, Brock. Thank you for telling me this yourself. I appreciate it.' As they walked to the front door Babington added, 'I'm supposed to be having dinner tonight with old friends. They've been very kind, wanting to help, but I just want to bury myself in here with a bottle of Scotch. Can't let them down, though.'

~

That evening, on the train down to Battle, Brock thought about Babington, coming back after the dinner with his friends to his empty house, slumping into his armchair with the Scotch and dwelling on the bitter truths that Nadya's scam email had exposed. And he also thought about his own Merz, wondering if it too had simply been a scam. If Molly was right that Schwitters never lived in Stepney, then surely Walter Crab had lied to him, and the only explanation he could think of was that Crab had himself been involved in art forgery, and his Merz was a fake. Brock was surprised that the idea pained him so much, apart from the evaporation of its financial worth. It was as if it somehow contaminated his whole career—his first big case, fondly symbolised by that little artwork, built on a fraud.

Suzanne was upstairs doing the books on the dining room table. She was bubbling with excitement, as was the glass of champagne at her elbow.

'I sold the *Adoration*!' she cried, standing up to give him a big kiss.

'Oh, fantastic! Congratulations.' Brock hugged her and took the glass she offered. *The Adoration of the Magi*, a small bronze relief of 1800 by the sculptor John Flaxman, had been a stubborn fixture in the shop for years. It was too expensive for her usual customers, but Suzanne had refused to pass it on to the London dealers who wanted to take it off her hands for much less than it was worth.

'A Belgian couple,' she said. 'Real collectors. They were so happy to find it.'

'Maybe you're moving upmarket,' Brock said.

'Maybe I am. Perhaps I should be more ambitious. The trouble is I'm not knowledgeable enough when it comes to antique artworks.'

'And from what I hear, the art market is a minefield. You should talk to our expert in art fraud, Molly Fitzherbert. She'll give you the lowdown. I told her about my Schwitters and it took her no time to work out it's probably a fake.'

'Oh no.'

'Seems like it. She got me an appointment to see the Schwitters experts in Hanover on the Monday morning of our trip to Germany, but that may be a waste of time.'

'So you've had a disappointing day.'

'Worse than that,' and he told her about finding Callum McAdam's body.

'That place,' she said. 'You'll be having nightmares about the Hoo. So they were lovers, were they? How sad.'

~

Brock did dream about Callum that night, though it wasn't a nightmare. He was in the painter's studio, watching him working on a canvas, and the mood was rather sad and elegiac. At one point Callum turned to him and said, 'You see, the trouble is, you didn't ask me the right question.'

The next morning, still filled with the feelings of regret that had permeated his dream, Brock told Suzanne that she should look at taking a day off and coming up to town to talk to Molly and perhaps also the art dealer Rosa Lipmann, whom he'd met at Nadya's memorial service. She checked her diary and said the following Friday would be best and she could then stay up in London with Brock to catch the flight the next day to Bremen. Brock said he'd make arrangements.

9

Friday night, home from work, Kathy set about some neglected housework, her mind preoccupied by Ashley Osborn's failure to show up for her interview. On Monday she would have to bring matters to a head, and she was debating what exactly she should do when her door buzzer sounded. She was in the middle of cleaning her bathroom, and she hurried out, pulling off her rubber gloves to answer the intercom. A man's face she didn't recognise was looking into the viewer.

'Hello, is that DCI Kathy Kolla?'

'Yes.'

'My name's DI Matt Stone.' He held his police ID up to the camera. 'I'm from Fraud, ma'am, a colleague of DCI Brock. I apologise for calling at this hour, but I wondered if I could have a quick word with you about an urgent matter.'

This was very odd, and the only explanation Kathy could think of was that Brock had got himself into some kind of trouble that was best dealt with outside of normal channels.

'Okay, yes. Come up.'

She pulled off her apron and threw it and the gloves into a cupboard and checked herself in the mirror. There was a rap on the door and she opened it to a man of about forty, six foot, lean, dark hair, black trousers and leather jacket, a blue scarf around his neck. 'Hello. Come in.'

'Thanks.' He entered and looked around. 'Mm, great flat.' He walked over to the window. 'Spectacular view.' He stood there, taking it in, the great sweep of the river from Big Ben and the Houses of Parliament over to the right, to Pimlico and Chelsea on the left.

His manner was disconcerting and Kathy was wondering if she'd made a mistake letting him in. 'You work with Brock?' she prompted.

'Yes.' He swung around to face her. 'We're in the same office. He hasn't mentioned me?'

'I'm afraid not.'

'Oh, I'm disappointed.' He gave a little smile. 'I think he misses his time in Homicide with you. You worked pretty closely together for years, didn't you?'

'Yes, we did.'

'But I suppose you still see a fair bit of each other?'

'Not much now. The occasional lunch.'

'Ah.' His smile faded. 'This really is a beautiful flat. Makes my place look pretty pathetic.'

'Can I get you anything? I was about to have a glass of wine.'

'I'd like that very much, but, under the circumstances . . . better not.'

'What circumstances? What's happened?'

'I could have phoned you, but I thought it would be better to see you in person.'

'Is Brock in trouble?'

'Brock? No, not as far as I know. This is about you. I've come to ask you to attend an interview on Monday morning at eight at New Scotland Yard with myself and DCI Bernard Crouch.'

'Crouch?' She'd heard the name before but couldn't place him.

'DPS,' Stone said.

Directorate of Professional Standards. Now Kathy thought she understood. She mustn't be the only one investigating Ashley Osborn. Someone else must have lodged a complaint and the DPS were on to it.

'Oh, right. Yes, fine—I'll be there.'

'Good. I'll see you then.' He wandered over to the other side of the living room. 'That's some kitchen. Two bedrooms?'

'Yes.'

'How long have you been here?'

'About three years.'

He nodded as if that confirmed something. 'Well, I won't keep you any longer. See you Monday. Report to the front desk and they'll tell you where we are.'

She closed the door after him, wondering what that was all about. It was as if he'd only come in person in order to check out her flat, and she felt as if she'd been intruded upon. DPS—corruption and complaints; if they were involved, things could be getting nasty. She retrieved her gloves and apron and tried to shake off the feeling those initials always provoked, taking it out on the shower screen.

~

It didn't take Kathy long on Monday morning to discover what Inspector Stone's strange visit to her apartment had been about. She was now sitting in a tiny basement room in New Scotland Yard, trying to focus on making notes on a pad she'd been given, her own notebook having been confiscated. A young woman constable was sitting on the other side of the table, looking as uncomfortable as Kathy felt. She had been there since 7.50 am, sent down to this ridiculous bare little room where Stone and Crouch had joined her precisely at eight. They were crammed together at a small table on which the two men set up their laptops, and the overheated space soon filled with their odours—BO from Crouch and Armani from Stone.

Crouch got to the point abruptly. 'DCI Kolla, we are investigating a complaint made against you by another police officer, who claims that you have attempted to pervert the course of justice. I must caution you that you are not obliged to say anything, but it may harm your defence if you do not mention, when questioned, something which you later rely on in court. Anything you do say may be given in evidence.'

Kathy's first thought was that this was some kind of stunt, but the expression on their faces told her otherwise.

Crouch reached into an attaché case at his side and slid a document across to her.

'This is your copy of our warrant to search your office and changing room locker; your flat, garage space and car; and your locker at the Vauxhall Leisure Centre. Will you please now give me your keys to all of these places and the relevant entry codes.'

Stunned, Kathy reached into her bag for her keys and handed them over, then began to write down the entry codes on the notepad they'd supplied.

When this was done, Crouch continued, 'We also require that you empty your bag and pockets. On the table, please.'

He flicked through the contents spilled on the table, setting aside her phone, notebook and iPad before telling her to take back the rest.

So this is how it feels to be on the receiving end, she thought. She'd done it to others often enough, but she hadn't really appreciated what it felt like, this mental stripsearch, the overwhelming feelings of outrage, helplessness and guilt that came flooding in, making it hard to think clearly.

'Have you any other phones?'

'One—no, two old mobiles in a drawer in my bedroom. And the landline in my flat.'

'Computers?'

This went on for a while, until they had everything they wanted. Finally Crouch said, 'Right, we'll leave you here for a few hours with another officer. In the meantime, you are not to attempt to communicate with anyone else. We'll get back to you as soon as we can.'

The two men closed their laptops and got to their feet. Stone had said nothing, and as he turned to leave he gave Kathy a look that might have conveyed sympathy, or perhaps disappointment. The constable was brought in to supervise her.

At midday they brought her a sandwich, a mug of tea and a bottle of water. The constable escorted her to a toilet down the hall, and when they returned the constable's place was taken by another woman officer, equally young and equally bored. Kathy asked her if she could have a newspaper and magazines to read, and after a while some were brought in. At 5.20 pm Kathy was reading a highly improbable article in a scandal sheet about Meghan Markle's career playing Rachel Zane in *Suits* when the door was flung open, the constable jumped to her feet and Crouch marched in.

'Right,' he barked. 'Detective Chief Inspector Katherine Kolla, I am charging you with conspiracy and incitement under the *Criminal Law Act 1977*, section one, part one. You will be free to leave under police bail, subject to the following conditions.' He handed Kathy her keys and an unfamiliar mobile phone. 'You may use this phone and no other until further notice. You are now suspended from duty until further notice. You may return to your flat and must apply to my office for permission to travel outside a radius of one mile from that address. Your commanding officer, Commander Torrens, has been advised of the situation and will brief the members of your team in Homicide. They will be instructed not to discuss work matters with you. Do you understand?'

'Yes, but you haven't told me what I'm supposed to have done.'

'I would advise you to consult a solicitor. Constable, please escort DCI Kolla off the premises.' He turned on his heel and left.

She felt slightly light-headed as she got into a taxi. It was all very serious, of course, yet it was so stupid and melodramatic that it was really rather funny. She imagined Commander Torrens' reaction, her team's stunned whispers. Hilarious, really. It might be instructive, she thought, finding out who her real friends were. Then she thought of Brock and Bren and felt sick. No, she didn't want them to know. She hoped it would all have blown over before they heard about it.

10

Monday morning; Brock had barely settled at his desk when there was an unexpected call on his mobile. A deep voice with a strong foreign accent said, 'Chief Inspector Brock? This is Egor Orlov.'

It took Brock a moment to remember the stocky figure at Nadya's memorial service, bristling with hostility. 'Yes, Mr Orlov. What can I do for you?'

'I want to apologise to you for my unfriendly words at Nadya's funeral. I was upset, and I wish to offer you my humble apologies.'

'Thank you, Mr Orlov, but there's no need. It was a very sad day.'

'But still, to make amends I would like to offer you a meal at my restaurant, Alexandrov's in Canary Wharf, as my guest.'

'Oh, that's very kind of you, but—'

'Would you be free today? Julian told me of the new development in the case, and he gave me your number. I might be able to give you useful information.'

'I see. Well, in that case, yes, I'd like to come and see you.'

'Good. Shall we say one o'clock? Just you, okay? I will reserve a table.'

Brock ended the call, feeling as if he'd just received a summons from a character in a John le Carré novel.

~

Later that morning he took the Docklands Light Rail across East London to Canary Wharf, emerging from the station into bright sunlight among the skyscrapers surrounding Reuters Plaza. He was early for his appointment at Alexandrov's and strolled for a while around Middle Dock, enjoying the fresh chill of the day and the vision of this Venetian Manhattan, the winter sunlight sparkling off the water and the steel and glass of the towers. Though the temperature was cool, office workers crowded around the tables set out along the edge of the broad quay, sunglasses on beneath the café umbrellas, filling the air with boisterous chatter. Brock imagined Stone here, viewing these potential suspects with a malignant eye. He found a free table and sat down, ordering a coffee from a young waitress with a Central European accent. On one side of him two lads who looked too young to be out of school were debating the price of tantalite, and on the other a girl was describing last night's embarrassing date. Brock sipped his cappuccino, the sun on his face, and felt good.

At the appointed time he returned to the plaza and wove his way through the hurrying crowd to where he could see the sign for Alexandrov's, between Carluccio's and Smollensky's bar. As he stepped inside, Orlov broke off his conversation with a waiter and came bustling across.

'Chief Inspector, come in, come in. I'm honoured to have you in my modest restaurant. Let me take your coat. We will sit over here.'

He handed the coat to the waiter and showed Brock to a table in a quiet corner. 'Thank you for making time to see me.'

A waitress appeared with a tray and two tumblers of ice and a milky liquid.

'What's this?' Brock said.

'White Russian, what else?' Egor chuckled. 'But very mild, I assure you, not too much vodka.' He raised his glass. '*Za zdorovie.*'

'*Za zdorovie.*' Brock tasted the coffee liqueur and cream. 'You're busy.'

'Always busy. And you too are a busy man, sir. We should order.' He offered the menu but Brock asked for his recommendation. 'Well, you should have my borsch, perhaps. You like borsch? And then maybe the Olivier salad with chicken, or I recommend the beef shashlik.'

Brock went for the borsch and salad, and Egor continued, 'You see that girl that served our drinks? Seventeen years ago that was Nadya, fresh over from St Petersburg with a nine-year-old kid, first time out of Russia. Hard to imagine, eh? And within a year she'd captured the heart of a rich London gentleman. A fairy tale, yes? And then she falls in love with a poor fucking artist and blows it all away. Can you believe it?

It makes me so angry. But that was Nadya, a romantic. What can you do?'

'Had you ever heard of Callum McAdam?'

'Never. I had no idea. And yet, when Julian told me the news, I thought back and, yes, there was something different about Nadya recently. How shall I describe it? A glow, a sense of excitement, perhaps. Poor girl, she was in love. A tragedy. No fault of Julian's, I have to say, although . . . well, he is a very decent man, but no Don Juan, eh?'

The soup arrived, a glorious crimson colour. Brock tasted it and said it was delicious, then went on, 'I saw Nadya shortly before her death, after she received an email. Did Julian tell you about that?'

'Yes, he did.'

'It appeared to be a typical email scam demanding money, but it had a Russian URL, and that seemed to terrify her. Can you think of any reason for that?'

'Well, she had an unhappy time in Russia before she came over here.'

'Yes, but that was seventeen years ago. Why should it terrify her now?'

'Oh, you never get over something like that, I think. It was always in the back of her mind.'

'Did you have any contact with her ex-husband after she arrived in London?'

'Sergei? No, never.'

'What about Miki? It would be natural for his father to contact him for birthdays, Christmas.'

Egor shook his head. 'No, no, not a word. Nadya would have told me, I'm sure.'

'All the same, I'd like to speak to Miki. Do you have his contact details?'

Egor hesitated, then said, 'Let me check,' and got to his feet.

Brock finished his borsch, and the Olivier salad arrived together with a glass of white wine that he hadn't ordered but appreciated anyway. He'd almost finished when Egor returned.

'Sorry, sorry, I got caught up. I have spoken to Miki and he would be delighted to see you this afternoon, if you are free to go over there; he works in Hay's Mews in the West End.' He handed Brock a slip of paper with an address and phone number.

'Thank you, Egor. That was a delicious lunch. Now, you mentioned that you had some useful information for me.'

'Ah yes, well, it was just to tell you about Nadya's state of mind, her affair.'

'I see. And you have no current knowledge of her former husband, Sergei Semenov?'

'No, no. I'm sure he doesn't have anything to do with this.'

'Well, can I settle up?'

'I told you, Chief Inspector, you are my guest.'

'I'm afraid I can't accept, Egor. I might be accused of corruption.' Brock chuckled.

'Oh, well, I'll get the bill for you.'

He returned after a moment and Brock gave him his credit card. The amount seemed very modest.

As he walked back to the station he wondered what that was all about. It sounded like the family rallying around their official version of Nadya's death, maybe a little too pointedly.

He caught the train back into the city, then a taxi to Hay's Mews, a narrow lane not far from Berkeley Square once lined with stables and now with two- and three-storey townhouses. The DPF office was towards one end, detectable only by a discreet and stylish sign on its small window. Inside, an equally stylish receptionist showed Brock to a small room lined with framed prints signed by modern masters—Chagall, Matisse, Picasso. He sat at the glass table, said no to the offer of a cup of coffee and pulled out his notebook, jotting down notes of his lunch meeting.

After ten minutes the door swung open and Miki Babington came in. He sat abruptly in the chair opposite Brock, fixed Brock with an intense, rather quizzical look and thrust out his hand. 'Inspector.'

'Thanks for seeing me at short notice, Mr Babington.'

'Miki, please. You want to talk about Mum?'

'Yes, please. I'm very sorry for your loss.'

'Sure.' Miki's eyes dropped to his hands on the glass in front of him. The fingernails were bitten to the quick.

'When was the last time you saw her?'

Miki rocked his head back and stared up at the track lights overhead. 'Um ... that would have been the weekend before she died, Sunday morning. I dropped in for coffee, chatted about a few things, nothing important. Yeah ... that was the last time I saw her.' His face creased in a frown, as if this had just occurred to him.

'How did she seem?'

'Fine, great.'

'Can you remember anything in particular you talked about?'

'Oh ... Julian going to New York, where he was going to stay.'

'And where was that?'

'The Peninsula. He always stays there.' He shrugged, gave a little private smile.

'So she didn't seem different in any way from her usual self?'

'No, not at all.'

'Nothing was bothering her?'

'Nope.'

'You understand why I'm asking this. We believe it's possible that your mother took her own life.'

'Yes.' He sighed. 'But I saw her before she got that stupid email. Julian said it really spooked her. You met her that day she got it, didn't you?'

'Yes, I did, with another officer. We tried to reassure her that it was just a commonplace scam, but she was certainly upset.'

'Well, she would be, with a Russian sender.'

'Why exactly?'

Miki shot Brock a look as if he was dim. 'Mum ran away from Russia. She was twitchy about anything Russian—Putin, you know.'

'And your father.'

'My birth father, yeah.'

'Do you hear from him at all?'

'No.'

'You don't know what he's doing these days?'

'Nah.'

'He's never tried to contact you?'

Miki shook his head.

Brock said, 'But your mother left Russia a long time ago.'

'She was still scared of him. Terrified.'

'Enough to kill herself?'

'Well, that's all I can think of. Is that it?' Miki began to ease his chair back.

Brock reached inside his document case and slid a photograph across the table. 'Remember this bloke?'

Miki stared at it, saying nothing.

'Callum McAdam. He was at Camberwell with you. Remember?'

'Oh yeah, I remember.' He slid the photograph back to Brock. 'Why?'

'Callum was found hanged in his studio last Friday, not a mile from where your mother died.'

'Yeah . . .' Miki's voice was a whisper, and for a moment he looked genuinely upset, but then the mask came back down. 'Julian told me. He said they might have been having an affair.'

'What do you think?'

He shrugged. 'Could be, I suppose.'

'You had no inkling of that?'

'No.'

'How would they have met?'

'Mum met him when we were at art school. Maybe they bumped into each other again.'

'Surely she would have mentioned that to you?'

'Not necessarily. Not if they were having an affair.'

'When was the last time you were in contact with Callum?'

'Oh, years ago.' He shook his head. 'Years.'

'They both died at a place called the Hoo Peninsula in Kent, near Gravesend and Rochester. You know it?'

'No.'

'You've never been there?'

'No, never heard of it.'

'So you didn't know Callum lived there?'

'Right.'

Brock hesitated, then took out his wallet. 'Here's my card, Miki. Call me if something occurs to you, something that may have slipped your mind.'

Brock stepped out into Hay's Mews to find that it had begun to drizzle, and he went across the street to a doorway, looking up at the dark clouds and wondering how long it would last. Miki was a bad liar, and he was surprised that an outfit like DPF, which presumably depended on smooth and convincing presentation, would employ him. He had that odd air of indifference, answering Brock's questions as if Uncle Egor had told him exactly what to say.

As he waited, he saw the DPF front door open and Miki step out. He too looked up at the sky, then he turned up the collar of his black leather jacket and hurried off, head down, without noticing Brock, who began to follow at a distance as the young man headed west along Hill Street towards Park Lane.

Miki disappeared around a corner, Brock falling further behind. He saw the trees of Hyde Park up ahead but Miki had vanished. Brock ran, in front of him the roar of traffic on Park Lane and to his right the forecourt of the Dorchester hotel, but there was no sign of Miki. Chest heaving, he hurried over to the hotel entrance and went inside. He caught sight of Miki at the reception desk, and he made his way cautiously towards him, keeping in the background as Miki, clearly impatient, turned away from the desk and started pacing back and forth.

After a few minutes he straightened as a man approached from the lifts. He stepped forward and the two of them embraced briefly and started talking, Miki gesticulating urgently. Brock pulled out his phone and began to film them, studying the man. He had the appearance of a businessman, in a dark suit, of late middle age, heavily built, clean-shaven with short cropped hair. To Brock he might have been an older version of the man in the photograph that Julian Babington had given him the day they had first met. His well-groomed appearance was certainly different from the bearded, shaggy-haired image of the man in the photo, but he had the same build and belligerent look of Sergei Semenov, Miki's natural father, who supposedly had never entered the UK.

The pair had found seats now, leaning in to one another as they talked. There was no possibility that Brock could get close enough to overhear them, and he waited until finally they got to their feet. The man gave Miki a heavy thump on the shoulder and ruffled his hair, then strode away, back towards the lifts, while Miki headed for the entrance doors.

When they had both gone, Brock went over to the reception desk and explained that he was a police officer and wanted to see the registration details of the hotel guest Miki had met. The receptionist studied his police ID and looked pained.

'I'm afraid I shall need more than this, sir,' he said. 'Do you have a warrant?'

Brock leaned closer and said, 'I don't want to see his credit card details, just the name and address he gave you. If you're not sure, call the Met and ask to speak to Detective Inspector Matt Stone in Fraud. I'll give you his number.'

The receptionist raised an eyebrow. 'Fraud, you say?'

'That's right.'

'I don't think that will be necessary. That was Mr Pavel Gorshkov, from St Petersburg.'

'He's stayed here before, has he?'

'Oh yes, several times. For three weeks this time; he's due to check out tomorrow.'

Brock thanked him and left.

~

As he sat in the taxi taking him back to his office, he thought what an odd investigation this was. It might be something, it might be nothing. He had no one to report to or discuss it with, no team to dig into all the details that he was missing. He was an investigator in limbo, and it obviously couldn't go on. Sooner or later someone would pull the plug, and what would he have to show for it? He'd have liked to talk to Kathy about it, see what she thought, but she had so much on her plate, running her own homicide team, that it would feel like an imposition. He thought fondly of their cases together at Queen Anne's Gate, and his heart sank as the taxi drew in at the kerb outside the bland office building where he was currently posted.

On the way back to his desk, he passed Matt Stone, who was studying his computer screen. Beside him was a file in which Brock caught a glimpse of a photograph of a woman's face. It struck him that she resembled Kathy. As he paused to take another look, Stone noticed him and quickly closed the file. Brock continued on his way. Of course it couldn't have been Kathy, for why on earth would Stone have a file on her?

He sat down and put in a request to UK Border Force for information on Pavel Gorshkov, and soon had a response confirming that Gorshkov had entered the country three weeks previously, and not for the first time. He used a Russian passport and gave his occupation as 'businessman'. Brock asked for a complete record of their information.

11

The next morning, Brock had a call from Will Holt in Gravesend. The post–mortem on Callum had found no evidence of foul play, and his boss had told him to drop it and move on to more urgent business. Brock asked about the key to the back door of Callum's workroom, and Holt said they hadn't found it. 'But that doesn't prove anything,' he added. 'If there had been an intruder, he would have been able to leave by the front door on the other side of the studio, which has a deadlock, and pull it shut and locked on his way out.'

'What about the bicycle track on the path to where Nadya died? Was it Callum's?'

'The print was too degraded by rain to make a positive ID, Brock. I'm sorry, but that's about as much as we can say. Oh, I did get a result on the satnav in Nadya's car. It had made a number of visits to the Hoo previously. I'll send you the dates. And we have the time when the engine was switched off beside the pond—three forty-six on Tuesday morning, the thirteenth. The pathologist says that's compatible with physical evidence of time of death. Looks like a lovers' quarrel, don't you reckon, Nadya Babington and Callum McAdam?'

Brock thanked him and rang off. Suicide was the obvious conclusion, but after his run-in with Miki he was uneasy. He retrieved the timeline diagrams he'd been playing with earlier and checked 3.46 am; if Julian Babington had followed her out to the Hoo that night there would have been enough time for him to kill her, then return to London, get cleaned up and make the 8.20 am Delta flight to New York.

He sat thinking for a while, did some research on his computer and ordered a car. He drove south across the river on Vauxhall Bridge, passing Kathy's flat over to the right, and continued on to Camberwell and the College of Arts on Peckham Road. Two students were struggling up the front steps with some kind of installation as he approached, and he waited for them to manoeuvre the fragile structure through the doors and followed them in.

Inside, he found several desperate-sounding young people arguing with the woman behind an inquiries desk. When they finally moved away, he stepped forward. 'Big day, is it?'

The woman gave a rueful smile. 'Submission day. How can I help you?'

He showed her his police ID. 'I'd like to speak with someone who would remember two men who were students here eight or nine years ago.'

'I've only been here three years,' she said, 'but Terry Franks should be able to help you. I saw him pass here a little while ago.'

She gave directions, and Brock followed the corridor she'd indicated until he emerged into a large bright studio space in which students were pinning work up on the walls and arranging three-dimensional pieces on tables. At Brock's request, one of them pointed out a middle-aged man peering at an elaborate construction made of wire coat hangers. 'That's Terry.'

Brock approached a tall, lean man with a greying beard and introduced himself. 'I'm hoping you might be able to tell me about a student who was here a few years ago. A Scots lad, Callum McAdam.'

Franks frowned. 'I remember Callum all right. He's not in trouble with the police, is he?'

'I'm afraid he's dead, Mr Franks.'

'Oh no. I'm very sorry to hear that. Not suicide, was it?'

'We're not quite sure of the circumstances at present. Why do you say that?'

'Only that he was inclined to be rather intense and melancholic. Took everything very seriously. He'd already studied at Glasgow and was a bit older than the other students and much more technically accomplished. A brilliant draughtsman, but a bit of a loner, an outsider.'

'No particular friends then?'

'Don't think so.'

'There was another student here at about the same time— Miki Babington.'

'Oh yes, of course! I'd forgotten that. Oh God, Miki!'

'What about him?'

'Well, I mean they were chalk and cheese. Callum was a hard worker, a worrier and a bit of a radical, organising petitions and the like. Miki was the opposite, lazy and unreliable. But somehow they seemed to strike up a friendship.'

'Did you ever have contact with their parents?'

'Um ... I don't know anything about Callum's. Up north, I assume. The office will probably have their contact details.'

'How about Miki's family?'

'Yes, his mother used to come to all the student exhibitions, I remember. Well, you couldn't miss her—beautiful lady, very striking looks. Russian, you know. I'd have liked to have met his father, too, but I don't think he ever came. Julian Babington has a fantastic art collection. Yes, chalk and cheese. I've no idea what they saw in each other—well, purely physical, I suppose. The odd couple.'

'Mr and Mrs Babington?'

Franks shook his head. 'No, no. I'm talking about Callum and Miki.'

'Physical? You mean they were gay?'

'Well, Miki certainly was. I was never sure about Callum. I remember an end-of-year party—they had a row and Callum threw a brick at Miki.'

'A brick?'

'Yes, from somebody's installation. Missed him, fortunately. Miki had something of his mother's good looks and could be a charmer when he wanted to be, but he could also be a real pain. I'm very sorry to hear that Callum's dead. He had a rare talent ...' An idea struck him and he said, 'Look, I can show you, if you've got time.'

'Yes, please.'

'We keep one or two of the best pieces of our students' work each year, and I'm pretty sure we kept something by Callum. Follow me.'

He led Brock up a set of stairs to a storeroom filled with plan chests and racks. He checked an index in a fat record book. 'Here we are, Callum McAdam.' He took a note of a number then went to one of the plan chests. After searching through a drawer he held up a pencil drawing of a seated figure for Brock to see.

'Isn't that just amazing? People talk about being able to draw like an angel, but Callum really could. Except for the sitter's modern clothes, this could be a drawing by Ingres—it's as good as that. I'd been hoping to learn of him doing really well after he left us, but I've heard nothing. Any idea what his recent work is like?'

Brock showed him some images of Callum's black paintings in his studio and Franks looked puzzled. 'Oh, goodness. Not the Callum I remember.'

~

At home that evening, after a quick defrosted dinner, Brock went down to the small storeroom below the stairs. There, from beneath a stack of novels, he hauled out the large box containing his old police notebooks. Over the years the style of cover on the Metropolitan Police notebook had changed, but its purpose—to record events as they happened—remained the same as when they were introduced by Robert Peel at the time he founded the modern police, equipping them with notebook and pencil, truncheon and whistle, a badge and a tall hat for added presence.

Brock searched through the small books, looking for the oldest, flicking through their pages for dates and pausing from time to time as the names of long-ago witnesses, informers and suspects sparked memories of past cases. Finally he found an entry that read: *21 Grove Lane, Stepney. FOS, woman in lvg rm bleeding bad throat wound, neighbour Vera Weech ID Emily Crab.*

He remembered now: the ambulance had been sent to the wrong address and he was FOS, first on scene, and Emily was leaking her life's last blood. Her neighbour Vera, who had found her, screamed the house down while he was on the floor with Emily, his only suit getting covered in her blood as she died. He had a vivid memory of the living room, the faded furniture and carpet, an ancient radio and small TV on the sideboard, and that amazing thing hanging over the mantelpiece, completely out of place: the Schwitters Merz where there should have been a print of a Peter Scott flying duck.

It was later that day, when Vera Weech had finally calmed down, that she first raised the suspicion that Walter had done it, saying that she had heard a violent argument earlier, and not for the first time. They had found Walter at his sister's house in Hackney, but she said that he'd been there since the early morning, doing some wallpapering for her. Walter had said that he believed Emily had a lover and that it must have been him arguing with her and cutting her throat.

Brock turned the pages and came to notes from three days later, when Walter's sister had come to the old police station in Lower Clapton Road and made a formal statement confirming Walter's alibi. At the end of his entry, Brock had written *NARW*, not a reliable witness. Two weeks later he had interviewed Walter again, and it was then that they had discussed the Schwitters. He found the page, with the brief comment *(discussed German artwork)*, and that afternoon Walter had finally broken down in tears and admitted to killing Emily.

Brock poured himself a whisky and sat down, going through it all again, picturing the murder scene at 21 Grove Lane, a place where, it seemed, Schwitters had never lodged. It occurred to him that he'd assumed that Walter had inherited 21 Grove Lane from his mother, though he couldn't remember him actually saying it. Thinking about it, he decided that it was probably the ancient wireless set and the Schwitters collage that had planted the idea in his head that his mother had lived there. But what if she hadn't? What if she had lived somewhere else altogether, in Barnes for example, where Schwitters was living in 1943 when the work was done? He would have to find out.

12

Kathy stood at the window of her flat, staring out at the grey clouds moving in from the east and streetlights coming on across the river. It was astonishing how slowly time crawled along when you had nothing to do. She couldn't remember ever having been so paralysed with inactivity. That morning, long hours ago, she'd called the Police Federation and put in a request for legal assistance. They'd promised to get back to her, but she'd heard nothing more. At first she'd expected that someone from her team—Judy Birch, maybe, or Peter Sidonis—would have been in touch, but as the hours dragged on she'd tried to resign herself to the silence. Finally, she used the phone she'd been given, assuming it would be monitored, to ring Judy's number and, when that produced only silence, to call Peter. He at least did answer.

'Hi, boss.'

'Peter.' She hardly knew what to say. 'Is Judy there?'

'No, we haven't seen her. Torrens was in here yesterday and told us all that you and Judy were both suspended pending a review of a current matter. He didn't explain what it was all about, but people from headquarters came and removed a load of files and your computers. Then today . . .' He hesitated.

'What?'

'We were told that you'd both been charged with . . . with corruption.'

'That was the word they used, was it?'

'Yeah.'

'It's about that death at Titmus Street we attended—Ahmed Majeed. Judy and I were doing a background check on the PC involved, Ashley Osborn. Was her name mentioned?'

'No.'

His tone told her that he didn't want to know any more. Corruption was like a disease; the very word made people back away to avoid contagion.

'Okay, Peter, thanks. Bye.'

'Cheers, boss.' The line went dead.

She put on a coat, left the phone she'd been given on the kitchen bench and went down to the river walk. For a while she stood staring at the dark current of the Thames, then she turned and made her way under the rail viaduct to get cash from an ATM before continuing on to the Vauxhall Leisure Centre. She opened her locker and saw that it had been turned over all right, her gear stuffed back in untidily. She straightened it and sat down and waited, watching the people come and go. After almost two hours a young woman came in and gave Kathy a wave. Kathy went over to her and said, 'How's it going, Phoebe?'

'Not bad. You?'

'Are you still selling Blackphones?'

Phoebe blinked. 'How did you know that?'

'I need a couple.'

Phoebe quoted an excessive price, but Kathy didn't argue. She stood waiting while the girl opened her locker, drew out two phones and handed them over.

Kathy thanked her and set off for the tube station and a train to North London.

~

The house was in darkness and the doorbell echoed inside without response, so she dropped one of the phones through the letterbox and turned back for home. She was in the tube when the phone in her pocket started ringing. She got up and went to a quiet corner of the carriage then answered it. 'Hello, Judy. Go out into the garden.'

She heard a shuffle, a door unlocked, and then, 'Is that you, boss?' Judy's voice sounded faint and anxious.

'Yes. You alone?'

'Yes. They told me not to contact you.'

'Me too, but they can't intercept that phone. They may have bugged our houses.' She thought how paranoid that sounded. 'You okay?'

'They charged me with conspiracy and incitement.'

'Me too.'

'I don't understand. How can this have happened?'

'Ashley Osborn,' Kathy said, and heard Judy groan.

'How could she do that?'

'I've no idea, but whatever stunt she's pulled won't stand up to examination for long. We just have to keep our nerve. Are you getting a lawyer?'

'Yes, I contacted the PFEW for legal assistance, but I haven't heard anything yet. What can I do?'

'I want you to write down in as much detail as possible everything you discovered when you looked into her past history—every name, date, event.'

'Good, it'll give me something to do.'

'I'll pick it up on Friday after dark, okay?'

'Okay.'

For a while the buzz of doing something made Kathy feel a bit better, but then the bleak sense of isolation settled on her again. She knew she'd have to fight it.

~

Kathy's first session with her solicitor on Wednesday morning did not go well. She had met him in his office, a small room in which every surface was covered with chaotic heaps of files and books. Rory Buchanan appeared overworked and overwhelmed. He seemed to have made no preparation for her appointment, and she had to give him her own pen for him to make notes. He told her several times how busy the Police Federation solicitors were, as if she should be grateful for whatever small assistance he could spare her.

Finally she said, 'Maybe if you've got too much on I should get a private solicitor.'

He peered at her over the top of his glasses. (Hadn't he heard of multifocal? Kathy thought.) 'Well, that's entirely up to you, of course. Perhaps I've given the wrong impression. We are a bit snowed under at the moment, but you will have my full attention, I can promise you that. And sometimes it's helpful to have someone who's in touch with what's going on inside the service. I have already heard something of your case. There are three officers involved, is that right?'

'Possibly. I believe that DS Judy Birch from my team in Homicide is, and the third might be a PC Ashley Osborn, whom we were investigating.'

'Have you been in touch with either of them since you were suspended?'

'No.'

Buchanan asked her to spell the names and scribbled them down on his pad. 'And why were you investigating PC Osborn?'

Kathy told him about the death of Ahmed Majeed and her suspicion that Osborn had interfered with the crime scene in order to protect Majeed's wife. She didn't mention anything about Osborn's previous history.

'And Birch was assisting you in this investigation?'

'Yes, under my direction.'

'Mm, conspiracy and incitement,' he mused. 'Any idea what that's about?'

'No, none at all. I can only imagine that Osborn is trying to smear us. But I'm just speculating. When I asked, they refused to tell me exactly what I'm supposed to have done. All I know for sure is that I've been charged with conspiracy and incitement under the *Criminal Law Act 1977*, section one, part one.'

'Yes, that's what I've been advised. That was detectives . . .' He flicked through pages of his file.

'Stone from Fraud and Crouch from Professional Standards.'

'Ah yes. Fraud . . .' He scratched his head, puzzled. 'What might that be?'

'I don't know.' It's what had been bothering Kathy. What possible connection did her investigation of Osborn have with *fraud*?

After her frustrating meeting with Buchanan, her mind kept returning to that question, and to the strange coincidence that DI Stone worked with Brock. How had he described himself? A *colleague* of Brock. Why had he brought it up in the first place? Had Brock said something, inadvertently perhaps, that had sparked this? Or was it spite? Some kind of office feud? Was Stone punishing her in order to get at Brock? She remembered how Brock had described his awkward position in Fraud, outranking his team leader Stone. Did Stone resent that? She would have loved to ask Brock himself, but again she baulked at letting him know that she was in trouble. Apart from her humiliation, she could imagine how he might react, attacking Stone, raising hell, and where would that lead? To Brock being kicked out, perhaps, and herself a pariah.

~

Two days later she was called to an interview with Stone and Crouch. As they waited for it to begin, Buchanan briefed her. 'You don't need to speak. Let's just see what they have to say.' Didn't he realise how many such interviews she had conducted herself over the past twenty-odd years?

Finally, a constable took them through to the interview room, and she sat facing the two detectives, Buchanan at her side, fussing with his papers.

'Chief Inspector Kolla, we want to talk about an investigation that you have been conducting into the death of Ahmed Majeed on the twelfth of October of this year.'

As usual, Crouch was the speaker. And how appropriate his name was; he was crouching forward on the other side of the table like a predatory animal, a raptor, studying its prey.

He went on, 'Have you now completed your inquiries in connection with that investigation?'

'No.'

'Why not?'

'There were certain features in the crime scene that didn't correspond to Mrs Majeed's account.'

'What were they?'

'Majeed's throat was cut, and the blood spatter pattern indicated that someone else had been in the room at the time when it happened. Also, the pathologist was of the opinion that the throat was cut from left to right, as a right-handed man would do it. But Ahmed was left-handed, whereas both his wife and the attending police officer, PC Osborn, the only other people who had been in the room, were right-handed.'

'And did you query these results with the crime scene analyst and the pathologist?'

'I did.'

'And didn't they concede that their concerns were not sufficient to contradict Mrs Majeed's account?'

'Yes, but I wanted to be sure.'

'So what did you do?'

'I interviewed Mrs Majeed again.'

'Yes, on November the thirteenth and PC Osborn again on the nineteenth. During the latter interview you accused Osborn of a criminal act to protect Mrs Majeed, didn't you?'

'Yes.'

'And on the following day PC Osborn reported sick with gastroenteritis. In fact, she's now admitted that she was suffering from extreme anxiety and fear as a result of your threats.'

'If you've watched the recording of that interview, you'll have seen that my questioning was not excessive, and certainly milder than what she would face in a courtroom. I considered it important to try to establish the truth.'

'What did you do immediately after that interview?'

'I spoke to DS Birch and told her to escort Osborn out of the building.'

'And what did you tell Birch to say to Osborn?'

'Nothing.'

'Really?' Crouch stared hard at her, and Kathy, puzzled, stayed silent.

'Fortunately, we also have a visual recording of that . . .'

He pressed a remote and the screen on the side wall came alive. A security camera, Kathy guessed, covering the rear entrance to their building. Judy appeared and, turning to Osborn, who'd followed her out into the yard, began talking to her. There was no sound, and Judy had her back to the camera, so that it would have been impossible to read her lips, but it was obvious that she was talking in an insistent, even aggressive way, leaning forward towards the other woman and gesticulating with her hands.

'What is she saying?' Crouch demanded.

'I've no idea.'

Crouch clicked the remote again, freezing the image as Judy took a piece of paper from her pocket and gave it to Osborn.

'And what is that?'

Kathy shook her head, wondering what on earth Judy was up to. 'I don't know.'

'Well, we do.'

Another image came up, a crumpled piece of paper on which two strings of digits were written.

'Do you recognise these numbers?'

Kathy had stopped breathing. 'The top line is my mobile phone number.'

'Yes. And the other?'

It was a long string of mixed numbers and letters.

'I haven't the faintest idea.'

Crouch gave a little smile and eased back in his chair. 'Really? That piece of paper has been analysed and found to bear the DNA and fingerprints of both Birch and Osborn. Birch has admitted that the handwriting is hers and that she gave it to Osborn. That second line of digits is the number of a bitcoin account. Osborn says that Birch offered, on your behalf, to clear her of any fault in the Majeed case provided she deposited the sum of twenty thousand pounds into that account. Otherwise you would make sure that she was tried and found guilty of Majeed's murder.'

Kathy stared at him, then at Stone, who lowered his head and studied his notepad.

'Do you have anything to say?' Crouch barked.

Kathy's solicitor said quickly, 'I need time to confer with my client.'

'By all means. I am now terminating this interview. In view of the seriousness of the offence I am revoking her present police bail. She will be taken into custody after you have finished *conferring.*'

'*No!*' Kathy's voice stopped Crouch as he gathered up his papers. 'This is a complete fabrication. I had genuine grounds for doubt about the circumstances of Ahmed Majeed's death, but I didn't put undue pressure on PC Osborn. I believe that this accusation of hers is a desperate attempt to block my investigation. Clearly she has something to hide. Sir, I have over twenty years as a homicide detective in the Metropolitan Police and have never had any doubts cast on my integrity. I demand that I be allowed to remain free to defend myself.'

Crouch looked stunned for a moment, then quickly recovered. 'Very well, I shall postpone revoking your bail for the time being. Meanwhile, you will not attempt to make contact with either DS Birch or PC Osborn.'

When they had gone, Kathy's solicitor shook his head. 'I'm not sure that was wise.'

She turned on him. 'I shouldn't have needed to do it, Rory. You've got to bloody stand up for me. Now I need you to find out everything you can about Osborn's accusations and what Judy Birch had to say about this.'

The solicitor shook his head. 'I fear that will be difficult, Kathy. They seem to be keeping a very tight lid on this. I wasn't going to mention it, but I've heard a whisper that they're putting a lot of manpower on to it. I'm afraid that they intend to make an example of you. What I don't understand is why they're so confident. Is there anything I should know?'

'What do you mean? Like what?'

'Is there any . . . dirty laundry they may have dug up about you?'

'No. Absolutely not.'

~

Kathy returned to her flat, poured herself a stiff vodka tonic and sat brooding. Buchanan was hopeless and she was friendless. It was a novel feeling, being utterly alone. She'd always been happy with her own company, never craved constant companionship, but this was different—to be utterly isolated, cut off, an outcast. She'd never really appreciated what that might be like.

When her glass was empty she made to pour another, then stopped. She could feel a sickening self-pity seeping through her. She put on a coat, picked up her keys and headed for the door; she needed fresh air.

Down on the riverbank she stood staring at the flickering reflections on the water. She was suddenly overwhelmed by a thought that up till now she had resisted—that her career, her reputation, her life were crumbling in front of her eyes. She wondered at what point someone in her situation would opt for the dark water.

'Not yet,' she whispered. 'Not by a long chalk.'

She stepped back into a shadowed corner where she couldn't be observed, took out the Blackphone and called Judy.

It took a long time for the other woman to answer, and when she did she was panting. 'Hello?'

'Judy, I need to talk to you.'

'Yes, okay. They've told me not to speak to you, but it doesn't matter. Where shall we meet?'

'Go for a walk. When you're certain you're not being followed, make your way to the King's Head in Larwood Street. You know it?'

'Yes.'

'I'll be there in an hour.'

~

Kathy was sitting in the snug bar at the back, tucked into a dim corner with two glasses of wine on the table, when Judy arrived.

Kathy smiled at her. 'Hi, Judy, how are you doing?'

Judy sighed. 'Bloody awful. Did they show you the film of me and Osborn at the back of the station?'

'Yes.'

'I'm sorry, boss. I'm so sorry. I thought I could get a quick result.'

'How exactly?'

'I told her that I really identified with her record on violence against women, and explained what happened to my mum. Then I said we knew she'd tampered with the Majeed scene to protect Haniya, and if she came clean with us on that, you might drop our investigations into other cases she was involved with in the past.'

'Oh, Judy.'

'I know, it was a stupid thing to do, but she seemed to go along with it. I gave her a note with your phone number and told her to contact you and she said she would. So I was devastated when Crouch showed me the film and told me that Osborn had said we'd tried to blackmail her. He showed me a photograph of the note I'd given her and it had a line of code added to the number I wrote down.'

'You told Crouch that?'

'Yes.'

'What else did you tell him?'

'I said you'd asked me to get background on her earlier career because you thought she might have bent the rules before.'

'Those were the words you used, "bent the rules"? Not that she might have killed anyone?'

'That's right; that's all I told him. To tell you the truth, I was beginning to think that it seemed pretty far-fetched, the stuff we were imagining her doing. I mean, really bizarre.' She reached under her coat and pulled out an envelope which she handed to Kathy. 'Here are my notes of everything I can remember of the investigation I did for you, and also notes of my interviews with Crouch and the other bloke.'

'How many times has he seen you?'

'Twice.'

'Have you got a lawyer?'

'Yes. She ... she's advising me to say that I just did as you told me, nothing else, and I didn't know what you were thinking or planning.'

'But I didn't tell you to approach Osborn.'

'No, and I've told them that was entirely my idea.'

Kathy reached out and gripped her hand. 'I know how hard this is, Judy, but we'll get through it. Now we know just what she's capable of. She wouldn't be trying to frame us like this if she didn't have something very nasty to hide, and we're going to find out what it is.'

'But how?'

'I have friends in the force, good people. They won't let this happen to us.'

'Really?'

Kathy saw the desperate hope in the younger woman's eyes and forced confidence into her voice. 'Yes, really. We just have to stick to the truth.'

'Okay, good, yes.'

~

Kathy read Judy's notes on the tube on the way home. They included a number of sources for her information, mostly newspaper reports, and the names that she'd been able to identify of people involved in the events. It was all circumstantial, of course, but Ashley Osborn's attempt to discredit them now threw it into a harsher light.

13

That same Friday Suzanne came up to town, where Brock was waiting for her at Victoria as her train pulled in. They had decided to begin with a visit to the Lipmann Gallery in Cork Street, where Brock had made the appointment with Rosa Lipmann, and in the taxi he explained how he hoped that they could both benefit from their visit. 'Rosa thinks I'm a collector and potential customer. She doesn't know I'm with the police, so we'll keep it that way. I really just want some background—family history, gossip, you know—about the Babingtons. But the important thing is that she has a wealth of knowledge about the art market that could help you. I explained about your interest in historical art for your shop.'

'*Shop* sounds rather downmarket, doesn't it?' Suzanne said.

'I bet she doesn't think of herself as a *shop*keeper. Maybe we should call it my antiques *gallery*.'

The cab pulled into the kerb and they got out opposite Lipmann's, the name in gold letters against the black frame of the window giving an immediate impression of established quality and respectability. Brock could sense Suzanne taking mental notes. There was just one large painting in the window, a voluptuous still life of fruit and flowers in a simple gold frame. They went inside and introduced themselves to a young woman sitting at a table, who murmured into her phone. 'Rosa will be right down,' she said, and they took a copy of a catalogue and began to examine the works on display.

Rosa appeared and led them upstairs to her office, a small space crowded with paintings stacked against the walls. She was dressed entirely in black, her grey hair tied back in a bun, and Brock had an impression of wiry toughness.

'I'm so glad you came to see me, Mr Brock,' she said as they sat. 'Or should I say Detective Chief Inspector Brock,' she added with a little smile. 'I didn't realise until Julian told me that you were a police officer. He said how supportive you've been.'

'Ah . . .' Brock saw Suzanne suppress a smile. 'Well, it's a very tragic case.'

'Yes indeed. Are you investigating Nadya's death?'

'The coroner has decided it was suicide.'

Rosa looked at Brock, clearly aware of his evasion. 'Poor Julian,' she said. 'And Miki too, of course. He was obviously overwrought at the service.'

'But I'm not here in a professional capacity,' Brock said. 'I am very much interested in visual art, as is Suzanne.'

'Yes, tell me more about your business, Suzanne. In Battle, David said?'

They talked for a while about Suzanne's 'gallery' and the Flaxman bronze, and the kinds of prints and small artworks that she thought she might sell. Rosa offered suggestions, giving her the names of specialist London dealers she might source work from.

'Tell them I've sent you, Suzanne,' she said, 'and they'll give you a good deal.' She turned to Brock. 'But you're more interested in twentieth-century work, David? Schwitters?'

Brock, who had done a bit of homework in preparation, said, 'Yes, Schwitters certainly, but also all of the Weimar artists—Grosz, Dix, Beckmann and so on. A fascinating period.'

'Indeed, and in preparation for your visit I looked out this . . .' She got to her feet and disappeared through a door into a storeroom, returning with a small lump of bronze which she placed carefully on the table in front of him. 'Do you know what it is?'

Brock hadn't the faintest idea, and from the sharp glint in Rosa's eye he sensed that this was a test. He was saved by the girl from downstairs appearing with a tray of coffee cups. When these had been distributed, Suzanne said, 'It's not Käthe Kollwitz, is it?'

Rosa turned to her in surprise. 'It is indeed! A preliminary study for her *Mother with Children*.'

'Yes, I thought so. Didn't you, David?'

'Well, yes, I did wonder,' Brock murmured. '*Mother with Children*, of course.'

'I'm afraid I can't sell it to you,' Rosa said. 'It's the only thing I've got left of the artworks my father and mother managed to bring with them when they fled from Vienna in 1938. They lost the rest when the gallery they opened here was hit by a bomb in 1940.' She was talking to Suzanne with a new respect.

'Oh dear,' Suzanne responded. 'Were they hurt?'

'No, they were down at Schmidt's delicatessen in Charlotte Street at the time, haggling over the price of sausage.'

They both laughed while Brock kept quiet in the background.

'I suppose their story is not unlike Nadya Babington's, fleeing to London to escape an impossible situation,' Suzanne said.

'Well, in that respect perhaps, but Noam and Avigail Lipmann had to work their way up from nothing to make a success of it here, while Nadya was rescued by a rich man.'

Brock caught the veiled note of disparagement, as did Suzanne, who said, 'I suppose Julian spoiled her terribly.'

'Oh goodness, yes. She was very pretty, of course, and took it all for granted.'

'She was lucky. And he looked after Miki, too, didn't he?'

'He tried to, but that boy is a law unto himself.'

'Does Miki have a girlfriend?'

'Hardly.' Suzanne arched an eyebrow.

'Oh, I see. A boyfriend then?'

'No doubt many. I wouldn't know.' She waved a hand, dismissing the subject.

'But, Rosa,' Suzanne said, 'why on earth did Nadya do it?'

'I honestly have no idea. Unless there was something going on that we know nothing about.' Another arched eyebrow and then a shrug. 'Anyway, life must go on. And you, David, are you looking for Weimar art at the moment? Or perhaps thinking of selling your Schwitters?'

'Possibly, but I need to do a bit more work on its provenance first.'

'Ah yes, very important. Perhaps I can help you.'

Suzanne said, 'We're going to Hanover this weekend to do some research.'

'Ah, the Sprengel Museum? Excellent. You must let me know how you get on.'

Brock checked his watch and said they would have to go.

'But you must come and see me again, David—and you, Suzanne. Let me know how your researches in Hanover turn out. I'd certainly be interested in selling your Schwitters for you.'

As they made off down Cork Street, Brock said, 'Käthe Kollwitz? That was bloody impressive, Suzanne. You won her over. I didn't realise you were so knowledgeable.'

Suzanne said nothing for a while. Then, as they reached the Burlington Arcade at the end of the street, she said, 'When she plonked it down on the table the label fell onto the floor at my feet.'

Brock roared with laughter.

~

Molly was waiting for them at the entrance to the Royal Academy. Brock introduced her to Suzanne and the two women hit it off immediately. It turned out that they had both done courses at the Courtauld Institute and could share stories about some of the characters there, including a man with whom Molly had had a disastrous affair. By the time they reached the Senate Room restaurant for lunch, they had exchanged the key facts from their respective histories.

'And what did you make of Rosa Lipmann?' Molly asked.

'Formidable,' Suzanne replied. 'How old is she?'

'Nobody knows. I'd guess early seventies.'

'And is she married?'

'Her husband died some time ago.'

'Only I wondered if she was carrying a torch for Julian Babington.'

'Really?' Brock interrupted.

'Yes. She certainly had no time for Nadya and Miki.'

They ordered salads and a bottle of prosecco and Molly told them that she had uncovered some information about Pavel Gorshkov. 'He's a director in an outfit in New York called I.I. International. The initials stand for the Russian words *izobrazitel'noye iskusstvo*. Bit of a mouthful. It means "fine art", and the parent company is an art dealership in Moscow.'

'So he's in the art business too!' Suzanne exclaimed.

'Yes,' Molly said. 'And it seems they have some tie-up with DPF where Miki works, so that would explain why Miki was going to meet him at the Dorchester.'

'There's another possible reason for that,' Brock said. 'It seemed to me that Gorshkov resembled an older version of the image of Miki's father that I've seen. It was only a suspicion, but if it was him it would put a whole new complexion on things.'

They discussed the possibilities, and Molly said she would try to find out more about Gorshkov's background from

New York. After lunch she took them up to the room that was to become the Babington Gallery and described to Suzanne all the treasures that would be accessible to the public for the first time.

Brock said little, thinking of the two bodies in the Hoo.

~

On Saturday morning the Ryanair flight took off from Stansted in grey drizzle and landed in Bremen in bright sunshine. A taxi took Brock and Suzanne into the old town, where they'd booked a room, and after dropping off their bags they set out to explore the Altstadt, getting lunch in the vaulted basement of the old Ratskeller. Suzanne confined herself to the Keller-snack and a glass of riesling, but Brock went straight for the bratwurst and *Kartoffeln*, as he always did when he set foot in Germany, washed down with a tall glass of beer. It was enough to make him forget London and the Hoo for a while and take him back to younger days, wandering in Europe.

In the afternoon Miranda came to their hotel with her hosts in Bremen, Mr and Mrs Katzenschläger and their daughter Hanna, and they all went to the Katzenschlägers' home in the suburbs. Miranda's German hadn't improved as much as they'd hoped, mainly because Hanna insisted on prac-tising her English on her, but the two girls were good friends and they all had a pleasant evening together. Miranda seemed more grown up, Brock thought, more confident, and with a cunning sense of humour that he hadn't seen before. At one point she said something in German to the Katzenschlägers and Brock caught the words '*mein Opa*', my grandpa. She gave

Brock a little grin and he smiled back, delighted with the new title.

On the Monday morning, he left Suzanne in Bremen while he caught the train down to Hanover, his *Merz 598a* packed carefully in his bag.

He took a taxi from Hanover station to the long grey concrete rectangles of the Sprengel Museum standing alongside an artificial lake, the Maschsee, arriving early for his appointment. Leaving his bag and coat in the cloakroom, he set out to explore the museum galleries, and in particular the collection of Schwitters' work. After nursing his small piece for so long, he found the range and diversity of the collection a revelation, and especially the reconstruction of the extraordinary Merzbau, an expressionist grotto Schwitters had built in his apartment in Hanover. Brock was immersed in it when he realised it was time for his appointment.

After retrieving his bag, he went to the information desk and asked for the director. He was given a form to fill in, his passport and police ID were checked, and his bag was inspected. A short while later, Dr Stark appeared and welcomed him warmly, then led him through a labyrinth of corridors to the archive office. Like Molly Fitzherbert, she was intrigued by his account of his first murder case, and watched in anticipation as he removed the wrapping around his Merz and set it down in front of her.

He waited as she stared at it and said, 'No, I have never seen this before,' then began to study it carefully, examining the elements of the collage, the signature and title before turning it over to examine the back. Finally she said, 'If this is a fake it is a very good one. We know of many collages

from this period of his life, but very few with the title "Merz".
It would be wonderful to discover another, but we have to be
sure. He changed the style of his signature during the course
of his life, but this looks correct for that period. Have you had
any tests done on the materials?'

He told her no, and explained the problematic discrepancy
between Walter Crab residing in Stepney and Schwitters in
Barnes. She thought about that, then turned to her computer.
'The three volumes of the published catalogue raisonné of
Schwitters' work provide the definitive list, of course, but
we are always gaining new information, and we have a
complex and extremely detailed database, including the
London years. Let's take a look ...' She consulted her screen.
'This work is dated 1943 ...Yes, here is the reference to thirty-
nine Westmoreland Road in Barnes, where he moved in
August 1942 with his son Ernst, also with Ernst's friend Gert
Strindberg, a great-nephew of the playwright. What other
names ...? Ah, here we are, the name of the owner of number
thirty-nine ...'

Brock held his breath.

'... was a Mr Henry Rouse. Not Crab, I'm afraid.'

'Oh.' Brock frowned and made notes of the names and
dates.'Would it be possible to have a printout of that section?'

'Of course. I'm sorry, because I really do think the composition, the balance of tones, the whole *feel* of your Merz seem
very authentic.'

'Well, thank you for your help.' He thought of Babington's
Merz and wondered if the Sprengel had been involved in its
authentication. 'You obviously know the Merz works very

well,' he said, 'and I wonder if I could ask if you recognise another one I encountered recently.'

He brought up on his iPad the image of Julian Babington's Merz that he'd taken when he visited his house and showed it to her.

'Oh yes, I do recognise this one. It came up quite recently. It's from 1927, I think? Let's see . . .' She searched her computer again. 'Here we are.'

She turned the screen to show Brock an image.

'Ah, so it is genuine.'

'Oh, most certainly. We were asked to record the change of ownership last year.'

'To Julian Babington.'

'Let me see . . . No, *from* Julian Babington, not *to* him. Mr Babington sold it to an American, Mr James Beckenbauer of Palm Beach in Florida, in April of last year. We know Mr Beckenbauer, of course—one of the most important collectors of Schwitters' work.'

Brock was stunned. He asked Dr Stark to check again and she showed him the record on her screen.

'I see . . . Might I have a copy of that too?'

'You have an interest in this work?'

'Yes. Julian Babington is an acquaintance of mine. I'm sure he will appreciate seeing the documentation.'

'Oh, he will already have it, but I'll certainly make a copy for you. Chief Inspector, before you go . . .' She looked somewhat embarrassed and Brock wondered what was wrong. 'Merz collages are exceptionally fragile—discarded scraps glued on with anything that came to hand, often just flour and water.' She stared at the newspaper in which Brock had wrapped *Merz 598a*. 'Will you permit me to ask a member of my staff to wrap it for you to take home?'

'What a good idea. I'd be most grateful.'

~

On the train back to Bremen, Brock studied the pages that Dr Stark had copied for him relating to the sale of Babington's Schwitters, struggling to come to terms with what he'd just learned. It had been a chance impulse that had led him to show her its image, and the effect had been like opening a trapdoor beneath his feet. He thought back to that evening in Babington's house after Nadya's memorial service, and tried to recall exactly that moment when they had stopped in the hallway of the house to look at the Merz. What had Babington said? *Yes, that fellow really knew what he was doing. I'm very attached to this one.* Those were his words, as exactly as Brock could remember them. He had gone to the house in Montagu Square hoping for some enlightenment and been disappointed when it didn't eventuate; but here, surely, it was. Either Babington had misled Brock, or else had been completely ignorant that they were staring at a fake, or else he had deliberately sold a copy to the American collector.

When he got back to Bremen he called Suzanne, packed his bag and caught the next available flight back to London.

~

Brock and Molly rose to their feet as Matt Stone came into the room with Superintendent George Abidi. After flying back to London, Brock had discussed what he'd discovered with Molly, and together they had spoken to Stone. For some reason that Brock couldn't fathom, Stone had seemed oddly uncomfortable talking to them, and instead of making a decision himself had set up this meeting with his boss, the head of their section.

Abidi greeted them warmly, shaking hands and waving them to sit. 'So you've got something juicy for us, have you, Molly?'

'I believe we have, sir. But Brock's done all the ground-work on this one and he should be the one to tell you.'

'Excellent. Fire away, Brock.'

'Sir, I believe we may have discovered a fraud involving one of the most important private collections of modern art in the UK. This fraud may involve two suspicious deaths and may also implicate a Russian criminal who, unknown to Border Force, has been a regular visitor to this country under an assumed name.'

Brock began with the Babington Collection, bringing up images of some of its items.

'Molly has identified twenty-three major twentieth-century works in the collection, worth millions of pounds, although we know there are more. They belong to this man, Julian Babington, a well-respected corporate lawyer with offices here and in New York, and were collected by his father Derek Babington, now deceased. The president of the Royal Academy recently announced that Babington is going to donate the whole collection to the RA, which has set aside a room to be known as the Babington Gallery. In other words, this is a high-profile collection of great public significance.

'Now, we've just discovered that at least one work in the collection appears to have been the subject of a forgery. In itself, this would merit an investigation, but there are even more sinister possibilities. Julian Babington's wife Nadya was recently found dead in the marshlands of the Hoo Peninsula in Kent, an apparent suicide.'

Brock went on to talk about the possibility of Russian involvement, then paused for questions, and Abidi, looking worried, immediately began asking about Gorshkov's criminal connections, about the involvement of Kent Police and about possible future lines of inquiry.

Molly replied, 'Sir, at this stage we haven't raised the subject of forgery with Julian Babington, and we feel we should keep that to ourselves until we've made further inquiries. The suspected forgery has been sold to an American collector, a Mr James Beckenbauer from Florida. Pavel Gorshkov also has links to a fine art dealer in New York, and we think it highly likely that there is an American angle to this. I have made preliminary contact with our colleagues in the FBI's Art Crime Team, and they are very interested. Before we go any further, I would suggest that DCI Brock and I go over to the US to find out what we can from Mr Beckenbauer and to liaise with the FBI.'

Abidi nodded. 'Yes, absolutely. As soon as possible. We don't want this blowing up in our faces, eh, Matt?'

Brock noted that Stone had seemed startled at first by Molly's suggestion, but his face immediately cleared and he agreed enthusiastically, almost as if he couldn't wait to get rid of them.

'Well,' Molly said when they'd gone, 'that went well. I'll

book our flights to the States, shall I?' She rubbed her hands with glee. 'I love Miami. And Art Basel's on.'

Brock was heading back to his desk when he got a call from Bren, wanting to arrange their next lunch date.

'I've got to go overseas on a case we're working on, Bren, and I'm not sure when I'll be back.'

'Somewhere nice?'

'The US—Miami first.'

'Lucky bastard. Perfect place at this time of year.'

'I'll try to suffer it gracefully. Apologies to Kathy.'

'Have you heard from her lately? I've been having trouble getting through to her. Her people just say she's out of the office but don't know where, and she's not answering her phone or texts.'

'Maybe something hush-hush?'

'Maybe, but you'd think she'd answer her bloody phone.'

'When I get back we'll have our lunch, Bren.'

'Sure. Have fun.'

~

Twenty-four hours later, Brock was gazing out of the window as the plane banked over the Florida coast. Below him he saw the stripe of pale yellow sand stretching away into the hazy distance, like a dam wall holding back the mass of towers pressing towards the dark blue of the Atlantic. On his knee was one of the books that Molly had given him to study on the flight from Heathrow, a memoir of the FBI's Art Crime Team written by its founder, Robert K. Wittman. It was fascinating reading, but it had brought home to him how ignorant he was, an amateur in a world of cutthroat professionals.

Once clear of immigration and customs, they caught a taxi to the hotel Molly had booked on Collins Avenue, South Beach. After the winter skies over London, the light here was dazzling, the temperature hot. The hotel claimed ocean views, though they were a block away from the beach, and it was true that from Molly's room it was possible, by hanging out of the window, to catch a distant glimpse of sand, though Brock wasn't so lucky. After a shower and a change into lighter and looser clothes, as Molly had advised, they headed out into South Beach. She obviously knew the place well, taking him to see the Art Deco buildings overlooking the ocean, before strolling back to the bars and restaurants on the palm tree-lined promenade of Lincoln Road. Molly chose a bar that boasted three hundred types of tequila. This was a different Molly from the one Brock knew in London—with stylish clothes, her hair loose and wearing sunglasses, she looked startlingly younger than that studious, mole-like creature in her office cave. He was amused and slightly disconcerted by the transformation.

As they sat watching the young crowd drifting by, she sipped her drink and sighed. 'I could live here, I really could. I'd become a different person, more laidback. Why don't we just stay here, Brock? Run away together. Don't look so worried. Are you and Suzanne married? You're not on Facebook or Instagram, are you? I tried to hack into your personnel file without success.'

'No, we're not married, but we're happy together the way things are.'

'Oh dear, what a shame.'

'I'm flattered, Molly, but you need someone younger. Someone like those two.' He pointed to a couple of young Latino men who flashed their perfect white teeth at her.

She laughed. 'The sun's going down. We should finish these and go on.'

They walked further along the boulevard to the Lincoln Road Garage, and up to Juvia, its rooftop bar and restaurant with views out over the city, where they were lucky to get a table. It was only six, but it was eleven in London and it had been a long day. Molly ordered cocktails and asked for menus.

Brock said, 'Well, I didn't manage to break into your file either, so why don't you tell me how you got into this life.'

She'd desperately wanted to be an artist, Molly said, and went to art college, but gradually came to realise that she wasn't as talented as she'd thought. At the same time, she became fascinated by art history, and when she finished her degree she moved to the Courtauld Institute and did postgraduate courses in the history of art and in conservation. One of her tutors had her own business as a conservator and offered her a job. It was at the time that a team from the Courtauld discovered that *The Procuress*, a seventeenth-century masterpiece in their own collection, was in fact a modern forgery by Han van Meegeren.

'It was so exciting to watch them at work, uncovering the awful truth,' Molly said. 'I was absolutely riveted, and knew I'd found my way forward. After that I worked in a private forensic lab authenticating artworks, mostly paintings, and after a couple of years I saw an advert for a job in art fraud at the Met, and applied. I've had some interesting cases, but this one is tops. I mean, I knew about the Babington Collection, but then the tragic deaths of Nadya and Callum ... Do you think they could have been murdered?'

'I'm trying to keep an open mind.'

'Well, if they were, the obvious suspect is Babington, isn't it? The cuckolded husband, the guilty lovers.'

'I really can't see Babington killing his wife just for having an affair. There would have to have been something else. But it's possible. At first it looked as if he was on a plane to New York when it happened, but now that alibi is looking shaky.'

'Or maybe he hired someone,' Molly said. 'Pavel Gorshkov, perhaps! If he really is Sergei Semenov, then it would be a case of Nadya's two jilted husbands getting together to exact their revenge. And Babington pays Gorshkov with a fake Schwitters, which Gorshkov then sells on to the Beckenbauers, using Babington's provenance documentation.'

Brock thought about that. It seemed bizarre and unlikely, but this was all foreign territory to him. He realised what an innocent he'd been all these years, treasuring his little Schwitters.

14

By the time she was called to another interview on Wednesday, Kathy was quietly confident that its purpose was to let her off the hook with the minimum of apologies and fuss. She was in for a nasty shock.

The beginning was encouraging enough—Crouch actually smiled at her as he took his seat. True, it wasn't a very nice smile, as if his facial muscles were unfamiliar with the expression, and Stone by his side looked as stony as ever.

'DCI Kolla,' Crouch began. 'Kathy ... shall we call you that?'

'If you like, Bernard.'

'Well now, Kathy, you've had a chance to think over what we spoke about at our last interview. Is there anything you'd like to change in your statement?'

'No.'

'Really? You still deny knowledge of that bitcoin account?'

'Yes.'

'Come on,' he said, in a rather gruesome attempt at playfulness, 'what's the password?'

'I've no idea.'

'What about the'—he consulted his notes—'the twelve-word wallet recovery phrase?'

'I don't know.'

'Does anyone else have access to the computer in your flat?'

'No.'

'Well, that is very odd, since the bitcoin account number, password and recovery phrase were all in a file on that computer of yours. Or at least they were, until the file was deleted the day before we took possession of the computer. Fortunately, our technicians were able to recover it.'

'No, that's not possible.'

'I'm afraid it is.'

At her side, Rory Buchanan cleared his throat and said, 'I'd like to consult with my client.'

'Good idea, Rory'—another ghoulish smile—'because we've got plenty more to talk about.'

Crouch switched off the recording equipment and he and Stone got to their feet and left.

'Kathy,' Buchanan said, 'I strongly advise that you reply "no comment" to all further questions.'

Kathy was thinking how glibly people used the phrase *this is a nightmare*, but this really did feel like one, a place where reason and logic were suspended. How could Osborn have planted a file in her computer, *and then deleted it*?

'I want to hear everything they've got,' she said. 'String them along. Tell them we need coffee and aspirin.'

Buchanan did as she said, and they sat alone for ten minutes while Kathy tried to make sense of it. Could Osborn have hacked into her computer remotely? Or broken into her flat? But how would she have bypassed her computer's password? Finally she nodded to Rory and they began again.

'So, Kathy,' Crouch said, brisk now and deadly serious, 'what do you have to say?'

'I can only imagine that Osborn hacked into my computer. I have no knowledge of any bitcoin account.'

'Oh dear.' Crouch shook his head and opened his file. 'Let's turn to another matter then—that luxurious Thameside apartment of yours, purchased three years ago. A very big step up from that little hutch you had in Finchley. How did you manage that?'

Rory intervened quickly. 'I advise Kathy not to answer that. It has no relevance to the matter at hand.'

'No relevance! The Metropolitan Police places the utmost importance upon rooting out corruption among its officers. If I decide it's relevant, then it's relevant. Answer the question.'

'My aunt and uncle died four years ago and left me a few shares.'

'Uncle Tom and Aunt Mary, yes. We all wish we had elderly relatives like Uncle Tom and Aunt Mary. They were very humble people, weren't they, living in an old industrial district of Sheffield in a tiny terrace house which sold upon their death for a mere fifty-seven thousand, three hundred and fifty pounds. Yet they left their favourite niece a fortune in shares.'

It was true. Kathy thought of that little house where she and her mother had sought refuge after her father killed himself, and the contrast with her present digs was indeed jarring. But Crouch was showing off, letting her know how much research they'd done. *Well*, she thought, *come on—tell me what else you know.*

'I advise you not to respond to that,' Rory murmured desperately, his tone suggesting that he knew that this was spinning horribly out of control and he could do nothing to stop it.

'I don't imagine they had any idea what they were worth,' Kathy said. 'They were blue chip shares acquired a long time ago when they were probably worth only a few pounds.'

'And where did they come from?'

'I believe my father must have given them to them.'

'Ah, your father . . .' Crouch peered at his notes. 'An undersecretary in the Department of Trade and Industry who committed suicide while being investigated for corrupt dealings with property developers.' He gave Kathy a bleak smile. 'Corruption seems to run in the family.'

Rory, looking pale, cried, 'I object!'

Crouch waved a dismissive hand at him. 'And he died when?'

'Thirty years ago.'

'Which unfortunately doesn't fit the fact that the shares came into your relatives' possession only five years ago.'

That did throw Kathy. There had been no explanation in Tom and Mary's will as to where the shares had come from.

Kathy couldn't think of any other source and had prepared herself for accusations that her father had acquired them corruptly. 'Then I don't understand . . .'

'Oh, come on, Kathy, we're not stupid. Who died five years ago?'

She shook her head, trying to think. 'I don't know.'

'Why, your dear close friend Martin Connell. Remember him? You were lovers, were you not? Or can't you remember the names of all your criminal lovers?'

'Martin was a lawyer, not a criminal.'

'A very fine distinction in his case—lawyer to Gregory North and Spider Roach and the pick of London's underworld, as you well know. You were investigated over your relationship with Connell, weren't you?'

'Yes, and cleared.'

'By David Brock'—Crouch let that hang in the air for a moment—'who became a close colleague of yours, guiding your future career.'

Kathy felt a surge of anger, wanting very much to reach across the table and smash her fist into that sneering mouth. Instead she stared at him, unblinking, until he dropped his eyes to his file and pretended to examine his notes.

When she felt she could speak with a steady voice, she said, 'Do you know for a fact that those shares came from Martin Connell?'

'Yes, we do.'

'I had no idea.'

'A final thank you to his old girlfriend, no doubt, for services rendered.'

'It must have been blood money. The last time we met he almost got me killed. Me and David Brock. You can check that too.'

'We shall, Kathy, believe me. We check everything. As you might imagine, that could take a long time. It can be very hard for the suspect, waiting in limbo, so when you decide to cut the waiting and come clean with us, we'll be here to listen to the truth.'

'I've told you the truth.'

Crouch terminated the interview with, 'Don't forget that your bail is conditional. Behave or you'll find yourself in jail for the next six months,' and left, followed by Stone, who had made notes throughout but, as usual, hadn't said a word.

Rory Buchanan was looking downcast and Kathy asked if he'd been involved in many similar cases. He shook his head. 'None quite like this. Is there anything you want to tell me?'

Kathy shrugged. 'What can we do to speed up the process?'

'Short of a confession, nothing. Nothing at all. I've heard of cases like this dragging on for years. Are you married? Partner?'

'No.'

'Maybe that's just as well. Most marriages don't survive this. You should think about getting psychological support.'

'People top themselves, do they?'

'Oh yes.' Then he added quickly, 'But some come out of it stronger than ever.'

His afterthought lacked conviction.

'Do you know if they're investigating PC Osborn?'

'I'll try to find out, but that business with the bitcoin details on your computer sounds pretty damning. Are you sure you don't want me to talk to them about a plea deal?'

'No, Rory! Not on your bloody life.'

~

When she got back to her flat she looked around and saw it in a new light. This was a parting gift from a man she had loved and then loathed for years, who had, in the end, betrayed her and almost caused her death. This was his reparation, his atonement. She'd thought that she had freed herself from him, but all this time he had surrounded her in his corrupt bounty.

15

On Thursday morning, Molly and Brock visited Art Basel Miami, a maze of partitioned spaces inside a vast exhibition hall displaying thousands of contemporary paintings, sculptures and installations for sale. There were enormous abstract paintings, gaudy portraits, startling photographic images, virtue-signalling illuminated slogans. Then there were the novelty pieces, like one-line jokes—a black box that gave off an intermittent knocking sound as if someone was trapped inside and begging to be let out, or the two elderly men with shaved heads clomping around in golden frocks and high heels. Brock wasn't impressed; it all seemed rather pretentious and silly. He wondered if the Nazis had thought the same about Kurt Schwitters, then realised that of course they hadn't—they had taken him very seriously indeed.

In those days, modern art was dangerous and seditious and, for Schwitters, a matter of life and death.

At 3 pm they caught a cab to keep their appointment with Bob and Edith Beckenbauer, who lived in an apartment in a tower at the southern end of South Beach. The couple welcomed their visitors warmly but also slightly anxiously, Brock thought, as if the detectives might be bringing a bomb into their home—a vast penthouse apartment with spectacular views over Miami. There was some chatter about their journey and what they had seen in the city, and then they took seats on a balcony with a view across Biscayne Bay to the towers of the CBD. Edith asked if they would care for coffee. 'Or something stronger?' Bob suggested hopefully. 'Champagne?'

'That would be marvellous,' Brock said, and everyone looked relieved.

Bob, long and lanky and rather stiff in his joints, heaved himself to his feet and went over to a large cocktail cabinet, where he filled four glasses. 'Now, you must tell us what makes Scotland Yard interested in our collection,' he said as he distributed them.

'Well, first,' Brock said, beginning the story that he had agreed with Molly, 'I should explain that I have a personal interest in Schwitters.' And he told them his Walter Crab story, which was received enthusiastically. They were now fellow collectors.

'So when I came upon a Scotland Yard investigation into a forgery ring that might have included Schwitters' work, I got involved. We discovered that you had recently bought a Merz, and decided to come and talk to you, among others.'

Bob looked worried. 'It must be pretty serious if you've come all this way. You mean there's a forgery ring producing fake Schwitters?'

'Quite possibly not. We get many tip-offs that come to nothing, but we had to come over here on another matter and thought we should take the opportunity to talk to you.'

Molly asked how they had started collecting Schwitters. It was a tale that Bob had obviously told many times, about his grandmother growing up in Germany before the war, in a house just down the street from Waldhausenstrasse 5 in Hanover, where Kurt Schwitters lived with his wife Helma and son Ernst.

'Grandma told me these great stories of the strange artistic people and their even stranger friends and visitors and their amazing house, and she showed me a sketch of her as a girl, done by Kurt himself. To me, a small boy, it was like a fairy tale, a magic faraway land across the ocean. When she died, she left me the sketch and her diaries and a photograph album of those days, before her family came to the States. Then one day I noticed this little thing in the window of a gallery in New York, and straight away I knew what it was—a Schwitters collage. I went right in and bought it, and that's how the collection began. Would you like to see it?'

'Very much,' Brock said, and Bob topped up their glasses and led the way through to the room they had set aside especially for their collection. On the walls were a number of collages, which Molly and Brock studied carefully, as well as sketches, including the 1928 drawing of Bob's grandmother. There were sculptures on plinths and an unexpectedly naturalistic

oil painting of a snowy landscape, done during Kurt's exile in
Norway before he escaped to England. Bob agreed that Brock
could take photographs, which he did, including of the little
Merz that he recognised from Babington's house. It was rather
eerie to see it here, the doppelgänger. Was it real or fake?
He couldn't tell, and neither could Molly, who peered long
and hard at it before giving Brock a shrug.

Brock asked how they had come to buy that particular
Merz.

'Well ...' Bob turned to his wife. 'When was it we heard
from Carl, honey? Over a year ago.'

'Just before Christmas, year before last. Remember the
weather in New York?'

'Oh yes, that's right. An art agent we know in New York,
Carl Nilsson, contacted us because he'd been approached by
a dealer who had a Schwitters, and of course Carl knew we'd
be interested. So we flew up there to view the work in Carl's
office in Manhattan. We both loved it, a classic 1927 Merz,
and we told him we'd definitely be interested if the price was
right. It took, what, six weeks to agree a price and sort out
the provenance?'

'Three months,' Edith said.

'Yes, I guess you're right, three months. And we finally got
it in ...'

'April,' Edith supplied. Then, to Brock and Molly, 'I can
give you Carl's details.'

Molly said, 'Do you know who the dealer was who
approached Carl?'

'No, he wouldn't say.'

'What about the seller?'

'Not at first,' Bob said. 'All he told us was that it was a well-respected English collector. You know how it works: the seller goes to his dealer and tells him he wants, say, one million for the piece; the dealer goes to the agent and says he wants one point five; and the agent goes to his private client and says he can get it for two million. It's the usual thing—the agent doesn't want to disclose his sources because he's afraid that next time you'll buy directly from them and cut him out of the deal.

'Of course, once the deal was done and we had access to the provenance documentation we learned that the seller's name was Babington, but Carl said that Mr Babington didn't want contact with us and insisted that the sale remain confidential. That often happens, as I'm sure you know; the seller doesn't want other people—competitors, creditors, family members—knowing they're disposing of an asset.'

Molly said, 'How about a forensic examination of the Merz?'

'Oh yes, we're always very careful. We had Walter Hardinger of FIF examine it, as we do with all our purchases. But in any case, we just had to look at the work to know it was the real thing. People think that forging a Merz would be easy, sticking some tram tickets and newspaper cuttings together any old how, and we've seen plenty of those. But Schwitters' compositions, his combinations of colours and textures, are very subtle; you can tell the real thing right away, believe me.

'As for Carl, of course you're welcome to speak to him yourselves, but I doubt he'll tell you who his dealer was. Unless you're allowed to waterboard him these days.' Bob laughed. 'I'll show you our document file, if you like, with the provenance documents and all our correspondence on the purchase.'

Molly and Brock examined these and then thanked the Beckenbauers and left.

Over a Cuban meal in Little Havana, Molly asked Brock what he thought.

'The change of ownership was registered with the Sprengel archive. How could that be done without Babington's knowledge?'

'Through an agent, perhaps? Or maybe Nadya intercepted his mail and forged his signature on the papers of sale. He was away a lot. Maybe DPF were the mysterious London agent and Miki fixed it up. Or maybe it was the real deal, and Babington's been secretly selling off the family treasures, keeping fakes on his walls.'

Brock shook his head. 'Sounds tricky.'

'Maybe Rudi in New York can help us.'

~

They left Miami the next day, catching a plane up to New York, where Molly had arranged to meet Rudi Spector from the FBI's Art Crime Team. She had met Spector before, and immediately pointed him out as they emerged from the arrivals gate, a big man in a thick winter coat, collar up, studying the passengers with a quizzical lift of an eyebrow. A grin lit up his face as he spotted Molly and he opened his arms to give her a hug.

'Rudi,' she said, and Brock noticed that her face was slightly flushed as she turned to him, 'this is my colleague David Brock—everyone just calls him Brock.'

They shook hands and Rudi said, 'How was Miami?'

'Hot,' Molly said. 'Hot and sunny.'

Rudi chuckled and led them out through the doors to be blasted by an icy wind that took their breath away as they ran to his black SUV. The big console between the driver and the front passenger had been customised, Brock noticed, with an impressive array of switches, and when they hit congestion on the Long Island Expressway Rudi flicked a couple of them to unleash a howling siren and strobing light. The traffic parted instantly in front of them and they accelerated smoothly down into the Queens–Midtown Tunnel, surfacing again in midtown Manhattan.

The city looked cold and dark after the warm glow of Florida. A few pedestrians scurried along the sidewalks, heads down against the cold wind. They drove down Broadway and into the underground car park beneath the FBI building on Federal Plaza, then took the lift up to the twenty-third floor, where Rudi hung their coats and organised coffee.

'So,' he said, as they settled around a conference table, 'what did you learn in Miami?'

Molly did the talking, describing their meeting with the Beckenbauers and how their suspicion that the Merz in Miami was a fake now seemed wrong.

Rudi said he knew Carl Nilsson, the agent who'd sold it to them, and as far as he was aware he was straight. 'Or as straight as anyone is in this game. He's not like most of them, putting on a flashy front for the rich collectors. His office is in Little Italy, Mott Street, with the old iron fire-escape stairs on the front like you see in the movies. He's up on the third floor above a Chinese grocery and a bespoke tailor, and what you see is what you get. And I'll bet he won't tell us the name of the dealer he got it from, not if they've asked for confidentiality. So, either Babington is quietly selling off the farm, or someone's screwing him, yes?'

'That's right,' Brock said. 'I think it's time I talked to him again.'

'Well, he's here in New York City—I checked. Flew in yesterday, staying at the Peninsula on Fifth Avenue.'

Brock took out his phone and called Babington's number. It went immediately to voicemail, and Brock said, 'Hello, Julian, David Brock here. I'm in New York at the moment and I need to see you. Can we meet tomorrow? Give me a call.'

They talked with Rudi some more and made their plans for the following day.

~

After breakfast the next morning, Saturday, Brock and Molly met Rudi in their hotel lobby and set off, planning to go through the Art Crime Team's blacklists of dealers and agents to look for possible connections to Julian Babington. However, Brock was puzzled that Babington hadn't returned his call and asked Rudi to stop off at the Peninsula so that he could try to make contact in person.

Rudi headed up to Fifty-Sixth Street then across to Trump Tower and down Fifth Avenue. As they approached the baroque stonework of the Peninsula, Brock noticed a man with a bright red suitcase standing outside the hotel. 'That's him.' He pointed as the man got into a cab, which set off down the avenue. They followed close behind as the cab worked its way across to Seventh Avenue, heading south, until it signalled that it was pulling over.

'Penn Station,' Rudi said. 'He's going into the station.'

'Okay,' Brock said. 'Drop me off. I'll try to catch him. I'll meet you back at the office.'

By the time Brock reached the station entrance, Babington had disappeared down the flight of stairs leading to the upper concourse level. Brock had never been here before and looked around, trying to get his bearings. Signs announced *New Jersey Transit*—was that where Babington was heading? But no, he caught a brief flash of the red suitcase disappearing into the crowd going down to a lower level, and Brock hurried after it. And there was Babington, on the lower concourse, at a window marked *Long Island Rail Road Ticketing*. Brock wondered whether to approach him, then decided to wait and see. He turned up the collar of his coat and went to another window.

'Where to?'

'What's the end of the line?'

'Babylon.'

For a moment he wondered if this was a joke, then realised the man was serious. 'Yes, of course, Babylon. Return, please.' As he used his credit card he saw Babington going down another flight of stairs. Brock grabbed his ticket and ran after him.

The stairs led down to a platform scattered with waiting passengers. He hung back against the wall until a train arrived and Babington went to get on, and Brock slipped into the rear door of the same carriage. They moved off into the long tunnel beneath the East River and surfaced in Queens, heading east into Long Island. Brock followed their progress on his phone and out of the window—Forest Hills, Kew Gardens, Jamaica . . . Sections of the track were elevated, much like in London, Brock observed, looking down into the backyards of suburban homes. Rockville Centre, Baldwin, Freeport . . . At Merrick, Babington rose to his feet, took his suitcase from the rack and moved towards the door.

As the train pulled to a halt, Brock quickly made his way to the carriage's other door then, hanging back, he followed Babington to the exit, where he raised a hand to wave to someone standing beside a car. A woman, fifty perhaps, attractive in a smart black coat and gloves, boots. Brock watched them hug and kiss in what certainly didn't look like any kind of business greeting, then he went over to a taxi waiting nearby and said, 'I'd like you to follow the white Audi over there.' The driver nodded and put the car into gear.

They drove down a long avenue, the shops and businesses giving way to white clapboard and shingle-roofed houses, some embellished with seasonal decorations, others with flagpoles and the Stars and Stripes. Turning into a side street, the Audi slowed and came to a stop outside a two-storey house remarkable for the exuberance of its illuminated Christmas decorations. Babington and the woman got out of the car and stood together, his arm around her, admiring the giant Santa with waving arm over the front door, the plunging reindeer and sleigh on the roof, the strings of multicoloured lights and flickering Christmas trees. Babington pointed at something and they both laughed, and then the front door flew open and two teenagers ran out, a girl and a boy, and charged down the path to greet them. Behind them an older youth, in his early twenties, appeared at the door and waved. All three were dressed in outdoor jackets and identical-coloured scarves and caps. The girl began jumping up and down impatiently, tugging Babington's arm and pointing at her watch.

The taxi driver said, 'That'll be thirteen-fifty, sir,' but Brock told him to wait. He got out his phone and photographed the group, then called Molly.

'Is Rudi there?'

'Yes, we've just got started. How are you doing?'

'Ask him who lives at number twenty-two West Franklin Avenue in North Merrick, Long Island.'

There was a pause, then Rudi Spector came on the line. 'The house belongs to a Mr John Sargent.'

'Family?'

Another pause, then, 'Wife, Sharon Sargent, forty-five. Three kids: Charles, twenty-one; John, seventeen; Amy, fourteen. They've lived there since 1997.'

'Okay. What do we know about John Sargent?'

'Age sixty-two, born Albany, New York . . . Apparently he's a registered fine art dealer with an address here in the city. Can't say I've ever heard of him. Let's check . . .' After a pause: 'Nothing much. Member of the Art Dealers Association of America since 2005. Never been on our radar. Why? What's going on?'

'I've followed Babington to Sargent's house. He seems to be very friendly with the family. Something's happening. I'll be in touch.'

The Sargents were all bundling into their mother's car with Babington and moving off. Brock told the taxi driver to follow. After a couple of miles of comparatively empty streets, they suddenly found themselves in the middle of crawling traffic.

'Ah!' the taxi driver said. 'It's the game!'

'The game?'

'Long Island Football Championship,' the driver explained. 'The big game against Garden City. They're gonna crush us.'

Ahead of them, Brock saw the others piling out of the Audi, and he quickly paid off the taxi and dived into the crowd to follow them. Around him most people seemed to be wearing the same colours as the Sargents. Then the two younger children, Amy and John, both carrying bulky bags over their shoulders, waved goodbye and disappeared into a wooden pavilion building. Brock continued following Babington and the others as they moved towards a food stall. They bought bagels and cups of steaming coffee and pushed on, Brock following at a distance. It occurred to him that they were probably going to meet up with the father, John Sargent, and he phoned Spector again and asked for Sargent's picture.

They emerged into the open, and Brock realised that they were on the edge of a large playing field, surrounded by banks of raked seating, and he watched as the three of them climbed up and found seats. His phone buzzed with a message from Spector, Sargent's driver's licence photo attached. Brock gazed at it for a moment, frowning, then climbed up the stand to a level above the others, so that he could watch them.

The sun broke out and the mood of the crowd galvanised into loud cheers as a school band appeared with their instruments and set up on the edge of the field. Brock saw Sharon Sargent wave to one of them, and realised that it was her son John, carrying a large trombone. He dipped his head with a grin and pretended not to notice. There was more clapping as the cheerleaders, Amy among them, appeared in breathtakingly chilly costumes. The band struck up and the girls began their routine. Finally, after another twenty minutes, the football players emerged from the pavilion, running out onto the field in two streams to more cheers and applause.

Brock knew nothing about American football and found it impossible to follow, with its continuous stoppages and changes of players. After a while his backside was aching on the hard plastic seat and he was relieved when everything came to a halt for a break. Some people in the stand got to their feet, among them Sharon and Charles, who made their way down to the exit. When they'd gone, Brock went down to their row. Babington looked up with a vague smile as he approached, and then the smile froze.

'Hello, Julian.'

'Brock. Good God,' he whispered. 'What are you doing here?'

'More to the point, what are *you* doing here, Julian? Or should I call you John?'

This time Babington's face paled, but then—and Brock had to give him credit for a quick recovery—he said, 'Jack, actually. It's Jack.' Then his eyes flicked behind Brock, and a woman's voice said, 'No luck, honey. I tried, but ...'

Brock turned to see Sharon, and Babington said, 'Darling, this is a ... friend, a colleague of mine, David Brock, from London.'

Brock gave a little bow. 'Hello, Mrs Sargent. I'm sorry to intrude.'

'Oh, it's a pleasure to meet you, David. I so rarely get to meet Jack's London friends. I'm Sharon.'

'Darling,' Babington said, 'David's come over with something urgent that I must attend to. I'm so sorry, but we'll have to leave you for a while.'

'Of course. Why don't you come and have lunch with us when you're finished, David?'

'Thank you, but I'm afraid I'll have to dash back to New York, Sharon.'

When they reached the exit from the sports ground, Babington said, 'I don't know about you, but I need a drink. There's a bar around the corner, okay?'

Brock nodded and wondered, seeing him stride rapidly away, whether he might make a run for it, but he made no attempt.

They took stools at a corner of the bar, a utilitarian sort of place, relieved by signed photographs of football heroes, indistinguishable beneath their helmets and body armour.

Babington called for two glasses of Jack Daniel's.

'This is how it began,' he said, pointing to the bottle on the shelf behind the bar. 'Twenty-three years ago, in a bar in Greenwich Village. I was with a business colleague, Richard, a lawyer. Some people he knew came in, and with them was this young woman, Sharon, his assistant. We got talking. At that time my life was pretty dark. My father was giving me hell as usual, and I was still married to my first wife, though I'd just discovered that she'd been having an affair with a chap I thought was my friend. Sharon was very nice and we hit it off. I relaxed and we chatted and when she asked me my name I noticed a Jack Daniel's bottle on the bar and

I just said, "Jack." I don't know why I did that, but afterwards I saw it as my first instinctive step towards freedom. Sharon seemed so fresh and optimistic and open and—well, the opposite of tired and disillusioned and cynical, like me. The next day Richard drove me to the airport and told me that she'd said I was really nice and she'd like to see me again. I told him I'd called myself Jack, and what a relief that had been, and he said, "Okay, Jack you shall be."

'The next time I returned to New York, Richard told me he'd arranged a date for me with Sharon. He also told me that my name was Jack Sargent, and he gave me a birth certificate and driver's licence to prove it. Richard's speciality was finding beneficiaries of deceased estates. He knew his way around every database and official record in existence, and he'd found a Jack for me—John Sargent, died in upstate New York of respiratory disease aged seven months in the very same year that I was born. It was still possible to do that sort of thing then, before nine-eleven. And the name he picked seemed like a portent . . .'

'Because,' Brock said, 'one of your favourite paintings in your father's collection was the watercolour of Venice by John Singer Sargent.'

'You remember. Yes, exactly. And you can't imagine how liberating it was, reinventing my story with Richard, creating my imaginary life as an American Jack Sargent. I felt free of my wife, free of the father who'd controlled every decision I'd ever attempted to make, including the choice of my wife.

'And then we fell in love, Sharon and I. It didn't feel like a deception. It felt completely honest and real.'

'But it wasn't, was it?' Brock said. 'It was a fraud, a forgery.'

'That's what I thought at first. But gradually I came to realise that it was my true life, the life that I was always meant to lead, and the other life in London was the fraud, constructed on compulsion and deceit. I was being given a second chance, a chance to be truly myself.'

He sighed, took a drink. 'And then Sharon fell pregnant, and I had to decide whether to stick with it or to disappear.' He smiled to himself, remembering. 'Sharon was over the moon, blissfully happy, and I knew I couldn't just walk away. She took me to see her folks. I thought they'd be a bit worried about the age difference between us—she was twenty-three and I forty, almost twice her age. But they just accepted me, warmly and openly, into a wonderful extended New York Irish family.'

Brock noticed that his accent had slipped into mid-Atlantic. 'You told them you were an art dealer?'

'Yes, that's what I'd told Sharon. She was very keen on art. I told them my family had moved to London for business when I was a boy and I'd been educated there, which explained my accent.'

'So Charles was born.'

'Chuck, yes. Back home, my wife and I divorced and I thought I'd just say goodbye to London, but then my father became very ill, and I was obliged to manage his affairs, and in particular his art collection, which he put into a trust, with myself as sole trustee. So I got into a routine of dividing my time between London and New York. And then John—Jack junior—came along, and then Amy.'

Brock said, 'And where did Nadya fit into this busy life?'

'Ah … Nadya.' Babington shook his head, called for their glasses to be topped up and raised his. '*Za zdorovie*. Nadya, 2001 … Dear old Dad was dead and I was stuck in London trying to sort out his affairs. I had business in Canary Wharf and quite often had lunch at Alexandrov's restaurant. One day Egor, the owner, introduced me to his new waitress, his niece Nadya, newly arrived from St Petersburg. Very attractive, very bright. I was having lunch there on my way to an opening at the Royal Academy, and when I mentioned this she told me she'd studied art at the St Petersburg Academy and said how much she'd love to visit the RA. The restaurant was quiet and Egor said she could have the afternoon off, so I took her along. Afterwards we had a few drinks, then went back to my place, and one thing led to another. I regarded it as a one-off thing, but Nadya had other ideas. Oh dear me, yes. We began to go out together, and my London friends said how envious they were, how perfect we were together and what a lucky old rogue I was. And I thought, well, this has nothing to do with Jack and Sharon Sargent in Long Island. This is that other guy, Julian Babington in London.'

'Exhausting for you, I should have thought,' Brock said. 'Expensive too, running two households. Is that why you sold your Schwitters?'

Babington stiffened. 'I'm sorry?'

'The Schwitters on your wall in Montagu Square. It's a copy, isn't it? Or did you sell the copy?'

He seemed lost for words, then, 'What are you talking about?'

'I'm a copper, Julian. I came across a record of the sale.'

'Oh.' He sipped his drink then said slowly, 'Yes, yes. I may have mentioned how expensive it is to house a valuable collection—insurance, security, maintenance. The firm does reasonably well, but the collection is an enormous strain.'

'Not to mention two households.'

'Indeed. I couldn't hand the collection over to the RA until Dad's estate was all settled, and that was going very slowly. So finally, when things were getting impossible, I decided to sell one or two things from the collection to maintain the rest. All quite legal—as sole trustee it was up to me to manage it as I saw fit.'

'How many things have you sold?'

'A few, nothing major. The RA will get what Dad promised them.'

'And you had copies made for yourself?'

'Yes. Frankly, I didn't want Miki or anyone else to know what I was doing. It might have cast doubts on the rest of the collection.'

'And you sold the originals?'

'Absolutely! I haven't cheated anyone, I promise you.'

'Who made the copies?'

'They were done very competently by a copy studio in China, but they wouldn't stand up to forensic examination. Nadya had no idea of the true state of our finances. She thought she'd married a very rich man, and I constantly had to restrain her spending. That church in the Hoo—I remembered after you mentioned it. She'd taken it into her head that we could be major benefactors, wanted to give them a hundred thousand! In the end I whittled it down to five thousand, but she was quite put out.'

'Yes, I can see how difficult it must have been for you, the financial problems, trying to keep both sides happy. How did you manage Christmas, for example?'

Babington groaned, shook his head. 'A nightmare.'

'And all getting harder, year by year. Which gives you a powerful motive for getting rid of Nadya, and not by means of an expensive divorce.'

'I didn't kill her, Brock.'

'Why did you change the time of your flight to New York that morning she died?'

'What?' Babington looked startled.

'You were originally booked on the Virgin flight at six twelve, but you changed to the Delta at eight twenty. Why?'

'I . . . I was working later than I'd intended. I needed extra time to prepare the documents I had to take to New York. Why are you asking?'

'Because we now know that Nadya's Range Rover reached the pond at the Hoo where she died at three forty-six am. By delaying your flight you gave yourself time to follow her there, drown her, and get away.'

Babington stared at Brock for a moment, then shook his head. 'No, no, no. I swear to you . . . I had no idea that Nadya had left the house. I assumed she was still asleep and I went without disturbing her. My God. I can't believe this is happening—Nadya dead and now you here in North Merrick accusing me of murder.' He rubbed a hand over his face. 'Look, can I ask you something? Before you haul me off to the local cops, come and have lunch with us. I want you to understand that I'm not making this up. I've told you everything, the honest truth. Come and see for yourself. Then you can do what you must.'

Maybe it was the whisky, Brock thought, or maybe it was that quality of empathy that a good detective needed to have; empathy with the victims, of course, but also empathy with the suspects, so that you could put yourself in their shoes and see the world as they saw it. Babington's life seemed bizarre, but all the more reason to understand what he meant by 'the honest truth'.

'All right,' Brock said. 'I'll come to lunch.'

As they stepped out into the sunshine they heard a roar from the football ground. Babington checked his watch and said, 'That's full time, I think. They'll all come pouring out now. Let's go and wait at the car.'

Eventually his family emerged from among the crowd and Babington waved.

'I've persuaded David to stay for lunch,' he said and introduced Brock to his children.

~

It seemed that the taxi driver's prediction had proved accurate, with a crushing win to Garden City, and the Sargents chattered on about the mistakes that had been made and the awesome power of the Garden City quarterback. Lunch was to be at Aunty Barbara and Uncle Artie's place, stopping at the Sargents' on the way to pick up dishes of salads and desserts that Sharon had prepared. When they arrived at Barbara and Artie's, they found a house full of adults and children, women carrying plates of roast meats and vegetables, Cousin

Jimmy pouring drinks. Brock joined a group of men who were discussing the game, and he commented on the impressive performance of the Garden City quarterback, which seemed to go down well.

It was all very companionable, with lots of laughter, and Sharon moving among them, vivacious, organising and obviously a powerhouse in the family. Then she came and sat with Brock and asked him about his line of work and how he'd come to know Jack. Brock hesitated for a moment but Babington, pouring himself another glass of wine, said, 'Oh, David works for Scotland Yard, honey. He's a police officer, investigates art fraud.'

'Really?' Sharon was fascinated, as were her son Chuck and Uncle Artie. 'That is so interesting! You haven't caught Jack trying to sell the *Mona Lisa*, have you?'

Everyone thought that was very funny.

'Not quite. I'm investigating a case with the FBI, and Jack's been helping us. I suppose you've all been over to the UK with Jack, have you?'

'We've been to Ireland a couple of times,' Sharon said, 'and to Greece, which was lovely, but not to London, although I keep begging him to take us. But he spends so much time there with work that it wouldn't seem like a holiday for him. I think art fraud must be such an interesting area of police work. It must take you all over the world.'

'Actually, I've only recently moved to art fraud. My real area is homicide.'

'Goodness. But surely there isn't much homicide in the art world, is there?'

'You'd be surprised, Sharon. The stakes are high, you see, the price of artwork being what it is.'

'Ah, of course. Jack hasn't mentioned any juicy murders in the line of his work.'

Babington looked at his watch. 'I should be getting you a cab to the station, David. There's a train to the city in twenty minutes.'

They went outside to wait for the taxi and Babington said, 'What did you think of them?'

'Lovely people.'

'Yes, they are. I wanted you to appreciate that. I know I've broken the rules, but I haven't hurt anyone or stolen anything. On the contrary, Jack Sargent has created and supported a fine family that loves and respects him. When you get back to the city, you may feel it's your duty to report my stolen identity to your friends in the FBI, and then they will have no option but to prosecute me and destroy our lives. I just wanted you to see what you would be destroying and beg you to think twice. What good would it do anyone? Nadya is dead, Brock; my other life in London is over. Please—don't destroy this one too.'

The cab drew to a halt at the kerb and Brock turned to him. 'Did you kill Nadya, Julian?'

Babington's face was pale and drawn, Brock thought, as if he wasn't sleeping much these days. He whispered, 'No, Brock. I swear to God, I did not kill Nadya.'

Brock held his gaze for a long moment, then opened the cab door and got in.

On the train back to the city he thought about the little lie—telling Sharon his name was Jack—which had transformed Babington's life. Spinning out of control, it had generated an affair, then a pregnancy and eventually a whole family of people whose understanding of themselves and their place in the world unknowingly depended on that lie.

~

Back in New York, he found that Molly and her FBI chums hadn't missed him a bit, engrossed as they were in discussing their cases and the very latest technical breakthroughs. Brock told them that he'd caught up with Babington and had lunch with him, during which he had asked him if he had sold the Schwitters Merz to an American collector.

'He admitted he had, and a few other works from the collection too, to pay for the cost of maintaining it. He said he had a copy made by a Chinese studio.'

Molly was disappointed. 'So much for my conspiracy theories,' she said.

Brock didn't mention Babington's other family, for a mixture of flawed reasons. In the first place, he'd been swayed by Babington's argument that the truth would destroy the family in North Merrick. Brock had seen that they were genuine and warm-hearted people who didn't deserve the scandal, heart-ache and financial problems that would follow Babington's arrest. Brock realised, too, that if he tipped off the FBI and Babington was arrested in America, he might never get him back to the UK to answer questions about what had really been going on over there. And that, for Brock, was the main issue, not Babington's familial misadventures.

All the same, he felt dissatisfied. Didn't Babington's explanation of the Schwitters sale to the Beckenbauers sound a
little improvised? What about the Russian angle? Were Miki
Babington and Pavel Gorshkov up to something illegal?

Most of all, he felt frustrated by an overwhelming sense
of impotence. As a homicide detective, he was convinced
that Nadya and Callum's deaths had not been investigated properly. Yet he wasn't a homicide detective; he was
an unskilled and ineffectual member of the Fraud Squad,
working in an area—art fraud—about which he knew next
to nothing.

And this sense of helplessness only grew during the following day, as he tagged along with Molly. They had asked for
the Art Crime Team's help to investigate Pavel Gorshkov and
I.I. International's activities, but so far they had found nothing.
While they waited, Brock went with Molly on visits to New
York galleries and museums and to presentations organised
by the FBI. On Monday there was a lecture by a specialist
from the Frick on Van Goghs which had been lost in Europe
during World War II and were now being 'rediscovered' in
various locations in South America. Another seminar looked
at new developments in detecting fingerprints on old canvases.
It was all very interesting, but also rather remote, and it was
with some relief that he was woken by his mobile at 4.30 am
on Tuesday by Bren, calling from London. Brock sensed the
urgency in his voice.

'Brock, hi. Are you back in town?'

'No, Bren. I'm still in New York.'

'Hell, sorry. What time is it over there?'

'Four thirty. Doesn't matter. What's the problem?'

'It's Kathy. I've been talking to someone from Sally Cameron's office. He asked if it was true that Kathy's in jail.'

'What?'

'Apparently Homicide is buzzing with rumours that she's been arrested on serious fraud and corruption charges. Nobody seems to know exactly what's happened, but they're saying your mate Stone at Fraud is one of the senior investigators.'

'*What?!* Bren, this is not possible.'

'I know, that's what I thought, so I got on to Commander Torrens' office. He wouldn't see me, but I've known his PA for ages, and she told me—in confidence—that Kathy was suspended from duty two weeks ago and hasn't been seen in Homicide since. She's not answering her phone and I've been to her flat several times and she wasn't there.'

Brock thought for a moment. 'Okay, I'll fly back today, as soon as I can. Keep me updated.'

'Let me know when you're due in and I'll pick you up at the airport.'

Brock immediately booked a seat on the 8.05 am flight from JFK to London, got dressed and packed. He texted Bren to say he'd arrive at Heathrow at 7.50 pm, and caught a cab to the airport, texting Molly on the way to tell her he'd been called back urgently to the UK.

16

It had taken a couple of days for Rory Buchanan to get back to Kathy. As far as he'd been able to establish, Crouch's team had carried out a brief background investigation into Ashley Osborn but taken it no further. It was what she'd been afraid of.

Buchanan went on to suggest that she write a comprehensive statement of her dealings with Martin Connell and a detailed account of her purchase of her flat, and she bought a laptop and printer and set to work. It took her a day. Then what? In the two weeks that had passed since her first interview with Crouch she had tried to keep busy. She joined a yoga studio but soon got impatient, then she tried a book group at the local library, but only attended one meeting. Only swimming seemed to soothe her for a little while. She kept the laptop with her at all times.

One night, returning from the pool, she arrived at the forecourt of her building just as another resident reached the front doors. She stopped and watched as the man tapped his six-digit entry code into the keypad, and it seemed to her that, if she stood a little further to the left, in an area of shadow beside the wall, she might be able to see the numbers he was keying. She followed him in and went up to her flat for her camera with a telephoto lens and returned to the spot. Soon another resident arrived, and Kathy zoomed in on the keypad and recorded his movements. When he had gone inside she examined the video closely then went to the entrance and tapped in the number that she thought she'd made out. The door clicked open. Each resident had selected their own entry code, both for the external door and for their own apartment door. In Kathy's case they were the same, and it occurred to her that it was also the number she had used as a password to open her computer. If Ashley Osborn had done what Kathy just did, she would have had access to everything.

She knew that she was becoming completely consumed by thoughts of Ashley Osborn. She was attempting to put together a file of information on her, but there was so little on the web and, as Judy had pointed out, nothing at all on social media sites. It seemed to her that Osborn was a ruthless obsessive, living, like Kathy herself, as a hermit with a single thing on her mind. Kathy briefly considered hiring a private detective to investigate her, but she decided it would yield nothing. Osborn wasn't an errant wife or a welfare cheat. She was, almost certainly, a highly competent murderer, and needed to be investigated by an experienced homicide detective, and the only one available was herself.

She went through Judy's notes, listing the missing pieces—
the people who had known Osborn and might have noticed
something; the places where she'd lived. And again and again
she found herself returning to that first case, the stabbing
murder of her sister's widower, Ryan Turton, in Leicester. It
was the case where Osborn had a powerful personal reason to
hate the victim, the man she had publicly accused of killing
her sister Gillian and who had got off scot-free. Why else did
she transfer to Leicester, and then transfer away again once he
was dead?

So she focused on Leicester, between the years 2002, when
Turton moved there, and 2009, when he died. But there was
little she could add to Judy's notes from this distance. She
needed to go there, to the places and people he knew, and see
for herself. Of course this was forbidden under the terms of
her bail and she remembered Crouch's final warning, but she
felt she had no alternative.

She would need a new identity, she realised, and wondered
what she should call herself. Something unremarkable, she
thought, but also a name that would mean something to
her but nothing to Crouch and Stone. She thought of what
she now considered a golden age in her life, her first twelve
years, before her father killed himself and brought it to a
brutal end. Who had her heroes been? And then she remembered Nancy Blackett, captain of the *Amazon* in *Swallows
and Amazons*, her favourite book. *Perfect*, she thought, *I shall
be Nancy Blackett.*

She visited an instant print office and had some business
cards printed with the name Nancy Blackett and her Blackphone number, then changed her apartment entry codes and

had a locksmith install an additional heavy-duty lock on her front door.

The next morning, very early, she placed the phone Crouch had given her in a drawer and slipped out into the dark and made her way to St Pancras station.

~

It was still dark when Kathy got off the train at Leicester that morning, the station buzzing with business types catching trains to London, Nottingham, Sheffield and all points north. She made her way out of the station and under the road viaduct, turning up her collar against the chill breeze, and walked into the city centre.

For several hours she just walked around, buying a city map from a newsagents, memorising the streets, getting a breakfast of sausages and scrambled eggs in a café, feeling that she was on borrowed time, waiting for the long arm of Crouch's law to reach out and grab her. Then she walked to the Central Library and settled down with a notebook and their computer and microfiches.

There was more than she'd expected on Ryan Turton's death, mainly because of his record as a player for the Leicester Tigers professional rugby union team. *Sporting Blue*, the weekly sporting supplement published by the *Leicester Mercury*, described his transfer in 2002 from the Nottingham Green and Whites to the Tigers, and his glowing record as a powerful second row forward in the 2002–03 season, when Leicester came sixth in the table. However, his performance seemed to decline after that. There was gossip of excessive drinking and non-attendance at training sessions until he was finally dropped by the Tigers in 2007. The *Mercury* picked up the theme of tragic waste in three articles relating to his death in February 2009. In the first, headed *Tigers hero's squalid death*, crime reporter Harley Mills described how Turton had been found in a doorway late at night in the Old Town area in a pool of his own blood and urine. Mills followed this the next day with an appeal from Leicester Police seeking information from anyone who was in the vicinity on the night of Saturday, 21 February and might have seen Ryan Turton. He was known to have been drinking heavily in the High Cross pub around eleven o'clock that evening and was found in a doorway in Pocklingtons Walk after midnight, stabbed to death. There was one further report from Mills, on the funeral service for Turton attended by players and celebrities associated with the Leicester Tigers, but nothing further on the police investigation into his murder.

Kathy picked up her phone and called the *Mercury*, asking to be put through to Harley Mills. There was a pause—a sign that he was still on the payroll, Kathy hoped—then a woman answered, saying that Harley wasn't at his desk right now. She refused to give Kathy his mobile number but said she'd pass on her request that he call. 'It's concerning the murder of Ryan Turton,' Kathy said as the line went dead.

She left the library and made her way to Granby Street, where she booked a room at the Grand Hotel, a flamboyant Edwardian building of orange brick striped with white stonework. The concierge gave her directions to the High Cross pub in High Street. From there she retraced Turton's steps on the fatal night, down Loseby Lane and

Grey Friars, walking slowly, as a drunk man might. She came to Pocklingtons Walk and followed it, looking for a likely doorway where he might have sought shelter. Nothing stood out, but she estimated it shouldn't have taken him more than half an hour of stumbling progress to get here from the pub, which put his time of death at sometime before midnight on that Saturday night.

Kathy returned to the High Cross, sat at the bar and ordered a wine. The barmaid was far too young to have been there in 2009, and Kathy asked if the boss was around. The girl looked at her doubtfully and told her there were no jobs here, but Kathy reassured her it was about something else. The manager came to see her, but he told her he'd only been there two years, and knew nothing about the death of any footballer called Ryan Turton.

Then Kathy's Blackphone rang.

'Nancy?'

'Yes, is that Harley?'

'It is, yeah. You wanted to speak to me?' He sounded pre-occupied and impatient.

'It's about the murder of Ryan Turton, remember him?'

'Ryan ... Oh, the rugby player. Yeah.' He laughed. 'I remember that one. What's your interest? You know who did it?'

'Maybe. Could you spare a few minutes? I'm in the High Cross, where he was drinking that night.'

'Oh?' He seemed to brighten at the mention of the pub. 'Yeah, sure. I'll be ten minutes.'

Ten minutes later a short, overweight, balding man in a cheap suit ambled in, looked around, then grinned at Kathy, the only single female sitting at a table. Kathy found the image of a veteran crime reporter rather reassuring. Knowing what a difficult time this was for regional newspapers like the *Mercury*, she had imagined that all the old hands would have taken a package and gone, leaving only young beginners looking for some quick experience before moving on to London. She stood and put out her hand. 'Hello, Harley. What'll you have?'

'Vodka tonic, please. Double.' He sat down and she went to the bar.

'So, Nancy,' he said as she returned and handed him the glass, 'what's your interest in Ryan Turton then?'

'I'm writing a book on famous sports people who came to a tragic end. You know: Andrés Escobar, who was shot dead by a fan because he accidentally scored a goal against his own team in the 1994 World Cup. Sarah Burke, the Canadian skier who fell on her head during a practice run when she was only twenty-nine. Stories like that.'

'Interesting.' Harley took a gulp from his glass and smiled appreciatively. 'Ghoulish, but interesting. What else have you written?'

'This is my first book. I've been overseas for a number of years, and want to focus on a new career. Tell me, why did you laugh when I mentioned Ryan Turton on the phone?'

The reporter chuckled. 'Well, I shouldn't have really, but you see, poor old Ryan was a heavy beer drinker, and he'd been hitting it pretty hard that night. He left the pub here sometime after eleven and began to walk home to his flat down in York Street, but by the time he reached Pocklingtons Walk he was bursting for a leak. What was the poor bugger to do?

He looked around and all he could see was the entrance to the Magistrates Court building, so he stepped in there, pulled out his walloper and was in mid-flow when the killer came up behind and stabbed him six times in the back!'

Harley roared with laughter then drained his glass. 'The cops asked me not to report that—they thought it might lead to a copycat flood of urination on the Magistrates Court building by grieving Tigers fans.'

Kathy grinned. 'Yes, I see. Six times, eh?'

'Yep. Frenzied, the cops reckoned, but they didn't want me to report that either.'

'Did they find the weapon?'

'Nope. In fact, there wasn't a single clue. Forensics came up with nothing, there were no witnesses, no CCTV, nothing at all.'

'Wasn't there a bag of heroin involved?'

'Yes, well, that's what lies behind most cases these days, isn't it? Drugs. But that didn't lead anywhere. The investigation hit a dead end.' He fingered his empty glass.

'Can I get you another, Harley?'

'Mm, no, better not.' He checked his watch. 'I'm due at a funeral.' He got to his feet.

'Who was the lead detective?'

'Detective Inspector Rick Waterman. Old school. Retired now.'

'Do you know how I can contact him?'

'No, I heard he moved down south somewhere when he retired. Anyway, you'd be wasting your time with him. Like trying to get blood out of a stone. You'd be better off talking to Wally Scanlon. He was in Waterman's team on the Turton case and he's still in the job. He's a DI now.' He checked his phone and gave Kathy a contact number. 'Tell him I put you on to him. Good luck with your book, Miss Blackett.'

Kathy watched him leave, then called the number.

'Scanlon.'

'Inspector, my name's Nancy Blackett. I've been speaking to Harley Mills, who suggested I call you. I was wondering if I could have a few minutes of your time.'

'You a reporter?'

'No, I'm writing a book on famous sports people who died tragically, and I wanted to include the Ryan Turton case. Harley said you were part of the investigating team.'

'Oh yes? Long time ago now. All right, let's see ... I can do five this afternoon. I'm away tomorrow and Thursday.' He gave her the address.

~

She found the office building in the north end of the town centre and checked herself in at five. Wally Scanlon came down to the desk to collect her, a big man, florid complexion, middle-aged, looking tired.

'Hi, Nancy, let's get a drink.' He led her over to a machine, pushed buttons and got a couple of bottles of water, then led her to a sitting area over to one side.

'So, you're writing a book?'

She explained her project and he said, 'Like that American pro golfer. What was his name—something Stewart? Got on a flight where the plane failed to pressurise and everyone on board was killed.'

Kathy had never heard of it and wasn't sure if he had invented it to test her, so she said, 'Right. Anyway, I came here to find out more about the Ryan Turton case. I believe you worked on it?'

'True enough. Rick Waterman was SIO, his last case—a big disappointment for him. All the publicity, should have been the crowning glory of his career, instead it just fizzled out. It was one of those frustrating cases that hit a brick wall— no forensics, no witnesses, no background that we could find.'

'Did Turton have a girlfriend?'

'Not at the time. He had a few mates, drinking pals, and he'd had a few romances, a couple with married girls that got him into trouble with their hubbies. But we checked them all. The truth was that people were beginning to avoid him by that stage. They were tired of him bragging on about his great days in rugby, now long over. He'd become a bit of a sad drunk.'

'What about the bag of heroin?'

'Yes, a little bag, probably cost not much more than five quid around here. But we couldn't trace the supplier and found no record of his ever using heroin—no traces in his system, no needle marks, no equipment at his home, not even a roll of foil. He was a big boozer, certainly, and was said to have indulged in cocaine in his days with the Tigers, but not heroin. Of course, you can't discount drugs, not today, but the fact was we couldn't find a single plausible suspect for the killing.'

'I see. I'd really like to put in some forensic type of details to make the story more vivid, and I was wondering if you might have a copy of the autopsy report?'

'You'd have to ask the coroner's office, but it was all very straightforward—six stab wounds in the back by a slim-bladed weapon, punctured his heart, lungs and liver. Death would have followed very quickly.'

'Could the killer have been a woman?'

'Certainly. The stabbing wouldn't have required great strength. But there were no angry jilted girlfriends on the scene. We couldn't find anyone with a motive, and in the end had to accept that it was a random attack, or maybe a case of mistaken identity.'

'Any specific details—from the post-mortem or the crime scene, say—to illustrate how thorough the investigation was?'

'It was certainly very thorough, but I can't think of anything specific.'

'Nothing forensic? No unexplained features?'

Scanlon rubbed his chin. 'The only thing I can remember was that there was a black hair found on Turton's jacket that wasn't his. We were very excited about that, until forensics gave us the bad news.'

'What was that?'

'It wasn't human! God, we were bloody annoyed, made them check it again. No good!'

Kathy laughed along with him.

'You're welcome to use that one,' Scanlon said.

'Thank you.' Kathy scribbled in her notebook. 'What sort of animal?'

'Oh, I don't think we ever bothered to find out. Turton could have picked it up anywhere—bumping into someone in the pub, or anything.'

'Could you recommend anyone else I might speak to? How about the pathologist?'

'The East Midlands Forensic Pathology Unit provided forensic services for us. Professor Maxwell. You might try him.'

'Thanks. I wonder, do you by any chance remember a young woman constable who was with you by the name of Ashley Osborn?'

Scanlon pondered. 'No, doesn't ring a bell. Why?'

'Oh, she was a name I came across, someone who was here at that time.'

'Not a detective. I suppose she might have been involved in the general duties. Someone who might know is Ellie Pierce, our office manager. But she's retired now.'

'Don't know where she lives, do you?'

'Sorry, no.' He checked his watch. 'I'd better get going.'

They got to their feet. Kathy thanked him for seeing her and gave him one of her Nancy Blackett cards. 'If anything else strikes you, do give me a call.'

After she left, Kathy called in at the Central Library again and tried to trace the former office manager. There were twelve E. Pierces listed in the phone directory and she managed to get through to eight of them, none of whom was the one she was after. She made a note of the other numbers and returned to her hotel. She told herself to be patient. Old cases like this took time, and it was a matter of patiently following up every possible lead until something emerged. Which was all very well, but how much time did she have before they realised that she'd gone?

~

Bren was waiting at the exit gate at Terminal 5 as Brock appeared.

'Bren, thanks for coming. Any news?'

'No, I've been tied up all day, but I've heard nothing. Still no answer on her phone.'

They decided to drive straight to Kathy's apartment. As they crossed Vauxhall Bridge, Brock looked out at the towers on the south bank, working out which windows belonged to Kathy's flat. 'I think her light's on,' he said.

When they'd parked the car they made their way to the front door of Kathy's block and pressed her buzzer. Then, getting no reply, they went to the concierge office, where they showed their police IDs to the man behind the desk.

'We're colleagues of Kathy Kolla in apartment twelve-oh-three,' Brock said, 'and we're concerned that no one has heard from her for several days. Has she left any information with you?'

The concierge checked his computer, looking worried. 'She changed her access code and got an extra lock fitted on Monday. We haven't seen her since.'

'We'd like to check her premises, with you present.'

The man hesitated for a moment, then nodded, getting to his feet. On the way up he mentioned the visits from the police with warrants a couple of weeks before, and Brock and Bren exchanged a glance. When they reached Kathy's door, Brock felt his heart thumping as they waited for the man to open up. Then they were inside. The light in the living room was on. They quickly checked the other rooms, and he felt relief flooding through him. 'Thank God,' he murmured.

Then Bren, opening drawers, came upon Kathy's phone, and his heart sank again.

Brock turned to the concierge. 'Your CCTV records people coming and going, doesn't it?'

'Yes.'

'Let's find out when she left.'

They returned to the office and entered a control room filled with screens and equipment. The concierge showed them how to access the relevant video records then left them to it as they settled down to search, working backwards in time. It didn't take long to find the image of Kathy exiting the building at four thirty that morning.

Brock sat back with a sigh. 'That was the time in New York when you rang me this morning, Bren.'

'So when I rang you she'd been gone five hours. Sixteen hours now. We'll be able to track her.'

But Brock wasn't so sure. She was wrapped in a coat and scarf, and if she didn't want to be tracked she'd only have to change the colour of her scarf and they'd probably miss her. And he was thinking of the river, right outside ... and then they might never find her. The choice was hers.

'What do we do?'

Bren's question roused him. 'Leave it till tomorrow. First thing, I'll collar Stone and find out what's going on.'

'I've got a monthly update tomorrow morning. Do you want me to get out of it?'

'No, Bren. Leave it to me. I'll get in touch as soon as I know anything.'

17

When Matt Stone arrived at the office the next morning, he found Brock sitting on the corner of his desk, reading the morning paper. Brock didn't appear to notice his arrival and Stone wasn't quite sure what to do. After a moment he cleared his throat and said, 'Morning. How was the States?'

Brock folded the paper and looked at him. 'Time we had a chat, Matt. Let's use the office.'

The 'office' was a closed room where private meetings could be held. Brock shut the door after them and they sat.

'What's this I hear about you arresting DCI Kolla?'

Stone coloured slightly but held Brock's gaze. 'It's confidential at this stage, Brock. I can't discuss it with you.'

'Bollocks. I'm a senior officer in Fraud and I've known Kathy Kolla longer than anyone else in the Metropolitan Police. Of course you can discuss it with me.'

Stone looked down at his hands. Finally he said, 'You may be implicated.'

'That's nonsense. Kolla is straight as a die, and if anyone says otherwise they're lying.'

'There's compelling evidence that she attempted to pervert the course of justice and extort money from a fellow officer.'

'No, no.' Brock shook his head dismissively.

'You investigated her yourself once, didn't you?'

'Many years ago. She was innocent then and she's innocent now.'

'She was having an affair at the time with a crooked lawyer called Martin Connell, wasn't she?'

Now Brock looked puzzled. 'Yes. Good God, you're not reopening that old case, are you?'

'Where did she get the money to pay for that expensive apartment of hers on the south bank?'

'I've no idea. It's none of my business, or yours.'

Stone gave a grim little smile. 'I'm afraid it is. It was paid for by Martin Connell.' He got to his feet and went to the door, then paused and looked back over his shoulder. 'Some friendly advice, Brock. You should think twice before barging into this.'

~

After a restless, dream-haunted night, Kathy left the hotel and made her way across the city centre to the Leicester

Royal Infirmary, looking for the East Midlands Forensic Pathology Unit. But when she reached the reception desk she was told that Professor Maxwell was at a conference overseas and wasn't expected back for a week. There was no one else she could speak to who had worked on the Turton case.

She walked back in heavy rain to the Central Library and tried to find the names of other people who might be able to help her—Turton's old teammates at the Tigers, for instance, who could shed more light on his private life. Had he known that Ashley had moved to Leicester?

When this didn't yield anything she made another attempt to contact E. Pierce, again unsuccessfully. She was about to give up when it occurred to her that there might be other ways of spelling the name. She found three possibilities— E.F. Pierse, E. and G. Pearse, and E.W. Pearse. She struck gold with the third.

'Yes, I'm Ellie Pearse.' The voice sounded friendly.

'Were you by any chance an office manager with Leicester Police?'

'I was indeed. How can I help you?'

Kathy told her about her book project and said that Wally Scanlon had given her Ellie's name. Could they meet? Ellie explained that she was about to leave for her bridge club, but she would be free later that afternoon. She gave Kathy her address and they arranged to meet at 4 pm.

It was something, Kathy thought, but she was becoming increasingly pessimistic. What had possessed her to think she could break into an intractable cold case with no more resources than a lame story about a book? She decided to give it twenty-four more hours and then return to London, hopefully before Crouch had discovered that she'd gone.

~

Brock was sitting in the outer office of the suite occupied in New Scotland Yard by Commander Steven Torrens, head of Homicide and Serious Crime Command, while his secretary, Jean, tapped away at her keyboard to hide her embarrassment. She had told him that the commander had no gaps in his diary today, and when Brock had insisted that it was urgent she had reluctantly spoken on the phone to her boss, who had told her to get rid of him. Yet there he still sat, unmoving.

Finally the inner door opened and Assistant Commissioner Sally Cameron appeared with Torrens at her shoulder.

'Hello, Brock!' Cameron said. 'How are you?'

Brock got to his feet. 'Well, thanks, ma'am.'

'Excellent. Well'—she turned back to Torrens—'I'll leave it with you, Steven.'

Torrens, looking harassed, glared at Brock, and when Cameron was gone, growled, 'Didn't Jean tell you, Brock? I'm busy.'

'This won't take long, sir.' He began walking straight towards Torrens, who, at the last moment, gave way and let him in, closing the door behind him.

'It's about DCI Kolla, sir.'

'Yes, I assumed so. And there is nothing I can tell you.'

'She's innocent.'

'I hope very much that she is, but this isn't some little matter where I can have a quiet word with the commissioner and sort it out. Good grief, man, this is the DPS we're talking about—the Ghost Squad, the Inquisition. She's in their hands now, and there's absolutely nothing that you or I or anyone else can do about it.'

He stared at Brock and must have seen the energy drain out of him as this registered, for he added quietly, 'If this turns out to be as bad as I think it is, it's going to be a disaster for all of us—everyone who's ever had anything to do with her, everyone in Homicide. We'll all be tainted. My advice to you is to get back to Fraud and stay there. Keep your head down and watch your back.' He took a deep breath. 'Now please go. I've got a lot on my plate at the moment.' He turned away to the file on his desk.

Brock left the building and crossed the street to stand on the Victoria Embankment, staring down at the dark water. Its endless current, inevitable and unstoppable, seemed like a metaphor for what was happening. He knew that Torrens was right, that there was nothing they could do except keep swimming and try to survive. His phone rang and when he saw Bren's name he knew what he had to say.

'Hi, Brock, I'm free now. Any progress?'

'I've just met with Torrens, Bren. He made it quite plain to me that we can't help Kathy now. She's in the hands of the DPS. You know what they're like. We have to step away.'

'Yeah, that's what he would say. So what are we going to do?'

'Just that, Bren. Step away.'

'What? You're joking.'

'No, I'm not. It's the same advice as Stone in Fraud gave me. I tried to ignore it, but I realise now they're right. Anything we do will only implicate ourselves and make things worse for Kathy.'

'Brock ... I can't believe I'm hearing this—from you of all people!'

'You've always trusted me in the past, Bren. Now, for yourself, for Deanne and the kids, I'm ordering you to drop it.'

There was a long silence on the phone, then finally a single bleak word from Bren—'Christ'—and the connection was cut.

Brock stared down at his phone, feeling sick.

~

Ellie Pearse was a plump, jovial woman living in a Victorian house not far from the university campus. When Kathy rang the bell the front door immediately opened and two young women rushed out, followed by Ellie.

'They're late for lectures,' she said. 'You must be Nancy. Come on in.'

She led Kathy to a sitting room in which a fat ginger cat lay curled on the sofa.

'And how is Wally doing?' she asked.

'Pretty well, I'd say. He seemed very cheerful. Busy.'

'Oh yes, always busy. I don't regret my days in the force— I had some good friends there—but I wasn't sorry to retire. You get to the point where you've gone through one too many new-broom management reorganisations. But I still get young women PCs coming and boarding with me here, along with the students.'

'You didn't have a PC called Ashley Osborn stay with you, did you?'

'Oh yes. I remember Ashley well. You know her?'

Kathy felt a great buzz of relief. 'I've met her. She told me about the Turton case.'

'You must give her my love. What's she up to these days?'

'Still a copper, but in London.'

'Is that right? She's moved around then. She left us to go to Derby, if I remember right. Lovely girl, but so serious. There was no light side to Ashley. I don't mean it as a criticism; she just seemed so old for her years.'

'Yes, she's still like that.'

'And she told you about the Ryan Turton case, did she? She was living here then.'

'Was she much affected by that murder?'

Ellie thought about that, then shook her head. 'No. In fact, she didn't seem much interested, while everyone else was eager to hear of any developments. To tell the truth, I don't remember ever discussing it with her here after work, although I tried to be sociable because she didn't seem to have any friends.'

She looked over at the cat and smiled. 'The only one she seemed to show any affection for was old Saturn, my cat. Ashley would sit over there with her and make her purr, stroking her.'

'That's Saturn?'

'Oh no, that's Maisy. Saturn died a few years ago.'

'Was she ginger too?'

'No, she was a Persian, jet black. People said she looked evil with those yellow eyes, but Saturn was ever so friendly. I miss her still.'

Kathy was interested. 'It's so sad when pets die, isn't it? Did you have Saturn cremated?'

'No, I buried her in the garden, beneath the hydrangea. It's done really well.'

They continued talking about the Turton murder and Ashley.

'Did she ever tell you why she came to Leicester?'

'I gathered that she'd had some kind of family tragedy back in Nottingham,' Ellie said, 'and wanted a change of scene.'

'And then she moved on to Derby. Why was that, do you know?'

'I think she just got restless. And now she's in London. Does she have a partner?'

'No, I don't believe so.'

'I used to wonder if that was the problem. I did try to get her to socialise a bit more, but she never seemed interested. And I suppose you've spoken to Rick Waterman about the Turton case, have you? He was in charge.'

'I haven't. Wally said he thought he'd moved down south.'

'No, he's still here, in that old house. His wife died a couple of months ago and I saw the notice in the paper and went along to the funeral. I said hello to Rick. He's walking with a stick now.'

'Harley Mills told me that he wouldn't talk to me. Like getting blood out of a stone, he said.'

Ellie laughed. 'He could be right. Tell you what, take him a bottle of Black Label. It was his favourite tipple. And tell him I sent you. Here, I'll give you his address. It's one of the old mill managers' houses on Frog Island.'

Kathy thanked her, promising to pass on Ellie's good wishes to Ashley, and said goodbye. As she walked back through the university campus towards the city centre, she thought about Saturn the black cat. Hair, she knew, didn't degrade like other body parts, and if Saturn's remains were beneath the hydrangea the cat's fur would still yield DNA that could be matched to the one found on Turton's jacket, if they still had that. She knew it was a very long shot, but it might be something her defence could pursue if things got desperate.

Evening was drawing in, the streetlamps on and daylight fading, as she followed Ellie's directions back through the city centre, stopping at an off-licence on the way to buy a bottle of Black Label. A light drizzle began to fall and she put up her umbrella as she crossed the bridge over the Grand Union Canal to Frog Island, once an industrial hub of the city packed with weaving mills, now deserted or demolished. As far as she could see, no one lived here now. But then, towards the end of the street and opposite a cluster of large steel-clad sheds, she noticed half-a-dozen red-brick Victorian houses in a cul-de-sac, and among them number 182a.

She rang the doorbell and tapped on the front door, but there was no response. Then, as she turned away, she saw a man walking towards her carrying a shopping bag and leading a dog. As they got closer she realised that both man and labrador were elderly, with greying hair and a slow, steady pace. The man had a walking stick. When they reached 182a he said, 'Hello. Can I help you?'

'I'm looking for Mr Waterman.'

'That's me.'

'My name's Nancy Blackett, Mr Waterman. Ellie Pearse gave me your address. I was hoping to have a few minutes of your time. I'm writing a book about famous sportsmen who met an untimely end, and I wanted to include the Ryan Turton case.'

'Not interested,' Waterman said, and made to move past her to the front door.

'Ellie warned me you might say that, so she suggested I try to bribe you with this . . .'

Waterman took in the label on the bottle in her hand and looked at her severely. 'I have never taken a bribe in my life, young lady. But it's a miserable night, so you'd better come in.'

He put a key in the door and the dog went in first, then Waterman, who switched on a hall light. The house seemed no warmer than the street, and Kathy wondered if he had central heating. She followed him to the kitchen, where he put down his shopping bag on the table and went to the pantry to fetch the dog a treat.

'We'll go next door,' he said, taking off his coat. He put out a hand for her coat and hung them both on pegs, then led her to a sitting room, where he switched on an electric fire and indicated a seat.

The room was immaculately tidy and seemed unused. There was no TV, no books, few ornaments. On the mantelpiece was a framed photograph of Waterman and a woman of similar age, lit by bright sunlight against the background of a beach.

'Ellie told me that you have recently lost your wife, Mr Waterman. I'm very sorry.'

He grunted and turned away stiffly to a cupboard from which he took two whisky glasses.

'That was in Australia,' he said. 'Last March. She'd always wanted to go.'

'Me too, but I've never been.'

'You should. You should do all the things you want to while you still have time.' He poured two glasses and handed one to Kathy, then sat facing her. The dog came in and lay down between them, in front of the fire.

'So you're writing a book.'

Kathy felt tawdry repeating the same stupid story once again, and Waterman obviously wasn't impressed.

'Who would want to read stories like that?' he said disapprovingly, and she felt chastened. He reminded her of an inspector she'd worked under before she got into Homicide, a stern man who always made her feel inadequate.

'I've spoken to Harley Mills of the *Mercury*, and to Wally Scanlon, but I thought I really should get your perspective.'

'It was a great personal disappointment to me, my last case, but that's how it is sometimes. A random attacker, never traced.'

He was trying not to sound defensive, she thought, but it didn't quite work. 'So you believe it was a motiveless murder?'

'Oh, there would have been some kind of reason—rage, frustration, psychosis. Perhaps Turton said something provocative, who knows. But it was random, I'm sure of that. Not much more I can tell you, I'm afraid.'

'I see.' Kathy watched Waterman drain his glass and sensed that he was about to wind up the interview. 'I wonder, do you by any chance remember a young woman constable who was with you at that time by the name of Ashley Osborn?'

'Ashley? Why yes, I do remember Ashley. My wife was a retired police officer herself, and she liked to welcome new women officers and help them find their feet. She arranged for Ashley to rent a room from Ellie Pearse, if I remember right. Do you know her?'

'Yes, I met her in London, where she's based now. That's what got me interested in the Ryan Turton case, him being her brother-in-law.'

'What?' Waterman looked surprised. 'You're saying Ryan Turton was related to Ashley?'

'Yes. As I understand it, Ashley's parents both died when she was young and her older sister Gillian raised her. She idolised Gillian. Then, when Ashley was eleven, Gillian married Turton. This was back in Nottingham, when he was playing for the Green and Whites. You sure you don't know the story?'

'No. No, I don't.'

'Well, they lived together, the three of them, and Ashley soon realised that Turton was abusing her sister, coming home drunk and bashing her. She felt helpless as things went from bad to worse. Eventually, when Ashley was sixteen, she came home from school and found Gillian dead at the foot of the stairs with a broken neck. The police investigated but didn't bring charges and it was put down to an accident. At the funeral, Ashley stood up and publicly accused Turton of murdering her sister.'

Kathy watched Rick Waterman absorbing this, playing it out in his head, the house very silent.

'You don't say. What happened to Ashley then?'

'As far as I can gather, Turton transferred to Leicester and Ashley was in care for a while, then she joined Nottingham-shire Police as a trainee.'

'Nottinghamshire Police.'

'Yes. Then she transferred to Leicester in 2007.'

'Why did she do that?'

'I'm not sure. I was hoping you might be able to tell me. You really didn't know any of this?'

He shook his head. 'No, I certainly didn't.'

'In 2009, four months after Turton was murdered, she moved on to Derby.'

Waterman looked disturbed. He said softly, 'And she told you all this?'

'She's a pretty private person, and most of it I had to find out for myself. I got interested in her because she was later involved in some high-profile domestic violence cases and I came across the connection with Turton and followed it up.'

After a long silence, Waterman said, 'You did well. You should have been a detective.'

'Thanks. Anyway, that's all by the bye. I just wanted to check nothing further had come up about Turton's death that I hadn't heard about. I think I've taken up enough of your time, Mr Waterman. I really appreciate your help.'

As they got to their feet he said, 'I'd like to have a look at what you write about the Turton case before you publish it. All right?'

'Of course.'

They exchanged details and she said, 'There are so many sad cases. I may not include Ryan Turton's.'

He looked relieved.

~

After he'd shown Nancy to the door, Waterman went upstairs to the little room he used as his study and opened the box file in which he'd kept all the consolation cards and letters he'd been sent when his wife died. It didn't take him long to find the beautiful card from Ashley Osborn with a note about how much she'd appreciated his wife's help when she came to Leicester. Beneath the message she'd written her email address.

~

Brock put a call through to Kathy's office and asked to speak to her deputy, DI Peter Sidonis.

'Just a quick word, Peter. Has anyone else been suspended from your team besides Kathy?'

There was a moment's silence before Sidonis came back with Judy Birch's name.

'Thanks. How about the accuser? You got their name?'

Sidonis said he didn't know, and Brock thanked him and rang off. He looked up DS Birch's details on the police intranet and rang the number. A woman's voice answered.

Brock said, 'Is that Judy Birch?'

'Hang on, I'll get her.'

Eventually another voice said, 'Yes?'

'Judy, I'm DCI Brock, a good friend of Kathy's. Has she ever spoken of me?'

'Yes.'

'You can trust me. I want to help you both if I can. How are you coping?'

'How do you think?'

'I'm sure it must be tough. Could you spare me a few minutes?'

'I suppose so.'

'I can be at your place in half an hour.'

'No, not here.'

She told him to meet her at the King's Head, where Brock found her sitting in the snug bar with another woman. When she saw Brock she said something to the woman and left their table and joined Brock at the bar.

'Thanks for seeing me, Judy. Have they brought charges against you?'

'Oh yes, same as Kathy.'

'Have you seen her lately?'

'No.'

'I can't find her. Can you help me?'

She hesitated a moment, then said, 'I don't know where she is.'

He had the sense that she had been on the verge of adding something but had decided against it. He went on, 'Could you fill me in on what's happened?'

She looked cautiously at the people around them queuing for drinks and they moved to find a quieter spot, and there she told him the whole story.

He took notes, asked questions and finally sat back, shaking his head. 'Good heavens.'

'Yes. We couldn't really believe it. Then she turned on us. She's bloody clever.'

'Where is Osborn now, do you know?'

'No idea.'

'What about Kathy? Is there any way I can get in contact with her?'

Judy lowered her head, then took a phone from her pocket. 'She gave me this. She said it's secure. It's got her number.' She handed it to Brock.

He found Kathy's number and pressed it, listened to it ring, and finally heard the familiar voice. 'Judy?'

'Kathy, it's me, Brock. I'm with Judy. Are you all right? Sorry, stupid question. I want to help.'

'You can't, Brock. Thank you, but you'll only entangle yourself in this. I have to sort it out myself.' She sounded exhausted.

'Where are you?'

No reply, then, 'Has Judy told you the story?'

'Yes.'

'I came up here to Leicester to see if I could find out more about the first murder, of her sister's husband. But I reckon I'm wasting my time. If nothing turns up, I'll come home tomorrow. Do they realise I've skipped town?'

'Not as far as I know. Where are you staying in Leicester?'

'The Grand, but stay away from me, Brock. I contaminate everyone I know.'

She rang off. Brock noted the number and handed the phone back to Judy. 'She's in Leicester, trying to find out more about the first murder. I'm going to see if I can help her.'

'What can I do?'

'Nothing, Judy. Just keep your chin up and do exactly what they tell you.'

He left her there with her friend and called a cab to take him to St Pancras. The concourse was busy with passengers just arrived on the 7.39 pm from Paris. He made his way to the ticket machines for the domestic routes and bought a single for Leicester. He plucked the ticket from the slot and turned to see a man in a black coat who was examining him with interest. Behind him, two other heavily built men were also scrutinising him.

'Evening,' the man said. 'You don't know me, but I know all about you, David Brock. My name's Crouch, Bernard Crouch, DPS.' He held up his ID. 'And you're under arrest.'

He reached forward, took the ticket from Brock's hand and examined it. 'Ah, Leicester.' He smiled. 'We've got a car waiting outside.'

~

That evening, Kathy was feeling deeply uneasy about her visit to Rick Waterman. He was surely depressed, grimly clinging to his routines after the death of his wife. His dog looked old and would be the next to go, and what would Rick do then? She had crashed into this sad scene, making him talk about the failure that had soured the end of his police career. Frustrated by her lack of progress elsewhere, she had deliberately taken him step by step through Ashley Osborn's story, hoping to use him to stir things up. Now she felt ashamed, remembering the look of shock on his face when she explained Ashley's connection to Turton. What would he do now?

Kathy hadn't gone back to her hotel, but instead walked the streets for a while, got a meal in an Italian restaurant and then went to the High Cross pub, from where Ryan Turton had set out on his final walk. It was after ten thirty when she returned to the Grand and was brought to a stop by the sight of two police cars with flashing lights parked outside. She joined a group of people standing watching, trying to see what was going on, when two cops emerged from the hotel. Kathy caught her breath when she recognised the bag that one of them was carrying. It was hers.

She turned and slipped away, walking quickly down narrow pedestrian streets, avoiding the main roads. What to do? If Crouch knew she was up here, they would certainly be watching the train and bus stations. She would have to stay here for the time being, but where? On the edge of the city centre now and moving into residential streets, she saw a sign for a bed and breakfast up ahead. Could she risk that? What if there had been a warning on the news? She would have to concoct some story about why she had no luggage. She walked on.

Had Rick Waterman tipped them off, or Wally Scanlon? She thought not. More likely it had come from London, that conversation with Brock and Judy. Crouch must have tracked them somehow.

It began to rain, and she thought enviously of those students going back to Ellie Pearse's cosy home. She had hardly been aware of her direction, but now emerged onto a broad ring road and saw a sign on the far side for Frog Island. She sprinted across the traffic lanes and followed the sign, emerging into an area of mixed industrial buildings. The streets were empty here, the buildings' car parks deserted, and she moved between areas of dark shadow beneath blank walls. The buildings became older, some sites demolished, and she recognised the old mills she had seen before. And there, at the end of the next cross street, was the cluster of mill managers' houses. There were no lights on in Rick Waterman's.

It was bitterly cold now, the rain getting heavy, and she looked around for shelter. Ahead of her was one of the deserted mills, four dark storeys looming up in the darkness, the door and window openings facing the street bricked up. Kathy saw a narrow gap in the fencing on the adjacent empty lot and slipped through, stepping as quickly as she could over the rubble-strewn ground. In the dim light she made out the rear of the mill, and saw that the openings there were less securely blocked, with corrugated metal sheeting that was bent and buckled in places where people had broken in. She picked one of these and eased and tugged at the sheet until she had made a gap wide enough to squeeze through. She pulled it closed behind her and stood still for a moment, panting, listening for any sound. Nothing. At least it was sheltered here, and dry.

Taking out her phone, she used its light to move cautiously into what appeared to be a broad space divided down the centre by a row of iron columns, the floor littered with rubbish. At one end she saw a stair rising to an upper level and she moved carefully towards it. The handrail had collapsed, but the stair itself seemed solid, and she climbed slowly up to the next level, which also appeared to be deserted. Light was shining faintly through a window in the end wall and she went over and looked out onto the street and, at the far end, the mill managers' houses.

It had been a long day and she felt exhausted. Her feet snagged against something and she shone her light onto a pile of old sacking. It would have to do. She formed it into a rough mattress, wrapped her coat tightly around herself and lay down.

18

Brock awoke at first light after an uneasy sleep filled with dreams of indefinable menace. He was at home—he could hear the rain dripping from the broken gutter—after Crouch and company had released him on police bail towards midnight. He could hardly complain that he hadn't been warned; both Stone and Torrens had told him to stay out of it, but he'd thought he could do better and had now made things worse for everyone, including Kathy. They had charged him with conspiring with another to pervert the course of justice, a common law offence in England and Wales carrying a maximum sentence of life imprisonment, but hadn't elaborated, releasing him on police bail to return for interview in the morning.

In that moment of clarity on waking, an uncomfortable thought came into his head. He had never doubted Kathy's innocence for one moment, and had acted accordingly. But supposing he was wrong? He'd initially dismissed that barbed comment of Stone's about Kathy's apartment—*It was paid for by Martin Connell*—but it had lodged in the back of his mind and wouldn't go away. What did he really know about Connell? What did he really know about Kathy?

No! He dismissed the idea. How could he imagine such a thing? It was as if all his certainties about truth and lies had been undermined, beginning with the discovery that his Merz must be a fake.

~

Kathy also woke at dawn, feeling chilled to the marrow. Above her the timber beams and boards were stained with age, and she imagined what this place must have been like in its heyday, the women working at the steam-powered weaving machines, the noise, the smells, the endless labour. She struggled stiffly to her feet and looked out of the window, the street slicked with rainwater, the dark sky, the few streetlamps still lit. There was a café she remembered passing just before she crossed the ring road, and she decided to see if it was open, climbing back out of the mill compound and jogging down the street towards the heavy traffic coming into the city. The lights were on, the café quiet, and she gave an order for a bacon roll and coffee and went to the little toilet at the back to wash herself and fix her hair—no make-up, which she'd left in her hotel room.

There was a copy of that morning's *Leicester Mercury* on the shop counter, and she took it and her breakfast over to a corner table. There was no mention of her, and she was almost disappointed that there wasn't a report from Harley Mills about his meeting with the wanted fugitive. She wondered if she could have mistaken the bag in the officer's hand outside her hotel, but then dismissed the doubt. It was hers all right. She decided she would go into the city centre and buy a coat and hat and make-up, maybe a wig, and then, later in the day when they might have given up looking for her, risk catching a train back to London.

~

She was in the Haymarket Shopping Centre in the city, trying on a green coat, when her phone rang. It was DI Wally Scanlon, and to Kathy's ears he sounded unnaturally friendly.

'Nancy! Glad I've caught you! How are things?'

'Fine, thanks, Wally. What can I do for you?'

'It's more what I can do for *you*! I've come across something on the Ryan Turton case that would really interest you.'

'That's great. What is it?'

'It's something I'd need to show you in person. It'll be fantastic for your book. When can we meet? I'm pretty free right now.'

This didn't sound right. Kathy said, 'Oh, that is a shame, Wally. I'm in Nottingham, to talk to people who played rugby with him here.'

'Oh ...' She could imagine him looking at Crouch for instructions. 'Well, are you coming back? We could meet later in the day.'

'I'm afraid my schedule is pretty tight. I have to go on later today to Newcastle.'

'Newcastle?'

'Yes. Maybe you could send a picture of whatever it is to my phone?'

'Um, look, where are you in Nottingham?'

Gotcha, Kathy thought. 'Sorry, Wally, here's my lift. Have to go. Thanks for all your help.' She rang off wondering if Crouch or Stone or whoever it was would fall for it. Either way, Crouch would be mad when they eventually did meet up. Obviously they hadn't been able to track her phone yet, and she silently blessed Phoebe's excessively priced device, but it was surely only a matter of time. She was deciding that she'd have to get rid of it when it rang again.

'Nancy? Is that Nancy Blackett?' Rick Waterman's voice was faint.

'Yes, Rick.'

'I've been thinking about our conversation. I would like to see you again. It's something important. Will you come to my house? Not now—later. At four thirty?'

It sounded like a repeat of Wally Scanlon's call, but Waterman's tone was very different, worried and preoccupied. Why did it have to wait until four thirty?

'All right, Rick. I'll be there.'

'Good.' He hung up.

Kathy hurried out of the shopping centre, dropped the phone through the grating of a street drain, and ran back to the vacant mill on Frog Island. Once again the area was deserted, no one in sight, and she quickly slipped through the fence and returned to her hiding place by the window on

the first floor, from which she could see the cul-de-sac
with the mill managers' houses.

She spent the next hours watching for unmarked cars or
vans that might drop people off, or stealthy visitors calling at
Waterman's house, but there was no sign of movement at all
until two thirty, when Waterman himself emerged from his
house with his old lab and departed on a slow walk. They
returned half an hour later, Waterman carrying a shopping
bag, and disappeared back into the house. It began to rain.

At three twenty a taxi appeared at the end of the street. It
drove slowly to Waterman's front door and someone emerged,
put up an umbrella and ran to the house. Kathy didn't get a
clear view of them beneath the umbrella, and couldn't even
be certain whether they were male or female.

She waited: four twenty, four thirty, four forty. The light
was fading, streetlamps coming on and no one else had
appeared. Making up her mind, she returned to the street and
walked quickly, hood up, head down against the rain, towards
the cul-de-sac. Waterman answered her knock immediately
and let her in, took her coat and led her to the sitting room.
There was no sign of the visitor.

'Take a seat,' he said, and gestured at one armchair, seating
himself, as before, in the other. Kathy was half expecting the
heavy drapes on the far wall to be flung open and men to
burst in from the rear garden, but everything was still.

'I was disturbed by what you told me about Ashley
Osborn's relationship with Ryan Turton, so I decided to
contact her myself.'

Kathy caught her breath. The visitor—Ashley? She glanced
at the doorway.

'Yes, she's here. We've had a good talk,' Waterman went on. 'She told me about you. You're Detective Chief Inspector Kathy Kolla, are you not? Currently on suspension on serious charges?'

'Yes, I am.'

'You needn't have lied to me, you know. It would have been better if you'd just told me the truth.'

'I apologise, but I thought it necessary. Did she explain that she's responsible for my suspension?'

'She did. And now she has something to say to you.' He turned to the door and called out, 'Ashley?'

After a moment Kathy heard footsteps in the hall and Ashley appeared in the doorway. She was still wearing her outside coat, her hands in the pockets. She looked sombre and pale.

'Hello, Kathy.'

It struck Kathy that the material on one side of her coat was pulled out of shape, as if there might be something heavy in the right–hand pocket.

'Rick told me that you brought him a bottle of his favourite Scotch. Smart research.' She smiled. 'How about a drink, Rick?'

He got slowly to his feet and went over to the cabinet, placed three glasses in a row and poured whisky into each. He handed one to Ashley and one to Kathy and then sat down again. Ashley remained standing and raised her glass in her left hand. 'Cheers.' She swallowed it in one gulp and seemed to relax a little. 'They're all in a panic about you in London, Kathy. Don't know where you are. But when Rick contacted me I wasn't surprised to learn you'd come up here. Find out anything?'

'Working on it.'

'Bet you are. Well, I think it's time to bring things to a close. Since you started probing, it's made me think about things, what I've been doing, and made me realise how pointless it's all been. So a few bad men met a premature end, but who cared? There were no lessons to be drawn because no one knew the reason why they died, until you worked it out, Kathy. And then my first reaction was to do everything I could to hide the truth. But why? Isn't that the only real point, to make people see the truth?

'So now I want to tell that truth. You've got your mobile there, Rick? Take it out. I want you to record this. I want you to take my confession.'

He did as she said, and she began talking in a flat, unemotional tone.

'I am Ashley Osborn, thirty-three years old and of sound mind. I make this statement to Detective Chief Inspector Kathy Kolla and Detective Inspector Rick Waterman of my own free will.

'I was born and grew up in Nottingham with my sister Gillian, who was nine years older than me. Our parents were killed in a car accident when I was eight, and my sister looked after us both. She was very pretty, and when I was ten she met and fell in love with Ryan Turton, who was just establishing a reputation playing rugby professionally for Nottingham RFC. They married the following year and we lived together, the three of us. Ryan was not abusive to me at first, but I soon became aware that he bullied Gillian and was becoming increasingly violent towards her. I used to hear him come home at night after he'd been drinking with his friends and shout and physically attack her. It was very hard to listen to. I know she often had to cover her bruises with make-up the next day and she suffered at least two fractures. I had a secret diary in which I kept a record of his abuse, and one day he came home unexpectedly when Gillian was still at work and caught me writing in it. He was violently angry and thrashed me with his belt and tore up the diary.

'When I was sixteen I came home one evening from performing in a school concert to find my sister lying at the foot of the stairs. I couldn't rouse her and called an ambulance and they said that Gillian was dead. I told the police that Ryan must have been responsible. He denied it. Of course the police all knew him because by then he was a big star with Nottingham RFC. I was interviewed by a woman police officer and a social worker, but no charges were ever brought against Ryan. He wept at Gillian's funeral, which made me very upset and I stood up and told everyone that he was responsible. They were all very embarrassed, and some of the women led me away and tried to comfort me, but I knew they suspected I was telling the truth. Soon after that he transferred to the Leicester Tigers and I was taken into care.

'When I was seventeen I decided to become a police officer and became a trainee with Nottinghamshire Police. I did this because I was determined that men who behaved as Ryan did should be held accountable. I had no contact with him, but I followed his progress in the sports news, and in 2007 I applied for a transfer to Leicester so that I could keep an eye on him; I was certain he wouldn't have changed his ways. Sure enough, I met an ex-girlfriend of his who told me the same old story of what he'd done to her. I tried to persuade her to make a formal complaint, but she didn't want to go through all that. Meanwhile, his career was in trouble and he was drinking heavily. There was a rumour of a rape that was covered up.

'Finally, on the night of Saturday the twenty-first of February 2009, I decided to act. I followed him from the High Cross pub to Pocklingtons Walk and stabbed him to death on the steps of the Magistrates Court. I acted entirely alone. Afterwards I remained in Leicester until the investigation was no longer active and then transferred to Derby, where I joined the domestic violence unit.'

And so it went on for almost half an hour, with her clear and precise confession to the murders of Mervyn Byrne and Victor Upshot in Derby, of Izad Patel in Luton and Ahmed Majeed in Clapham, with a catalogue of their unpunished crimes against women. She emphasised that she had acted entirely alone, though in the case of Ahmed Majeed, Kathy remained convinced that Haniya had been involved in some way.

'Regarding my accusations of corruption against DCI Kolla and DS Birch, I freely confess that I fabricated the evidence against them in order to protect myself. They never behaved in an incorrect manner towards me.

'The reason that I am now confessing to killing these men is that I realise that my actions have no meaning if people don't understand why those men died. Their deaths were a necessary and just retribution for their crimes, which had gone unpunished by the criminal justice system. I make this confession now so that people will understand how much remains to be done to curb male violence against women, and I hope this inspires them to act.'

Ashley took a deep breath. 'Did you get all that? Rick, I'm sorry that I ruined the end of your police career. I think I should have come to you then and confessed, and perhaps people might have acted back then and the other deaths would have been unnecessary. I am now surrendering myself into your custody. I want you to make the arrest.'

Waterman was clearly shaken by what he had heard. He made an effort to pull himself up straight and said, 'Ashley Osborn, I have heard your confession and I am arresting you for the murder of Ryan Turton.' He hesitated, then added, 'I'll call for a police car.'

As he bent to his phone, Kathy was watching Ashley draw her right hand out of her pocket, and saw the heavy thing she had been holding in there: a solid black pistol.

Ashley said, 'I've given you a hard time, Kathy. I'm sorry. In another life we could have been good friends.'

Before Kathy could move, Ashley put the muzzle of the pistol into her mouth and pulled the trigger.

For a moment they were paralysed and the scene seemed frozen in Kathy's head: the deafening bang in the small room, the spray of blood on the ceiling, the lifeless slump of the body to the floor.

Then Waterman lowered his head into his hands and began to sob.

19

They had arranged to meet for their long-delayed lunch together. It was Brock's turn to select the venue and to pay, and he chose the Ivy, the famous restaurant in Covent Garden which had recently celebrated its one hundredth anniversary. There they gathered, seated at one of the lamplit tables, competing to identify celebrities among the other diners. Kathy won on double points, spotting Elton John, looking solemn over by the window, having lunch with Jude Law. But she didn't smile at her triumph, and Brock was struck by how strained and almost gaunt she had become. She had lost weight, but also vitality, as if her struggle had exhausted all her reserves of strength.

He raised his glass of bubbles. 'Here's to you, Kathy. To persistence, endurance and smart thinking. You deserve a medal.'

Bren said, 'Hear, hear!' but Kathy shook her head.

'It would have been better if I'd left the whole thing alone.'

'No,' Brock said firmly. 'You didn't have that choice. The one with the choices was Ashley Osborn, and in the end she got exactly what she wanted.'

He was referring to the storm of debate which had erupted in the days following Ashley's death, for Rick Waterman's recording of her confession and suicide had been hacked or leaked within twelve hours of her death, and her spectacular confession had dominated newspaper headlines, blogging sites and Parliament while the fraud and conspiracy charges against Kathy, Judy and Brock had been hurriedly quashed.

'And Bren,' Brock continued, 'I hope you've forgiven me for keeping you out of it all. I wish I'd taken my own advice.'

Bren shook his head. 'You old bastard. I should have known you better than to think you'd walk away from it all. And I'll bet you enjoyed every minute of it.'

'I did find those long interrogations with DCI Crouch quite instructive. I thought I might send him a memo on how he could improve his technique.'

Bren laughed. 'Well, I hope they've all made grovelling apologies to you both.'

'Oh, Bren,' Brock said, 'you know the Met better than that. At the moment they're desperately looking for some-where obscure to park me out of sight and mind. What about you, Kathy? Have you rejoined your team?'

'Yes. The shrink said I wasn't ready, but I wanted to try to return to normality. But I'm finding it hard.'

'Well, I know exactly what you need—a good murder mystery. And it just so happens that I have one that I very much need your help with.'

He topped up their glasses and began to tell them the whole story of the Babington Collection and the deaths of Nadya Babington and Callum McAdam, and despite everything, Kathy found herself being drawn in, as one strange twist followed another. When their first course arrived—Argyle smoked salmon for Brock and Kathy and Bang Bang chicken for Bren—Brock was telling them about Babington's double life on Long Island and Bren was shaking his head and muttering about 'a glutton for punishment'.

'Anyway,' Brock concluded, 'the point is that we have two deaths which, in my opinion, have not been properly investigated, and since Kent Police have closed both cases I can't do anything about it. But Nadya was a Londoner, within the jurisdiction of the Met, and her death was preceded by her husband's appeal to Assistant Commissioner Cameron about the threatening email, so I was thinking that a resourceful officer in Homicide might very well have grounds for investigating further. Why don't you sound out Torrens, Kathy? He won't speak to me, but he must be feeling a bit vulnerable now, not having given you more support.'

'Okay.'

'But there's another angle, and I wondered if you could help here, Bren. Lurking at the back of all this is Nadya's past life and failed marriage to Sergei Semenov, and their dodgy offspring Miki. Now, if I'm right that Pavel Gorshkov, the man Miki met at the Dorchester, is in fact his father, then that blows the whole thing wide open. What are they up to?

Could Gorshkov be responsible for the threatening email and his ex-wife's death? Again I'm helpless, in limbo, no longer part of Fraud or anywhere else, supposedly on leave—but you've been involved with Operation Nexus, haven't you, Bren?'

Operation Nexus was a joint operation of the Metropolitan Police and the Home Office to investigate and deport foreign nationals who were suspected of coming to the UK for criminal purposes. It had been attacked by some critics for not being open to scrutiny.

Bren nodded. 'Yes, still am.'

'Good. Do you think you could get them to investigate him? I know the FBI in New York have been looking into his art dealings.'

'Possibly. But we might need to get someone in art fraud to advise us.'

'Yes, I think I can arrange that. But it's mainly his identity that I'm interested in. If he's been entering the UK under a false name, that makes him an obvious target for Nexus, and we could use that to pressure him. But I don't want to scare him off before we're ready to pounce. If he thinks we're on to him, he may just slip back to Russia and then we'll never be able to reach him.'

Their main course arrived, the Ivy's shepherd's pie for all three of them, and they turned their attention to that.

Later, when lunch was finished and they went their separate ways, Brock decided to return to the Fraud office. He'd been avoiding it since the investigation against Kathy and himself had collapsed, but he wanted to get hold of the notes still in his desk.

He was thankful to find that Stone wasn't around, then noticed a package lying on his own desk. He opened it and smiled to see a bottle of tequila inside. Stuffing it and the documents into his briefcase, he hurried out to the lift and was standing there, trying to look inconspicuous with the fat briefcase under his arm, when the doors opened and there stood Molly, whom he hadn't seen since New York.

'Brock!' she cried. 'At last! I've been trying to get hold of you. We must talk.'

'Yes, we must,' he said, looking back over his shoulder, 'but not here.' He bustled her back into the lift and pressed the button.

'What's happened to you?' she said. 'Why are you being so furtive?'

'I'm trying to escape before Stone sees me.'

'No one's seen him for a week. There was a rumour going around that he'd been investigating *you*, of all people! I told them that must be nonsense.'

'I'm afraid it was true, Molly. Fancy a coffee?'

The doors opened at the ground-floor lobby and they walked round the block to a café, where he told her what had happened.

'That's why everybody's been so strange,' she said. 'I'm sorry, Brock, they didn't tell me a thing. Can I do anything to help?'

'I hope so. I'm still not satisfied that we know enough about Babington's Merz, nor about Nadya Babington and Callum McAdam's deaths. I'm convinced that they're linked to Babington's art collection. Would you be able to help me with that?'

'Absolutely. I've got nothing on that can't wait. What can I do?'

'Did you find out anything more about Pavel Gorshkov while you were in New York?'

'Not much. The Art Crime Team say that he's never visited the US, although they have his name as a director of I.I. International in New York. Their office is in the Seagram Building on Park Avenue, so we're not talking about a low-rent outfit. They don't appear to operate in the same way as other art dealers in the city—they have no gallery, don't advertise and don't attend the big auctions at Sotheby's, and no one seems to know who their clients are. Rudi's theory is that they buy and sell through intermediaries and act as a confidential agent for Russian oligarchs wanting to buy big-dollar items anonymously.'

'We didn't ask Rudi about Sergei Semenov, did we?'

'No, we didn't.'

Brock took a file from his briefcase and handed it to her. 'This is all we know about him at present—not much—and an old photograph of him, taken about twenty years ago. It would be good if you could find out if the Americans have anything on him. Oh . . .' Brock drew the bottle out of his bag, 'and thank you for the tequila, Molly.'

'No, thank *you*. I really enjoyed our trip. I flew back the day after you mysteriously disappeared and I've been waiting to hear what's going on. Does this mean the Babington case isn't dead?'

'That's right. I'm out of Fraud now and I'm putting a new team together. It would be great if we could count on you.'

'I'm in!' she cried. 'It's been really boring around here since you disappeared.'

20

The following day, Brock woke to the sound of water splashing down outside his bedroom window. He got up with a grunt and shuffled from room to room, making sure that none of it was actually getting into the house, then got dressed, had a breakfast of toast and coffee, and sat wondering how to fill the rest of his day. He was free of all taint, but had no office or duties to perform. He listened gloomily as the radio warned him that there were only seven shopping days left to Christmas and he'd better get out there with all the other panicking shoppers jamming the stores. He turned it off and sat staring at the rain streaming down the windowpane. Then he took out his phone and called the roofer to accept his quote. They told him it would be a couple of months before they could do the job, but Brock felt better for having made the decision.

~

Kathy was in Hammersmith, at her desk in the glass tower of the Box, catching up on paperwork. Her team had welcomed her and Judy back with genuine relief, and now everything seemed as before, as if it had never happened, but she knew it would be a long time before she could feel that way. She found it difficult to concentrate on the routine matters and her heart gave a lurch each time her phone rang and she hesitated before picking it up, half expecting to hear Crouch's voice ordering her back for another interview.

When she had cleared the memos, she read the notes Brock had given her and put a call through to Detective Sergeant Will Holt in Kent Police. She introduced herself and told him that she'd been asked to write a report on the death of Nadya Babington and would appreciate his help.

'And you're in Homicide, ma'am?' he queried. 'I believe the coroner's office is inclined to accept that her death was suicide.'

'Yes, and we're not suggesting otherwise, but she was resident in our area and, between you and me, her husband is a cousin of one of our assistant commissioners.'

'Ah, right. Well, how can I help you?'

'Could I have a copy of the pathology report and your report to the coroner?'

'Certainly.'

'There was another suicide in that area soon afterwards, wasn't there?'

'Callum McAdam, yes. We suspect that there was a relationship between the two of them, and that one suicide led to the
other, but we have no direct evidence of that. They left no notes.'

'Did you check their phone records?'

'No, my boss ruled that wasn't necessary.'

Kathy picked up the tone in his voice, and said, 'But you
weren't so sure?'

Holt hesitated, then said, 'Have you spoken to DCI Brock,
from the Met? He alerted us to McAdam's death.'

'Yes, I have.'

'Well, he seemed to have doubts about it, and to tell the
truth, so did I. So I'd be happy to help you however I can. Do
you want copies of the McAdam reports too?'

'That would be good, yes.'

The first reports arrived within an hour, and as she sifted
through them she felt the old stirrings of excitement, the grip
of concentration brought on by the mystery of unexplained
death. It was why Brock had involved her, she thought; his idea
of therapy. She called his number and told him she wanted to
visit the Hoo.

'You'll need a guide, Kathy,' he said. 'I'll pick you up in
an hour.'

~

She was waiting in the office lobby as he drew up outside, and
she ran out through the rain to jump in beside him. The car
was warm, music in the background—Mozart, she thought—
and as they set off she felt as if she were playing truant. 'I've
never been to the Hoo,' she said.

'I hadn't either, and I'm afraid it'll be a pretty bleak place on a day like this.'

An hour later they turned off the A2 and set out across the estuary flatlands veiled by the pouring rain. Brock said he would take her first to Nadya's pool, but the track leading to it was so boggy and treacherous that he had to stop before they reached it and continue on foot. He had brought rubber boots and umbrellas for them both, but the penetrating rain had soaked through their coats and trousers by the time they reached the pond. Bleak was the word all right, Kathy thought, as she stood on the bank and wondered at someone choosing such a place to die. Why here, of all places?

'Enough?' Brock said. 'Let's see if the vicar's in.'

They returned to the car and reversed with difficulty back along the track to the road.

After a while she spotted the dark stump of St Chad-on-the-Marsh up ahead.

They parked, got out and hurried through the rain to the church door.

'Hello?'

'Hello there!' a voice called from inside.

'The vicar,' Brock murmured. 'The Reverend Alwyn Bramley-Scott. He sounds cheerful.'

The vicar stuck his head out from his vestry. 'Come in here and get warm. That east wind! There's nothing between us and the Urals. Ah, you're the detective, aren't you?'

They went in and Brock introduced Kathy. An electric fire was glowing in a corner of the little room, and from a pocket in his coat Brock drew out a bottle of sherry. 'Is it too early for a snifter?'

'Not at all! Very apt for such a grim day,' the vicar said with relish as he took three glasses from the cupboard and poured. 'Sit, sit.'

'I'm off duty now,' Brock explained, 'at a loose end, but I can't get those two deaths out here from my mind.'

'Yes, yes. So very sad. They had such a close relationship, yet they were such different characters—Callum so dour and intense and quite careless in his appearance, while she was vibrant and full of life and beautifully dressed. But I would say that she was a volatile person, perhaps given to spells of depression and despair.'

Brock nodded. Then he said, 'I was thinking about you the other day, Vicar. The roof of my house is leaking and the gutters are shot, and I got a couple of quotes and couldn't believe the prices. And I thought about what you've achieved here, without help from the church authorities. I've got to hand it to you, it's a miracle. How did you manage it?'

Bramley-Scott beamed at the compliment. 'As I think I told you, the community rallied round. Yes, it *was* a kind of miracle.'

'But there is no community, Alwyn! A couple of farms that look pretty rundown and a penniless artist. Talk about loaves and fishes!'

The vicar smiled and murmured, 'The Lord works in mysterious ways . . .'

'In fact, the only person connected with this place who had any money was Nadya Babington. It was her, wasn't it? She was your benefactor.'

Bramley-Scott looked as if he might deny it, but then he sighed and said, 'They—Nadya and Callum—believed passionately in saving St Chad's. You must understand how desperate the situation was. The foundations were sinking, the walls crumbling, the roof rotten and the whole structure on the point of collapse. Can you imagine? The oldest church in England, and the authorities bickered among themselves and did nothing. Callum and Nadya saved us. God brought them to us and they saved St Chad's. Now it will last for another thousand years.'

Brock gazed out through the archway into the body of the church, looking again at the massive oak beams of the roof, the timber brackets and rafters. 'How much are we talking about?' He thought about the quote he'd just accepted for his own modest roof. 'A hundred thousand?'

The vicar bowed his head and said nothing.

'Half a million?' Silence.

Brock bent closer to him and said quietly, 'Vicar, I work in an office with highly skilled young men and women who specialise in fraud. One phone call from me and they will recover the records for every penny you've ever spent.'

The vicar looked startled and stared at him for a moment before whispering, 'Seven hundred and twenty-six thousand, one hundred and fifteen pounds, as of the end of last month. But it was not from fraud, believe me, sir. Callum and Nadya raised the money and insisted on anonymity.'

Brock leaned closer. 'Then why are they both dead?'

'I don't know! We had discussed a service of dedication and thanks for the restoration early in the new year and they were both so enthusiastic! I can only think ... no, I mustn't say that.'

'Tell me.'

'This place—the Hoo, the church, Callum's studio—was a sanctuary for Nadya. She came here whenever she could. To escape.'

'Escape? From what?'

'Her husband. She was terrified of him. He brutalised her!'

'What?' Brock tried to reconcile this with his image of Babington. 'He abused her?'

'Not physically, I think. I saw no sign of that. But mentally, psychologically. She lived in daily terror of him and escaped here whenever she could.'

'She told you that?'

'Callum told me.'

Brock, still trying to come to terms with this, saw that the vicar's glass was empty and he topped it up. The other man reached for it and thankfully took a gulp and said, 'The funny thing is that apparently the husband is quite religious.'

'Really?' Another surprise.

'Yes, but I know nothing of the Russian church.'

'Russian?'

'Oh yes, he's Russian, you see, like her.'

Then Brock got it. 'She was terrified of her *Russian* husband.' He glanced at Kathy.

'That's right, and so you see ... I wasn't sure whether I should have mentioned this when you told me of her death, and then Callum's. I mean, I have no evidence against the man. And then Sergeant Holt told me that their deaths were being treated as suicide, and I thought there was no good to be done by mentioning it.'

Kathy said, 'You must have a record of their payments to you.'

'Indeed yes, I have a donations book.' He opened his desk drawer and handed it over to her. 'I hope you discover the truth behind all of this.'

Brock looked over Kathy's shoulder as she flicked through the book, whose pages were divided into three columns—dates, amounts and sources. Apart from a sprinkling of small donations from visitors and locals and a single payment from N. Babington of five thousand pounds, the bulk of the money came in the form of irregular payments spread over the previous three years, ranging from twenty to fifty thousand pounds, each with the initials C.M. against it.

'How did Callum pay you, Vicar?'

'Oh, in cash. Always in cash.'

'Which you deposited in a bank account?'

'No. Callum told me it would be best to avoid the banks. He said it was important that the donations be kept private.'

'But he didn't tell you who these donors were, or why they were giving you this money?'

'As I understood it, they weren't giving the money to me, but to him. He told me they were clients of his who were paying him for commissions he'd carried out—commercial work, he said, that paid well. He himself had little need for money and so he was giving most of it to the church for the rebuilding.'

Brock said, 'Have you been inside his studio, Vicar?'

'Yes, I did pay a visit. Callum gave me a copy of the key, if you want to look at it.'

'And you saw his work in there?'

'The Hoo landscapes, yes. He said they were his real work, as against his commercial work. For that, he said, he had another studio, but he didn't say where it was.'

They had a look at other documents the vicar had, mostly invoices for the building works, then took the key and donations book and thanked him and returned to Brock's car and set off for Callum's place. Brock was silent, preoccupied, and Kathy said, 'Sounds plausible, doesn't it? Callum had a day job that brought in a regular pay packet but wasn't what he considered his real work, so he handed the cash over to the church and spent his nights doing the dark masterpieces that nobody wanted.'

'Where's this other studio?'

'Maybe it's his employer's studio—maybe in the city. Could be digital, something that pays very well. Animation? Advertising?' She could see that Brock was frustrated—this wasn't the answer he'd been hoping for.

They reached the Smithy, looking forlorn in the streaming rain as Brock swung the car in behind the workshop at the rear where he had found Callum's body, and they drew on plastic gloves. The lock resisted his efforts to open it, as if the building resented his intrusion, then finally snapped open. Stepping inside, they took in the slightly sour smell in the air and the dark stain on the floor below where Callum had hung. Apart from that, there was no indication of what had occurred here, the rope now removed and the chair placed upright against the wall. Brock explained what he'd seen before, and they took their time examining the benches and floor, but the paint stains were ancient and there was no other sign that Callum had done any painting here.

The studio next door still had his great black abstract landscapes on display, one sitting unfinished on an easel with a paint-encrusted palette and brushes beside it. Brock noticed some mail lying on the floor below the letterbox at the front door. Apart from the junk mail, there was a receipt from L. Cornelissen and Son, art materials supplier, and Brock put it in his pocket to see if Molly could learn anything from it. They walked slowly around the room, Kathy's heels clicking on the concrete floor. There was a large paint-spattered drop sheet laid out beneath the easel, and when she trod on it the sound of her footstep changed to a hollow thud. She pulled back the drop sheet to reveal a section of the floor that was timber. Shifting the easel and sheet clear, they saw hinges and a recessed handle which Kathy pulled, swinging back the heavy trapdoor to expose a flight of steps leading down into a basement.

There was a switch on the wall at the foot of the steps, and when she pressed it a dazzling white light filled a substantial cellar room. What first struck Kathy was how neat and clean it all looked. There was another easel down here, an adjustable chair and a workbench filled with equipment—a computer, a large microscope and magnifying glass, racks of glass tubes, jars and bottles, and an electric oven. There was a fat book on the bench, *Art Forensics*, its pages well thumbed. Nearby there was a large steel plan chest, and when they pulled out the drawers they found sheets of different types of paper, and canvases, some of them old and stained with the paint of images that had been scraped off.

Kathy said, 'Could this be it? The other studio?'

'Maybe,' Brock murmured, 'but it seems more a science lab than a studio.' He pointed to a mortar and pestle holding traces of an ochre powder. 'Looks like he made up his own paints, experimenting with pigments.'

Kathy was turning over the sheets of paper in the plan chest, and now held one up, an unfinished sketch with a few broad strokes of watercolour over a light pencil drawing. Brock looked over her shoulder and said, 'Looks a little bit like a John Singer Sargent.'

'Really? I didn't know you were so knowledgeable about art.'

'You'd be surprised, Kathy.' He began taking photographs, then said, 'We should get Molly, and forensics. I'd like to know who else has been down here.'

'Yes,' Kathy agreed.

Brock tried to ring Molly, but her phone was engaged and he left a message. Kathy, meanwhile, had organised a forensic team for later in the afternoon, so they decided to drive over to Rochester for lunch.

Brock chose the Golden Lion on the High Street and ordered a pint of Ruddles ale for himself and mineral water for Kathy.

'You'd better drive,' he said. 'Of course, drinking sherry with the vicar was a necessary sacrifice in the line of duty.'

'Of course.'

She didn't smile, he noticed, and seemed subdued. He wasn't quite sure how to handle it. Finally he said tentatively, 'Flashbacks?'

She looked up, startled. 'Oh, sorry. Actually I was just realising that for the past three or four hours I haven't thought about it.' She smiled. 'You were right. What I needed was a good murder mystery.'

Brock noticed the waitress passing by with someone's

lunch. 'And a plate of cod and chips. You've lost too much weight.'

His phone chirped. Brock saw Molly's number and answered the call. 'Molly, we've discovered something interesting at Callum McAdam's studio. Can you get out here?'

'Yes, I'll leave right away. Sorry I couldn't answer your call—I was talking to Rudi Spector in New York about Sergei Semenov. Fascinating. Tell you when I get there.'

Brock gave her directions and turned his attention back to ordering lunch. He was pleased to see that Kathy seemed to have an appetite.

When they were finished they returned to Callum's studio to find that the crime scene team had just arrived, their previous job having finished unexpectedly early. Brock and Kathy let them in and showed them to the basement room, then returned to the car to wait for Molly. The rain had stopped at last and a pale sun was glimmering through the clouds.

Kathy said, 'Can I ask, why did you come back?'

'Back?'

'Into service again, into the Met. Why didn't you just enjoy being free?'

'Oh, I did try that, but it didn't work. I got terribly bored. I missed this ...' He waved his hand. 'Problems like this— tricky, complicated, life and death. You know what I mean.'

She turned away. 'Most of the murders we're getting now are either domestics or teenage gangs knifing each other. They're stupid and depressing, and I thought Ashley Osborn's case would be what you're talking about. Something challenging, something I'd never seen before. Well, it was that all right—challenging, like walking into a minefield.'

'But you stopped her, Kathy. And if you hadn't, others would have died, until eventually someone else like you would have had to stop her. They won't give you a medal for it, but I would.'

'Thanks.'

'But if we're being open and frank, then tell me, why *did* Martin Connell leave you all that money?'

'I don't know for sure, but I think it was something to do with the Spider Roach case, how he betrayed us to Roach. Apparently Martin had a nasty death—a bad stomach cancer. Maybe it put the fear of God into him, and he wanted to make amends.'

'Then why did he do it through your aunt and uncle?'

'To protect me, I think. He would have foreseen what would happen if the Met found out he'd given me money. I've been thinking that I should sell the flat and give his money to some worthy cause. What do you think?'

Brock smiled. 'No, keep your lovely flat. I reckon you've earned it.'

A car swung into view and came to a stop beside them. Molly got out and came to Brock's window.

He said, 'Crime scene are checking the cellar. Hop in and tell us all about Sergei.'

'You didn't find more bodies down there, did you?' she asked.

'No, no. They're collecting fingerprints and DNA. We want to know who else has been there.'

'Oh good, only after talking to Rudi Spector I wouldn't have been surprised.' She got into the back seat and pulled out her notes. 'Well, he was very interested when he pulled up Semenov's file. Assuming he is the same Sergei Semenov that Nadya married—born in 1962, lived in St Petersburg—he first showed up in America in 1993 on a business visa, working for a Russian import–export company called Baltic WFS—wholesale food suppliers. In the next few years he made regular trips to New York, until 1996, when he was arrested during a raid on Baltic WFS, which was suspected of being a front for the Russian mafia Shulaya clan in New York, importing heroin into the United States from the Golden Crescent through Kazakhstan and Russia. In the subsequent investigation, Semenov was charged with extortion and racketeering, illegal firearms, narcotics trafficking and wire fraud, and was jailed until 2001, when he was expelled from the US and never heard of again.'

Brock said, 'That was the year Nadya came to London with Miki. She probably fled Russia when she heard that he was being released.'

'Could be.' Molly took a deep breath, turning the page of her notes. 'So, Sergei Semenov was a member of what they call the Bratva, or Brotherhood—the Russian mafia. According to Rudi, they are ruthless, highly organised and look after their own, and for some time there's been a rumour that they have a team that services the high end of the art market, obtaining items for very wealthy collectors who are after a specific thing. Let's say you are a new Saudi or Chinese billionaire and simply must have a classic Modigliani nude for your collection. Most of them are in public collections and few ever come on the open market. You might wait a lifetime to bid for one at an auction. So you go to the Bratva and they find out who's got what you want, and they make them an offer that they can't refuse. This is a very specialised market for just a few clients, but the rewards are enormous. A Modigliani nude sold at auction in 2015 for one hundred and seventy million US dollars.'

Brock said, 'And Rudi thinks that's what I.I. International is doing?'

'Possibly. As I told you, Pavel Gorshkov is listed as a director of the company, but has never been to the States. His office address is in St Petersburg. So the thing is, are Semenov and Gorshkov one and the same person? The FBI have photographs, prints and DNA of Semenov, of course, but nothing on Gorshkov.'

Molly showed them the passport photographs of the two men. They were certainly similar, although Gorshkov was markedly older and fleshier and had a broken nose. 'Rudi's getting a facial recognition scan of the two images to check, and DCI Gurney is arranging to send him the fingerprints from Gorshkov's UK entry visa. So we should soon know.'

The door of the Smithy opened and a woman in crime scene overalls waved to them. They got out of the car and walked over.

'We're done,' she said. 'I'll get a report to you as soon as I can.'

Kathy thanked her and led the way into the workroom. Molly followed, looking around. 'Where did he ...?'

Brock pointed to the roof truss overhead and the stain on the floor, and she winced.

They moved through to the studio, where the last of the forensic team were emerging from the trapdoor with their camera equipment. Molly gazed at Callum's paintings around the walls and frowned. 'They're so dark and obsessive, aren't they? I wonder how he ended up here.'

'Minimal rent,' Brock suggested, 'and obscurity. He took his art very seriously. Come and take a look at what he's got.' He indicated the open trapdoor and led the way down the steps.

'Oh yes.' Molly looked around, then went over to examine the bottles and tubes. 'He has his own pigments and mediums, so he could mix his own paints.' She moved to the plan chest, examining the contents. 'He's got every type of paper—laid, wove, deckle edge, rag, cold-pressed ... And the canvases— linen, cotton, jute, rough and fine. Many are old, previously used. What about stretchers?' She opened a cupboard door. 'Yes, here we are, old and new. He was a real scavenger.'

Brock said, 'Why an oven?'

'You can use an oven for creating effects—cracking and ageing. He wasn't short of money; some of this gear is expensive.'

Brock remembered the envelope he'd picked up from the doormat and gave it to her. 'Yes,' she said, 'L. Cornelissen and Son is an art supplies shop near the British Museum.' She examined the list of purchases. 'Pigments, gums and resins. He knew what he was doing.'

They locked Callum's studio and returned to their cars, and a thought struck Brock. He told Molly to follow them and asked Kathy to return to the church. The vicar was still in his vestry, bent over his typewriter, when Brock tapped on his door and waved Molly in. She looked around at the cramped little room and Brock pointed to the icon of Christ's head on the wall. She smiled and nodded. 'Rouault,' she said. 'From 1937. It's in the Cleveland Museum. I remember it well.'

The vicar was looking at her oddly and Brock apologised and introduced her. 'I just wanted to show Molly your picture, Vicar. I thought at first it was a print, but it's not, is it?'

'Oh no. It's original. Callum painted it for me to celebrate the completion of the roof.'

Molly moved closer to the picture, then closer still, examining its surface, then finally stepped back and stared at Brock.

'Do you like it?' the vicar asked.

'It's amazing,' Molly said. She looked at Kathy standing in the doorway and said, 'It's perfect.'

Brock nodded. 'The perfect copyist.'

They went back out to their cars and Brock said, 'Okay, we need to do this properly, Kathy. We need a team and a base. Can you help us?'

'Yes, I can make a space available in my office in Hammer-smith, with access to everything we might need. What do you think?'

'Oh, that would be wonderful,' Molly said. 'I can't stand the thought of going back to my hole in Fraud. Is there a parking space?'

'Yes.' Kathy looked at Brock.

'Good idea, Kathy. And you should be senior investigating officer.'

'All right. Well, the most immediate thing is to discover if in fact a crime has been committed. I wonder what that computer can tell us. I'll get our tech people to take a look at it.'

~

Molly followed Brock's car to the parking garage below the Box, where Kathy took them up to her office and introduced them to the members of her team. There was an awkward moment when she came to DS Andy Alfarsi, since it was he who had arrested Brock in the Hampstead murders case.

Brock smiled and stuck out his hand. 'Hello, Andy.'

Alfarsi gave a rueful grin. 'No hard feelings, boss?'

''Course not. All part of the game.'

Desks, computers and a conference table, whiteboards and a screen were arranged for the newcomers in a corner of the office with a view down over the endless flow of traffic on the Hammersmith flyover. Kathy knew that Judy Birch was having the same problems she'd had getting back into things after the Ashley Osborn debacle and thought it might be good for her to work with Brock for a few days. She asked her to help him to write up a report on everything he'd done connected with the Babington case so far, a chore that Brock had neglected.

After an hour of this he was getting restless, when he heard Kathy take a call from Bren, who had been in touch with Rudi Spector in New York. When she finished she said, 'Right. We have a match. The fingerprints of the Sergei Semenov arrested in New York in 1996 and the Pavel Gorshkov now in the UK are one and the same, which is presumably why Gorshkov has never visited the States.'

They discussed what they should do now and Brock made the final decision. 'Let's find out as much as we can of what he's up to before we act. We need to follow his movements, track his phone calls. Bren should handle this through Operation Nexus, so if we have to pull him in he doesn't suspect the surveillance is linked to Homicide.'

They all set to work, collating the information from Kent Police, from America and Brock's notes, preparing for a start the following morning.

21

The next day it was Molly's turn to make progress. She had been working hard, studying the material that Zack had found on Callum's computer, and she now presented her conclusions as they sat around the conference table.

'Callum was a mystery to me,' she began. 'I mean, artists are expected to be eccentric, but I just couldn't understand what he thought he was playing at. Brock told me that his tutor at Camberwell said he was the most talented in his year, yet here he was living like a hermit in the Hoo, painting the same gloomy landscapes over and over and selling nothing, engaged in some kind of secret mission with a wealthy lover to save a ruined church. I mean, it didn't make much sense to me.

'So I started with his family background. Kent Police gave me the contact details for his parents in Glasgow, to whom his body was returned, and I spoke to his mother. She said he'd always been a difficult boy and was diagnosed with ADHD when he was ten. In his teenage years he performed badly in everything at school except for art, the only subject that interested him. His art teacher was the sole person he would cooperate with, and she helped him to get a place at the Mackintosh, where he did well. However, his relationship with his parents deteriorated, to the point where he and his father were estranged. His mother knew he'd gone to London, but she didn't know where he was living until Kent Police contacted her.

'Brock mentioned that his tutor at Camberwell had called him a bit of a radical, organising petitions and so on, and I wondered what that was about. Well, Zack found a file on his computer which made it clear. It turns out that Callum was a Screamer.'

'A what?' Kathy voiced the query on everyone's faces.

'A Screamer. In Callum's final year at Camberwell, Edvard Munch's pastel *The Scream* was sold at auction by Sotheby's in New York for just shy of one hundred and twenty million dollars, the highest price ever paid at that time for a work of art. A group of art students in London picketed Sotheby's to protest against the obscene prices being paid for art, pointing out that the money paid for *The Scream* could have sent ten thousand students to art school. They all wore masks like the screaming figure in Munch's painting and called themselves the Screamers, and they got quite a bit of publicity. Their manifesto was published by *The Guardian*, and it turns out that it was written by Callum McAdam. It wasn't just a prank; Callum's files show that he was dead serious about the issue. The manifesto is rather long, but here's an extract.'

Molly handed out pages and they read:

'The Screamers' Manifesto

'We protest at the corruption of art by the art market.

'The greatest artworks are unique in having been stolen by the obscenely rich. Great works of literature, poetry, plays, music are all accessible to everyone, but today the finest art is snapped up by the mega-rich and hidden from public view. Why is that? Because the art market demands scarcity in order to inflate the price of art for the benefit of the obscenely rich.

'When a pastel drawing by Edvard Munch sells to a financier for $120 million, or $115,000 per square inch, the corruption of the art market is exposed for what it is: a parasite on the soul of art.'

Molly went on, 'You get the idea. Of course their protest made no difference whatsoever. Art prices had been rising steadily since 1987, and they've kept climbing ever since. The highest so far is Leonardo da Vinci's *Salvator Mundi* for four hundred and fifty million.'

Kathy said, 'When you say he was dead serious, what are we talking about?'

'In his computer there are lots of drafts of letters written to the press in the name of the Screamers. I've checked a few of them, and it seems that at first some were published, but as time went by and prices kept rising his letters became more angry and aggressive and weren't printed. In fact, the Screamers pretty much disappeared from public view within a few months, but Callum kept up his protest, running a Screamers website and blog, and sending letters to the billionaires who'd bought expensive artworks, demanding that they give them to public galleries.'

Molly turned over her notes. 'There was another passage in Callum's manifesto that stood out for me. Listen to this . . .'

She found the page she was looking for and read: '*If a play by Shakespeare is performed in a thousand different bizarre ways, it is still a Shakespeare. If a novel by Dickens is reproduced a million times, even with mistakes, it is still a Dickens. If a building designed by Michelangelo is erected years after his death, it is still a building by Michelangelo, but if a painting by Michelangelo is painted years after his death it is not a Michelangelo. Why is that?*

'*I may make an exact copy of a painting by Picasso using precisely the same materials, the same techniques as Picasso did. It is a perfect copy, indistinguishable from the one Picasso painted. It is his concept, his style, his colours, his brushstrokes, but it is not accepted as a Picasso. Why is that? Because the art market demands scarcity in order to inflate the price of art for the benefit of the obscenely rich, so that they can flaunt their wealth for all to see.*

'See what I mean? He makes forgery sound like a moral duty.'

Brock said, 'And was Miki Babington a Screamer?'

'Yes, he was; at least, to begin with.'

'Their tutor seemed to think they might have been lovers.'

'No, there's no indication of that, and the relationship seems to have been a stormy one. Callum was very serious and intense, whereas Miki was lazy and unreliable. Callum was also keeping up an email correspondence with Miki's mother, Nadya. It starts at the time of the Screamers, and continues with long exchanges about the philosophy of art. They talk about their favourite artists, especially current landscape painters—he loved

John Virtue's London paintings, and David Tress's Welsh land-scapes. They also talk about saving the ancient church, whose fate symbolised to Callum everything that's wrong with the world today.'

'Do they discuss how they can save it?'

'They talk about helping the vicar to raise funds. Callum had an exhibition of his landscapes in a small gallery in Rochester, with money from sales to go to the church, but apparently he only sold one work. Then, about four years ago, he emailed Nadya to tell her he'd had an idea for a way to solve their problems with the church and they must meet to discuss it. And that's where their correspondence ends.

'Apart from that there's pretty mundane stuff—records of bills and orders to L. Cornelissen and Son and other artists' suppliers. He was buying a wide range of colours, far more varied than the dark monochromes of the paintings in his studio.'

Kathy took over, reporting that Gorshkov/Semenov was still in the UK and being monitored by Bren through Operation Nexus. She also reported that she had received a response from a forensic pathologist she had asked to look at the post-mortem reports and photographs of Nadya and Callum. He raised a couple of queries. There appeared to be some bruising on the back of Nadya's neck that would be consistent with her head having been forced down into the pond. In Callum's case, there was extensive bruising and abra-sions on his throat, as if he'd struggled against the noose while he was hanging there.

Brock said, 'I'd like to know what Miki Babington is up to. When I saw him he said he hadn't seen his father in years, then when I'd gone he went straight out and met him at the Dorchester. Whatever they're up to, they're in it together. I don't want to give him any hint of that, but I think we should have another word with him.'

'Right. Do you and Judy want to do that?'

~

They decided to go straight to the DPF office in Mayfair without phoning ahead. Judy squeezed the car into a parking space in the mews outside the sign for the Dufort-Poirier Foundation and they went in. The receptionist was on the phone, talking in French, and she gave them a brief smile while she finished her call.

'Sorry about that. How can I help you?'

They showed their ID and Brock said, 'We'd like to speak to Mr Babington, please.'

'Of course.' She murmured into her phone, then looked up. 'I'm so sorry, sir. Mr Babington is tied up. Would you like to make an appointment? He suggests one day next week.'

'This is urgent, I'm afraid. We'll wait.' Brock turned to Judy. 'Maybe you'd better switch the police warning light on in the car outside.'

The receptionist looked startled. 'Oh, surely that isn't necessary?'

'We don't want any accidents, do we?'

'Only he may be some time ...'

'Is he with someone?'

'I ... I'm not sure.' She blushed.

Brock smiled at her. 'Look, we don't have any time to waste. Which room is he in?'

She hesitated, then whispered, 'First floor at the back.'

Miki was alone in the room, seated at a desk flicking through a copy of *Fast Bikes* magazine. He looked up, annoyed, as his door opened, then jumped to his feet. 'What the fuck?'

'Sit down, Miki. You remember me, DCI Brock? And this is Detective Sergeant Birch. We're trying to finalise the report to the coroner on your mother's death, and there're a few things that don't add up.'

'Oh, really?'

Brock took out his notebook and slowly turned the pages. 'When I spoke to you on the twenty-sixth of November, you told me that you had never visited the Hoo Peninsula in Kent. Would you like to reconsider that answer?'

'Um . . . I dunno. Why?'

'You also said you hadn't seen Callum McAdam in years. I'm giving you a chance now to reconsider those answers, and I have to remind you that lying to the police can have serious consequences, as I'm sure you're aware.'

'Bloody hell.' Miki sat up straighter in his stylish office chair. 'I've just lost my mother and you come in here and threaten me because I might have forgotten something or other. Yeah, maybe I have been there and seen Callum. Maybe I was stoned or not paying attention. So what?' Then his eyes widened. 'Oh . . . has Julian been making out I'm respon-sible for what Mum did? Has he? Well, I'll tell you one thing—if he'd spent less time sodding off to America every five minutes and more time with her, maybe things would have been different.'

'Did she feel he neglected her?'

'Maybe she thought he had a girlfriend over there, who knows? Personally I don't think so—all he cares about is his bloody collection. The rest of us don't count.'

'Do you think he resented you?'

'Well, I've had to make my own way, haven't I?'

'Perhaps you wish you'd stayed in Russia with your own father?'

A look of caution came into Miki's eyes. 'Bit late for that.' He glanced at his watch. 'Anyway, I'm waiting for a call from an important client, so you'll have to go now. If I can remember anything about Mum or Callum, I'll let you know.'

As they left, Judy said, 'Bit of venom there when he talked about his stepfather, wasn't there, boss?'

'Yes, you're right about that.'

~

Back at the Box, Kathy and the others were discussing preliminary forensic results that had come in from the search of Callum's cellar, confirming that Callum, Nadya and Miki Babington had all left prints there, as had at least one other unidentified visitor. Brock described the visit to Miki, and they agreed to apply for a warrant to monitor his phone calls. They were now accumulating information, yet so far the only crime they had uncovered was Sergei Semenov's fake identity as Pavel Gorshkov.

Kathy sensed the group tiring and losing momentum, breaking down into separate couples speculating vaguely about timing and motives. Brock had said little and was standing alone over at the windows, hands in pockets, staring out at the darkening sky. It was time for her to take control and somehow reinvigorate the team.

She called out, 'Listen, before long I'm going to have to report to Commander Torrens, and if we've got no evidence of a homicide he'll tell me to pass the whole thing over to UK Border Force and Nexus. Semenov'll be sent home and that'll be the end of it. We need a theory at least that'll convince the boss it's worth giving us more time. So, ideas, please.'

There was a long silence. Then Brock turned away from the window and came back to the table and sat down.

'You want a theory, Kathy? I've got a theory. It begins like this. On the twelfth of November last, Nadya Babington receives a stupid scam email demanding money that sends her into a state of high panic. When we try to help her she refuses to let us examine her computer. In other words, she's hiding something so desperate, so overwhelming that she can't share it with us or with her husband. Why was she so frightened and what was she hiding? Those are the questions we have to answer. Her fear was real and justified—she would be dead within twenty-four hours.

'She was scared to death because the scam email had a Russian origin, and she was terrified that it was a warning from her Russian former husband, Sergei Semenov, to behave. But she had left him seventeen years ago, so why was she so terrified now? It could only be because she knew that he was here, in London. And she couldn't tell us that because, whatever he was up to, her son Miki was involved in it too and he would come to grief.

'So what were they up to? There's really only one answer, isn't there?'

Brock looked around at them, but no one spoke, so he continued. 'Miki works for DPF and Semenov is tied up with I.I. International, both dodgy dealers in art—in the case of I.I. International, to high-end buyers. Julian Babington owns a fabulous art collection. Miki and his dad were stealing his paintings.'

There was a murmur around the table, then Kathy said, 'With the help of Callum McAdam?'

Brock nodded. 'Yes, with the help of Callum McAdam, the highly talented artist who couldn't sell his own works but could make superb copies of other people's. With Nadya's help he would have direct access to the originals for days on end while Babington was away on his regular visits to America.'

'Why would Nadya cooperate?'

'That's one of the things we have to find out. They were lovers and perhaps Callum told her some story—he was making copies as a little sideline to sell for funds to save St Chad's, something like that. But by the time she received that Russian email she knew that it was much more than that. Callum wasn't selling copies of paintings, not for the kind of sums we saw in the vicar's account book. His copies were going onto Babington's walls, and the originals were being sold on the black market by Semenov. Molly and I have seen one of those originals in a collection in Miami. When I put that to Babington he looked stunned, but recovered and claimed he'd sold it himself legitimately to raise funds to maintain the collection. I think he was lying.'

Molly explained, 'He'd be desperate to hide the possibility that the collection may be compromised.'

They thought about this, then Kathy said, 'So on the morning after she got the scam email, Nadya drove over to see Callum, to try to get him to put things right.'

Now Judy spoke up. 'Yes, only it was far too late. Maybe Semenov was there, and he knew they couldn't let her go telling people what they'd done. So he took her to the pond and drowned her. A few days later, either Callum killed himself or they eliminated him too.'

There was silence for a moment as they digested this, then Molly shook her head. 'No, Brock, it wouldn't work. I think he was telling the truth about the Miami piece. They wouldn't be able to sell the stolen originals, even with their genuine provenance documentation. Sooner or later Babington would hear of it and denounce them.'

'You're right,' Brock agreed. 'They wouldn't be able to sell them—as long as Babington was alive.'

They were silent for a moment.

Finally, Molly said, 'That's true. Once he's dead the buyers can openly claim that Babington sold the plums of his father's collection to them, and gave copies to the Royal Academy. And if each buyer had evidence of some tiny forensic flaw that Callum had inserted in the copy, they could prove that theirs was the original. It's perfect.'

'So,' Brock said, 'unless we take control of this situation, Julian Babington may well be about to have a fatal accident. That's what you have to tell Torrens, Kathy.'

~

By the following day Commander Torrens had agreed to at least some of Kathy's measures. He was sceptical of Brock's theory, and wouldn't authorise a full-scale police bodyguard operation for Babington, who was instead provided with a personal alarm and a list of private security specialists. Miki's phone would be monitored and Operation Nexus would step up their surveillance of Semenov. It wasn't enough for Brock, but he and Molly settled down to researching magazine articles, old auction records and other sources to try to compile as complete a list as possible of the artworks in the Babington Collection, which Babington himself seemed strangely reluctant to provide, saying that his father's records had been hopelessly disorganised.

At 11 am, as Brock and Molly were taking a coffee break, he got a call from DS Holt at Gravesend to inform him of a break-in at St Chad's earlier that morning. At around 6 am, over an hour before dawn, the vicar had been awake, making a cup of tea in his kitchen in the vicarage, a small house near the church. He thought he saw a flicker of light from the window of St Chad's vestry, and had gone to investigate. Opening the church door, he had been surprised by a dark-clad figure. There had been a scuffle, during which the vicar received a blow to the head. By the time he recovered, the intruder had gone and he found the vestry disrupted, with drawers open and papers scattered. Holt was at the scene now with a forensic technician. Brock told him he'd be there within the hour.

When he arrived, the Reverend Bramley-Scott had been visited by a doctor and had his head bandaged. He seemed remarkably buoyant as he looked at the mess.

'He took nothing of any value as far as I can see—a small cash box I kept in that drawer, only a few pounds. Honestly, you'd think they'd be bright enough to guess that this would be the last place to find anything worth stealing.'

'He seems to have been interested in your files,' Brock said.

'There's nothing much to see. I keep most of my parish paperwork in the vicarage.'

'But you had your book of donations here.'

'That's true, so that I could enter any gifts after each service in the church. But you borrowed that, didn't you?'

'Yes, that's right.'

Will Holt raised an evidence bag he was holding. 'Seems he dropped this . . .' He showed Brock the small flashlight inside. 'The vicar says it's not his. I'll get it checked for prints and DNA.'

Brock said, 'How long will that take, Will?'

He shrugged. 'There's a big backlog coming up to Christmas. Not till the new year.'

'Let me try,' Brock said. 'I might be able to do better.'

Brock phoned Kathy on the way back, and by the time he reached the Box a courier was waiting to take the flashlight away for analysis. By evening they had a result: a positive DNA match with Miki Babington.

~

A patrol car took Brock and a uniformed officer to the address they had in Primrose Hill, a pastel-coloured Victorian townhouse on a gently curving street not far from Regent's Park.

An elderly man wearing a silk dressing-gown answered their knock.

'Good evening, sir,' Brock said. 'Does Miki Babington live here?'

'No, he does not!' the man said, with some feeling.

'Do you know where I might find him?'

'On Fitzroy Road,' he said, waving a hand, 'back there. I don't know the number, but you can't miss it—it's pink,' he added contemptuously.

'Thank you for your help, sir.'

'Is the little bastard in trouble? Oh, I do hope so.'

'I'm afraid I can't say. You haven't seen him today then?'

'No.' The man closed the door.

They drove back to Fitzroy Road, found the pink house and tried again.

Another man answered, much younger this time, and raised an eyebrow at the uniform standing behind Brock's shoulder. 'Hello. Something wrong?'

Brock showed him his warrant card. 'Does Miki Babington live here, sir?'

'Ye-es,' he said cautiously. 'Why?'

'Is he here now?'

'Yes, I—'

'May we come in?'

The man hesitated, then said, 'I suppose so.' He stepped back, calling, 'Miki!' up the stairs, and showed them into a lounge room.

Brock introduced himself and said, 'May I have your name, sir?'

'Norman Gladwell.'

'Are you the owner of the house?'

'I am.'

They heard footsteps and Miki's voice. 'Norman?' He stopped dead in the doorway and stared at Brock. 'What the hell are you doing here?'

'Have you been to the Hoo Peninsula in Kent today, Mr Babington?'

'No, I have not. I've been here all day.'

'How about at six this morning, Miki?'

'I was here, wasn't I, Norman?'

Gladwell looked from Miki to Brock then, after a moment's hesitation, said, 'Yes, that's right.'

Miki smirked at Brock, who said, 'Miki Babington, I am arresting you on suspicion of break and enter and the assault of the Reverend Alwyn Bramley-Scott.' He recited the caution as Miki stiffened, face pale. The patrol officer led him away.

Gladwell looked startled. 'Did you say break and enter?'

'Yes.' Brock turned to him. 'I'd like you to accompany me to the police station, Mr Gladwell, to make a statement.'

'Were they lovers?'

'Now there's an interesting thought.'

~

When they got to West End Central, Brock had Miki processed and locked up for the night, to be interviewed in the morning. He sat down with Norman Gladwell, who was looking very worried.

'So, Mr Gladwell, could you tell me your name, age and occupation, please.'

'Norman Gladwell, thirty-two. I'm a registrar at University College Hospital.'

'And what were your movements from midnight last night?'

'I was working at the hospital all night until five this morning. Then I left for home—my house in Fitzroy Road, Primrose Hill. I must have got home at about five thirty.'

'Was Miki Babington there?'

Gladwell hesitated, took a deep breath. 'Actually ... no, he wasn't. The house was empty. I went straight to bed and would have been asleep by six. I woke again at about eight and heard him and went downstairs, where he was making toast. He seemed very jumpy and I asked him what was wrong and he said he'd had an argument with someone who owed him money and they'd had a fight. He said he didn't want anything more to do with it, and begged me to say that he'd been at home all night and hadn't left the house all morning. It sounded like a trivial quarrel and I agreed and went back to bed.'

Brock phoned Kathy and brought her up to date. There was nothing new to report from the church.

~

The next morning they attempted to interview Miki Babington, who refused to speak without his lawyer present. By a curious coincidence, the lawyer was from the practice founded by Kathy's one-time lover and benefactor, Martin Connell. For Kathy it was an unsettling discovery, as if Martin's malign influence was reaching out from the grave. For Brock it was

both disappointing and revealing, for the firm had a reputation for defending high-end crooks. He wondered how Miki
could afford them.

The lawyer's advice to Miki was to say nothing, which
was exactly what he did. He had been examined by a doctor
and his prints and DNA taken again, but no words passed his
lips beyond muttered curses. Brock wanted him to be held
in jail on police remand for the permitted ninety-six hours,
but his lawyer objected and demanded a court appearance
to test their evidence. In the end, the police accepted bail
on a surety of one hundred thousand pounds—provided, to
Brock's surprise, by Julian Babington—with a condition of his
bail that he remain at Babington's house in Montagu Square.

'He's a little shit,' Babington said to Brock, 'but he's Nadya's
little shit. I owe it to her. He shouldn't get into any trouble in
Montagu Square, though I'm afraid I won't be with him over
Christmas.' He lowered his voice. 'You asked me in America
how I managed Christmases, and they've always been a nightmare. I've faked illnesses and a mother at death's door, God
forgive me, but this year will be different. I'm flying to New
York tomorrow to be with Sharon and the kids. Miki will be
all right. His lawyers have warned him to behave while I'm
away.'

They were silent for a long moment, and then Babington
said quietly, 'I haven't thanked you for not saying anything
about my other life, Brock. I'm immensely grateful to you.
Once the collection has been safely handed over I intend
to sell up here and move permanently to the States to live
as Jack Sargent, but I'm keenly aware that I have put you
in a difficult position. If possible, I would like to set things

straight, and I wondered if you could advise me. Perhaps if I came clean with the Americans and threw myself on their mercy? I hate the idea of telling Sharon and the kids, but perhaps I must.'

'Yes, I think that would be best, Julian. I'm not going to commit a felony for you. At some stage I may be put in a situation where I have no choice but to tell the truth. It would be best if you cleared things up before then. To the extent that I can, I'll try to help with the American authorities.'

'Thank you, Brock. That's very decent of you. You're absolutely right, of course.'

Later Brock and Kathy watched Julian and Miki leave together in a taxi. Kathy said, 'Well, at least they'll be keeping tabs on him while we have a few days off.'

Brock almost asked her what she meant, then realised that she was talking about Christmas, only a few days away now. 'Yes, and I'm sorry, Kathy, I forgot to say that Suzanne asked me to invite you to join us, if you're free.'

'Thanks, Brock. That would be nice, but I've made arrangements. Sorry.'

'Oh Kathy, *please*. You must come. It'll just be the three of us: Miranda's in Germany and Stewart's going to stay with some university mates up north. Please. Suzanne will kill me if she finds out I forgot to tell you . . .'

Kathy laughed. 'Yes, well, in that case, thank you, I'd love to come—on one condition.'

'What's that?'

'My team's having a Christmas do on a party boat tonight, staff and guests. Will you and Suzanne come as my guests? Then you can stay overnight in my flat.'

'A party boat?' Brock looked doubtful. 'I'm not sure if she'll be game for that.'

'Try her.'

So Brock did, and was surprised by the enthusiasm of Suzanne's response.

22

The evening on the boat was a great success, and Kathy was glad to be able to repay Brock and Suzanne's hospitality by having them stay at last in her flat. The following day they drove down to Battle and a couple of days later, on Christmas Eve, they enjoyed a meal together at the Cut and Grill in the High Street before returning home for a nightcap and retiring at around eleven.

Shortly after 1 am, while Santa was climbing down chimneys and the faithful were making their way home from Midnight Mass, a couple walking in Montagu Square noticed a curious flickering light in the living room of one of the houses. They stopped and stared at it, thinking how delightful it was as a Christmas effect, when suddenly the window exploded onto the street, and almost simultaneously a volcanic eruption of flame and smoke burst in a roar out of the roof above.

It was almost 3 am when the call came through to Brock's mobile, and by 4.30 he and Kathy were in the square, standing with TV film crews, local police and neighbouring residents wrapped in blankets, watching the fire hoses still playing on the smoking blackened ruin that had once been the Babingtons' elegant townhouse. There was no sign of Miki and no response from his phone, and while Kathy set about organising a hunt for him, Brock phoned Julian Babington's number. It would be midnight in New York, he calculated, and Babington sounded happy, his voice hoarse. 'Brock! Happy Christmas! How are you?'

Brock hesitated at the blow he was about to deliver. 'Julian, I'm sorry to be the bearer of terrible news. There's been a fire in Montagu Square, at your home.'

'What? Oh no! Don't tell me ... Has there been much damage?'

'I'm afraid the house is in a bad way.'

'Dear God.' His voice had dropped to a whisper. 'The paintings?'

'I'm waiting to be allowed in by the fire brigade, but it doesn't look good.'

'Is anyone hurt?'

'No indication so far. We're trying to contact Miki. Do you know any other addresses where he might be?'

His 'no' was so faint that Brock hardly heard it, but then Babington's voice came back more firmly. 'What the hell has he done? . . . Look, I'll get a flight over as soon as I can. In the meantime, I know you'll do whatever's possible.'

~

Dawn cast a stark bleak light on the ruined shell. The hoses had been turned off and a foul odour filled the whole square. To Brock it seemed that the smell contained the taint of roasted meat, but he told himself that was just imagination. Eventually he and Kathy were taken over to speak to the head of the fire crew.

'We're pretty sure there was some kind of accelerant involved,' he said. 'Must have built up a terrific temperature down there, then spread quickly up through the rest of the house. The old dry timber floors and roof structure caved in.'

Brock asked, 'Is it possible anyone was in there?'

'Haven't seen any evidence, but the cellar is full of debris, still smouldering. We'll have to wait to examine it. Come back mid-morning.'

'One thing,' Brock said. 'The cellar contained valuable paintings and was supposed to be fireproof.'

The fire chief shook his head. 'The fire started *inside* the cellar. Whatever fireproofing it had was designed to protect it from an external fire, not this. Nothing down there has survived, I'm afraid.'

Brock thanked him and they turned away. He spoke to some of the neighbours who were standing nearby while Kathy went across the street to take pictures of the ruin. When she was finished, they walked north and found a café on Baker Street. They used the washroom to try to clean away the smell of the fire that seemed to have permeated their clothes. They sat down with coffees and Kathy said, 'The whole art collection! Well, I suppose Miki is suspect number one.'

'Yes,' Brock agreed. 'He must have had access to the cellar. What the hell was he up to?' He shook his head. 'All those treasures . . .'

'But why was he here on his own? I mean, why would Julian Babington go off to New York at this time of the year? Surely offices over there would be closed. Maybe Babington wanted an alibi while paying someone else to take care of Miki. That person then tried to cover it up with a small fire that got out of control.'

Brock sipped his coffee, then said, 'Actually, he has a very good reason for going to New York at this time of year, Kathy—one that I haven't told you or anyone else about.' And he described following Babington to Long Island and discovering his secret life in North Merrick. 'He wanted to be with his other family for Christmas.'

Kathy was astonished, trying to imagine it. 'He must have tied himself in knots telling his stories to two wives. Makes my life seem boringly simple.'

An hour later Brock's phone beeped with a message from the fireman and they returned to the square, where he told them that what appeared to be a burned and broken bone had been found among the basement debris; he had moved his crew off the site, declaring it a potential crime scene. He offered to take them closer, leading them up the steps to the threshold of the front door to view the scene inside. The hall floor had collapsed and with it the staircase and upper floors onto the remains of the cellar. A generator-powered floodlight picked out little details—the blackened end of a joist projecting from a sooty wall, a heap of white ash on a ledge—and among them Brock made out the corner of a charred picture frame still attached to the wall. It was all that was left of the Schwitters. The fireman pointed down to a red marker among the chaos of rubble, beside a pale stick that might have been bone.

'This is going to take time,' Brock murmured. 'They'll have to get engineers in first to make the site safe. How about the adjoining properties?'

'Mostly superficial damage, thankfully,' the fire officer replied. 'Blistering caused by the heat through the party walls.'

~

It was evening when Julian Babington phoned Brock, who relayed what little new information he had. 'We can't be sure until the place is safe for a forensic team to enter, Julian, but I'm afraid the firefighters think they may have found human remains in the cellar.'

'Dear God. Have you been able to contact Miki yet?'

'I'm afraid not.'

There was a pause, Brock listening to Babington's breathing as he took this in. He knew that it had been snowing in New York, and he imagined Babington's breath steaming in the freezing air.

'I had trouble getting a flight, but I finally managed to get a seat on the six o'clock United flight tonight, getting in to Heathrow at six twenty tomorrow morning. Can I meet you sometime tomorrow?'

'I'll pick you up at Heathrow.'

'There's no need, Brock, really . . .'

'I'll be there.'

~

Later, in the Box, Kathy saw Brock at his desk, poring over a document. How tired he looked, she thought—as if the fire had burned up his last reserves of energy.

'How's it going?' she asked in a cheery voice that sounded phoney to her, but seemed necessary for the circumstances.

'Not bad.'

'Brock, you hardly slept last night. Time for a break. Go home, have a good sleep. Nothing's going to happen for a while.'

He looked up and smiled at her. 'True enough. I'm picking Babington up at Heathrow at dawn.'

'You don't have to do that.'

'Oh, but I do. I think I've made a big mistake. Sit down, Kathy. I've been in touch with UK Border Force. Let me tell you the story.'

So she sat down, and he told her, and her eyes widened. 'Oh hell,' she said.

23

It was cold the next morning, Boxing Day, though not by New York standards, and Brock was wearing a heavy overcoat as he waited in the arrivals hall of Terminal 2. By contrast, Babington, pale with dark rings around his eyes and looking as if he hadn't slept on the flight, came through the gate without any coat or scarf. He stopped and gazed around as if disorientated.

Brock stepped forward and they shook hands.

'We've done this before, haven't we?' Babington said, his voice hoarse. 'It seems like a very long time ago. You should be with your family, Brock.'

'You too,' Brock replied, with a grim little smile. 'You've got a cold?'

Babington coughed, nodded.

'Why haven't you got a coat?'

'Left it in the lounge at Kennedy by mistake.' He coughed again. 'Any word of Miki?'

'I'm afraid not.'

~

At Montagu Square Brock stopped at the police barrier and they got out of the car. Babington stared wide-eyed at the blackened front where his house had been, its windows vacant holes like the eyeless sockets in a skull.

'I can't believe it,' he whispered.

'An engineer is on his way to make sure the structure's stable and then our forensic team will move in. Come, I'll show you.'

Brock went to the barrier and showed the uniformed police officer his ID, then took Babington up the front steps, watching his reaction as he stared at the hollow ruin of his home.

'How could this have happened?' Babington muttered. 'All gone.' He turned to Brock. 'I once heard my mother tell my father that his collection was a curse. I didn't understand what she meant, but it's true.' He was shivering from the cold in his thin suit, his face pale and drawn.

'Yes, that's what we need to talk about. Seen enough?'

They returned to the car, where Brock switched on the engine and turned the heating up. 'So, what do you think happened, Julian?'

'I was going to ask you the same thing.'

'You first.'

'Well ...' Babington seemed to have trouble concentrating. 'Sorry, I didn't sleep on the plane ... a nightmare.' He rubbed his face and roused himself. 'If ... if Miki really is down there ... well, he must have been doing something ...' He turned to Brock. 'Look, the place was fire-alarmed! Why didn't it go off? He must have turned it off!'

'Why would he do that?'

'I think there's only one explanation, don't you? Suicide! And suicide that would have the maximum possible impact on me. The destruction of everything I've tried to protect.'

'Would he really have gone that far?'

'He blamed me for his mother's death.'

'He told you that?'

'Yes he did. Apparently, after that morning when you came to our house ...' He hesitated, staring out at the ruin, as if the mention of *our house* had suddenly brought the reality of what had happened into focus. 'Sorry ... yes, about the scam email, Nadya spoke to him about it, said the police were useless and I wasn't taking it seriously. Apparently she was very distressed. When she killed herself he told me it was my fault.' He burst into a choking cough and fumbled in his pocket, bringing out an inhaler. 'Sorry, chest ...'

Brock waited until Babington was breathing more steadily, then said, 'Well, he might want to punish you, but why kill himself?'

'It was Christmas Eve, he was alone, rejected by his partner, more or less under house arrest, likely to go to prison ... He was always self-pitying, but who wouldn't be desperately depressed? I'll bet he got blind drunk and decided to go out in the most melodramatic way imaginable.

And I blame myself, Brock. I should never have left him alone at a time like that.'

He put a hand over his face. His shoulders shook and his voice was unsteady as he said, 'Since marrying Nadya, I'd hardly ever been able to spend Christmas with Sharon and our children. I had to make the most grotesque excuses. It was an agony, and so this year I thought *at last*! Then Miki spoiled it all, getting himself arrested, and I told myself that was just too bad; I couldn't disappoint Sharon again.

'And frankly, Brock, I blame the police and the legal system. He was too unstable to be out on his own with a criminal charge hanging over him. He should have been kept in custody.'

Brock nodded slowly, murmured, 'Hm ...'

'You see my point?' Babington asked.

'Oh I do. I see it very clearly. But I have a small problem.'

'What's that?'

'I checked with our border police and the airlines and discovered that a Mr John Sargent of twenty-two West Franklin Avenue, North Merrick, Long Island caught BA one-seven-eight from New York on the morning of Monday the twenty-fourth of December, arriving in London at seven fifty that evening. He then returned to New York at eight the following morning on United eight-eight-three.'

Babington's face had frozen. He stared unblinkingly at his ruined home. He didn't speak.

Brock went on, 'So when I phoned you on Christmas morning—midnight New York time—to tell you about the fire, you were actually still here in London, waiting for your flight out, weren't you?'

Babington hadn't moved, and Brock wondered if he'd heard him. 'Julian? Time to tell me the whole story.'

He watched as Babington sagged and cupped his face in his hands. Eventually, after a long silence, he sighed and sat up straight. 'Oh God, I'm so tired. I haven't slept for days. Just haven't been able to. Tried pills for the last flight but no good ...

'Yes, you're right. I'm afraid it was just a stupid mistake. It can be very confusing when you try to live two lives. On Sunday we had lunch together—me, Sharon and the kids— and I thought how perfect it was: the decorated tree with colourful parcels at its foot, the snow outside and Christmas lights everywhere. It was what I had always yearned for, yet I was overcome with grief and guilt. Nadya was dead, and her son was alone in the London house with his life in pieces. And I realised I had been wrong to come to America. I had been too impatient. It had been my duty to stay in London this last Christmas to support Miki.

'I got up from the table and made a phone call to book a flight to London, and when they asked for my name I automatically said John Sargent, because that's who I am in America. So that's how it happened ... a simple mistake.'

Brock shook his head. 'No, Julian, your story makes no sense—you booked a *return* flight for just twelve hours after you arrived. You had no intention of spending Christmas Day with Miki.'

'It was just intended as a fleeting visit ...' he began to mumble, but Brock cut him off.

'Julian Babington, I am arresting you for making an illegal entry into the UK on a false document.' Glancing in the rear-view mirror, he saw a car pull in behind them and Kathy and Judy get out. 'That'll do for now.'

They took Babington to West End Central, where he was cautioned and processed and led away to a holding cell. All the while he said nothing, seemingly turned in on himself, no longer aware of what was happening. Brock asked for a doctor to examine him, but the duty sergeant explained that there might be a delay, with a shortage of on-call staff, it being Boxing Day.

And then they returned to the Box, where they began the process of trying to discover what Babington's movements had been during those brief night-time hours when he had been in London under the alias of Jack Sargent.

Kathy asked how border security at Heathrow and New York hadn't picked up Babington's double identity, and Brock said, 'I believe the biometrics are intended to detect faces that don't match the passport identity or else belong to someone with a criminal record. Both Babington and Sargent had longstanding valid passport identities, dating back to before nine-eleven, when the systems were tightened up, and neither had a criminal record.'

They retrieved security camera footage of Babington arriving at Heathrow Terminal 3, carrying an overnight bag. Another camera at Heathrow had recorded him getting into a taxi, which they traced and discovered that it had dropped him at Piccadilly Circus, where he had disappeared into the crowds of Christmas revellers.

While they began searching camera footage from the surrounding streets, Brock phoned Suzanne and Molly Fitzherbert and told them what had happened. Molly was with her parents at their home in Sevenoaks and, stunned by the news, immediately said she'd come in. Suzanne, more used to dramatic events occurring at inconvenient times, was philosophical and said she'd keep the stuffed turkey roast till another time.

They were now tracking Babington's phone history and discovered that he had walked on a meandering route from Piccadilly Circus to Montagu Square, arriving there at 10.36 pm, and had stayed in and around the vicinity of the square for over three hours, until just after 2 am on Christmas morning, when the firefighting was at its height. He had then walked down to Oxford Street, where he'd stopped for a while outside Selfridges, then continued through Grosvenor Square and Berkeley Square to finish not far from the Royal Academy in Cork Street, where he stayed for a couple of hours before calling for a taxi and being driven back out to the airport.

'What's in Cork Street?' Kathy asked, and Brock replied, 'Rosa Lipmann.'

Kathy drove them to Cork Street while Brock, hunched in his coat against the car door, said nothing. He took a deep breath as they drew to a stop outside the gallery and said, 'Right,' and heaved himself out and rang Rosa's bell.

For a long while there was no response, but then the door opened and Rosa stood there in a pink dressing-gown and slippers. 'Ah,' she said, 'I wondered how long it would take you. If you're going to drive me to a police station I'll need to get dressed, otherwise you can come in and talk to me as I am.'

'You'll do,' Brock said and stepped inside and waited while Rosa locked the door again behind Kathy and led them upstairs to her office, where she switched on a coffee machine.

'Sit, sit.' She waved an arm. 'It's about Julian, is it? Yes, well, the bell started ringing and ringing and woke me up and I thought, *Christmas drunks!* But then I heard him calling out, "Rosa! Rosa!" I said, "Name of God, Julian, it's three am! And look at you!" I thought he must have been in an accident— hair wild, shirt out, leaning against the wall. I helped him up here as best I could and saw what a mess he was in—the arm of his coat appeared to be scorched and he was gasping for breath, having trouble breathing ... He suffers from emphysema, you know.'

She paused to pour them coffee, then went on. 'He said he'd come across some people who had been letting off fireworks, and there had been an accident. I asked if he was hurt, should we go to the hospital? But he said no, no, he just needed to clean himself up. So he took off his coat and went to the bathroom. I brushed and wiped his suit, but there was nothing I could do for his ruined coat.

'The odd thing though was the smell on his clothes— the smell of burning. It was a sickening smell close-to, and I couldn't get rid of it, though I did what I could with eau de cologne. Actually, I think that just made things worse. I offered to take him to Montagu Square to get some fresh clothes but he said no. There was no arguing with him, and I could see he was very disturbed by whatever had happened. Eventually he ordered a taxi and left, I'm not sure of the time, and I went back to bed but couldn't sleep. I turned on the radio for the early morning news and heard about a terrible fire in Montagu Square. *My God*, I thought, *what should I do?* I didn't know, so I did nothing until I heard more. And now you're here. But tell me, please—not the collection?'

Brock said, 'Yes, Rosa, the collection. All gone.'

She closed her eyes and let out a wail of grief. 'The Joan Mitchells? The Freud? Not the *Sunflowers*!'

'No, not the *Sunflowers*. Julian had already handed that over to the RA.'

'Ah, at least that's a blessing.' She shook her head, looking perplexed. 'What a tragedy. How on earth did it happen?'

'Julian says that Miki set the house on fire to punish him for Nadya's suicide.'

'Oh no, that crazy boy ...'

'But then, what was Julian doing calling on you with burns on his coat?'

'Yes,' Rosa said warily. 'What do you think?'

Brock looked around the office at the pictures hanging on the walls. 'When I spoke to Julian this morning, he described his father's collection as a curse. What do you think he meant by that?'

'It's true that it's been a great burden for him. Considering his father was a lawyer, he left his affairs in a terrible tangle when he died. Julian has spent years trying to sort out the trust his father set up.'

'Derek was a compulsive collector, was he?'

'He was totally obsessed with his art collection.'

'So he must have spent a great deal of money on it?'

'Oh yes! Julian used to joke that they had so little money for other things that he was tormented at school for wearing second-hand uniforms that he'd grown out of years before.'

'I imagine he would have been very sensitive about a thing like that.'

'Indeed. He was a very sensitive boy. And he lost his mother because of the collection.'

'How do you mean?'

'She got fed up at always penny-pinching when she was married to a wealthy man. Who could blame her? So when someone else came along she abandoned Julian along with his father, which was unforgivable.'

'And you stepped in?'

'Well, I did what I could. Poor boy, he was only ten.'

'And I imagine you were a great help to his father, too, in developing his collection.'

'I was one of the dealers Derek used, yes.'

'His principal dealer, I think?'

'Well, let's just say that our tastes were very much the same. I was able to help him find some bargains.'

'The Mitchells?'

Rosa tried to contain a modest smile. 'One of my triumphs. I saw them in a small gallery in New York before she became really famous. I phoned him straight away and he agreed to buy them. It's just so heartbreaking to think that they're gone.'

Kathy's phone buzzed. She stared at the screen, then handed it to Brock, who read the message: *Forensic team confirms presence human remains in basement.* He said, 'Thank you for your help, Rosa. We'll have to interview you formally in due course. In the meantime, it would be best if you kept what we've just discussed to yourself. You know what the press can be like.'

When they got back in the car, Kathy said, 'She didn't tell us the whole story, did she?'

'No, you're right. She was protecting him and she'd had plenty of time to work out what to tell us. How long was

Babington with her? Two hours? Longer than it takes to wash your hands.'

'Did you notice that she didn't ask how he was? Maybe she thinks he's still in America.'

She drove back to Montagu Square, where they put on hard hats and crime scene suits and climbed a ladder down into the cellar. Lifting gear had been set up to haul charred beams and debris out of the pit, and the forensic team had now cleared much of the space, exposing the tiled concrete floor. It seemed to Kathy more like the site of an archaeological dig than a modern crime scene, with the human remains that were being gathered up and bagged resembling ancient relics from Pompeii or medieval London, charred and shattered. The largest pieces that she could decipher were the pelvis, a section of the skull and a length of spinal column. The crime scene manager said, 'If he was dead before the fire started, I don't fancy our chances of establishing when or how.'

They returned to West End Central and found the detention suite in turmoil. The duty sergeant explained that Babington had collapsed while a doctor was examining him and had been rushed to hospital. The doctor, who was about to leave, said, 'He's got a fever and severe breathing difficulties.'

Brock said, 'I believe he suffers from emphysema. He has an inhaler.'

'Ah yes. Do you know what other medication he was taking?'

'Sorry, no.'

'Well, he's confused and doesn't appear to understand where he is. In fact, he doesn't even seem to know his own name.'

Brock said, 'Could he be putting on an act?'

'No. The man's ill—mentally and physically at the end of his tether.'

Back in the car, Brock said, 'Well, Kathy, it seems we've got our man, but for what exactly? Now we just have to wait for the supporting evidence to come in—the DNA of Miki's remains, more street camera footage, another session with Rosa Lipmann. Get a good night's sleep and we'll review it all in the morning.' He gave a weary smile. 'See you tomorrow.'

24

Their floor at the Box was deserted the next morning, except for Kathy's team working quietly in their corner. Molly was trying to complete a comprehensive catalogue of the lost works of the Babington Collection, while Judy was organising a team of people to cover all the technical and human resources that would build a detailed picture of what had happened. Kathy, meanwhile, had been called to Commander Torrens' office to report on the situation and work out a strategy with the press office. Brock sat alone, arms folded, feeling oddly detached from it all.

Kathy had barely returned when a call came in on her phone. She glanced at the screen, then put it to her ear and listened. She said, 'Would you repeat that, please?' She finished the call and looked across at Brock, a frown on her face.

The room fell quiet, and she said, 'It's not Miki. They've done a preliminary DNA match, and the body in the cellar isn't Miki's. It's not a match to anyone we know. We've no idea who it is.'

There was a moment of stunned silence, then everyone was speaking at once. Kathy tried to get them back on track. 'We'll have to wait for the pathologist's report. In the meantime, we'll follow up on everything else. Priority is finding evidence of mens rea, Babington's intention to kill or commit arson. What did he do on that meandering route from Piccadilly Circus to Montagu Square? Was he looking for somewhere he could buy a weapon or an accelerant? A hardware shop or a petrol station? We also need a psychological assessment. Why would he burn his own house down? For the insurance? Or to conceal a murder?'

~

Brock left them to it and drove out to the hospital where Babington had been transferred. There he waited, hoping to speak to him again, but finally the senior doctor came and told him there was no possibility of that for the time being. Apart from his mental state, Babington was physically very weak, his severe breathing difficulties apparently aggravated by the inhalation of toxic smoke. Brock thought there was tragic irony in that, Babington suffocated by his cursed art collection.

He returned to the Box with pizzas and energy drinks for the team, and while they were eating and planning new lines of inquiry into Semenov/Gorshkov's movements, a report came in to Kathy's computer from the pathologist. She had examined the body parts and concluded that they had a male victim, short in stature, perhaps five foot six or 1.65 metres, medium build, age approximately seventy years. She hoped to have computer images of the face developed from the skull fragments within seventy-two hours.

'How tall's Semenov?' someone asked, and Brock replied, 'Over six foot, a hulking great brute aged in his mid-fifties. It's not him.' He was disappointed. The Nexus people had lost track of Gorshkov and he had hoped that he might have tried to get his hands on the last genuine artworks left in Babington's cellar. Incineration in the cellar would have been an appropriate fate for him. If he had managed to leave the country undetected, their chances of having him extradited from Russia were nil.

'Who is it then?'

Brock said, 'If it's not the crook, maybe it's the cook. He's the only five-foot-six seventy-year-old that springs to mind.'

'Who?' Kathy stared at him.

'Nadya's dear old uncle, Egor Orlov, proprietor of the Russian restaurant Alexandrov's at Canary Wharf. Looks like he was in on it too.'

Kathy turned back to her screen. 'Wait a minute, there's more.' She read from the report. 'She says they've found the remains of two more victims right at the back of the cellar.'

It took several hours before they had made preliminary identifications of the deceased: Egor Orlov, Pavel Gorshkov and Miki Babington, the three generations of Russians.

'He got them all,' Brock said, getting to his feet. 'Come on, Kathy, it's time we roasted sweet little Rosa Lipmann over white-hot coals.'

~

Though West End Central didn't possess any instruments of torture, they did their best. They seated Rosa on a comfortable chair in the interview room and gave her a cup of tea.

'Now, Rosa,' Brock began, 'Julian is in a very bad way in hospital, but we are uncovering more and more of what happened. We know that he was present when the fire started in the cellar of his house in Montagu Square, and we know that he wasn't alone. We have discovered the remains of three people down there. So with every hour we are getting closer to the truth. I'm aware that you are very fond of Julian and want to protect him, but it's too late for that. This is your last opportunity to tell us everything before we discover it for ourselves and charge you with perverting the course of justice by withholding key evidence. You wouldn't want to be in that situation. So please, tell us the whole story.'

Rosa sighed, took a deep breath and began.

'The trouble with Julian was that he always needed to please everyone, and they all took advantage of him—his father, his first wife, then Nadya and Miki. I don't know about the American woman, I've never met her, but the way he talks about her she may be an exception. Anyway, I warned him about Nadya, calculating and manipulative, and that conniving uncle of hers, but he ignored me and she made him marry her.

'One day she came into my gallery with Miki and this other young man, a Scotsman, and they wanted me to sell his paintings. So dull they were, so gloomy, but among them was one that was quite different from the rest, an oil of an apple tree, very decorative, very striking. I said I liked it and would hang it in the gallery to see if it would sell. Well, it did sell, almost immediately, and when I phoned Nadya to tell her that the cheque was in the mail she was very pleased, and said she'd get the Scotsman to bring more like that to show me. But the thing was that the picture seemed somehow familiar, though I couldn't place it. Then it came to me—the style was rather like Klimt, though we tend to think of Klimt more as a figure painter than a landscapist. So I looked up images of Klimt's landscapes and there it was, *Apple Tree 1*, 1912, by Gustav Klimt. I had sold my customer a forgery. I was furious! I stopped the cheque to the Scotsman and gave Nadya hell, but she just said it was a mistake. The thing was, when I grovelled to my customer and told him what had happened, he said he didn't care, he loved it and wanted to keep it anyway. It was all most galling, I can tell you.

'I told Julian about it, and he didn't think it was funny, but he didn't do anything about it. So I decided to keep an eye on Nadya, especially when Julian was away in America. I had an excuse, because for years I had been acting as an unpaid curator for Julian's collection, cataloguing the works and sorting out the provenance documents that his father had left in such a mess, and he had given me a house key and the alarm codes so that I could come and go to do this work. So I started calling in at the house to keep an eye on things when Julian went overseas. I wasn't spying on Nadya, you understand, just trying to protect Julian's interests. Well, it didn't take me long to discover that Miki and the Scotsman had the run of the place when Julian was away. But I also discovered other things. One time I found the living room covered in drop sheets set up in front of one of the Mitchells and an easel and paints and a canvas with a half-finished copy of it. That Scotsman was copying works from the collection! So I waited for them to return and I confronted them. The Scotsman didn't say a word, but Nadya tried to fob me off with a tale about him making paintings of famous works to sell as copies to earn money for a good cause. She implied that Julian knew, but when I told Julian he said he didn't, but he wasn't concerned. I tried to warn him how dangerous such a talent was. "Remember van Meegeren," I told him, "who made perfect forgeries of the great masters and fooled everyone, including Hermann Göring!" But Julian just laughed.

'There was one other time I called at Montagu Place unexpectedly and found something disturbing. There were two men there in the living room examining the paintings. One I knew—Nadya's uncle Egor. Egor didn't introduce me to the other one, a big man, also Russian.'

Brock interrupted, showing her the image of Gorshkov.

'Yes, that's him. Who is he?'

'He calls himself Pavel Gorshkov. Does that name mean anything to you?'

'No. Well, I went and busied myself checking the collection catalogue I'd been preparing and Egor asked me what it was. I told him and he asked if they could have a copy, as his friend was very interested in art. I told him no, it was private and confidential, and he shrugged and they carried on looking at the paintings and speaking in Russian. I did overhear one phrase when they were looking at the Mitchells—*million dollarov*, that's what Egor said.'

Brock said. 'When was this, Rosa?'

'Let me think ... about a year ago? Maybe October or November of last year. I did warn Julian to be more careful about who he allowed in to look at the paintings, but I don't think he did anything about it. It disturbed me to see Egor there. What was he doing showing people the collection and talking about their value? Anyway, after that I stopped going to Montagu Square, and I didn't see so much of them, so it was a terrible shock when I heard about Nadya's death. At the time, suicide was the only reason I could think of.'

'But now you know better?'

'I should tell you about the fire. Can I have another cup of tea? That one was very weak.'

They took a break while Rosa gathered her thoughts, sipping a fresh, and stronger, cup of tea. She was a tough old bird, Brock decided, playing on her appearance as a harmless old lady.

'All right,' she said, placing the cup firmly in the saucer. 'Let's get this over. I must confess that I didn't tell you everything that Julian said when he came to my place on the night of the fire. I admit I was trying to protect him, but that's pointless now. The truth must be told.'

'Yes,' Brock agreed.

'When he'd had a shower, he asked for a big whisky and told me what had happened, starting with the day before Nadya died. After she got that scam email she was in a terrible state, and she finally confessed to Julian that she had allowed the Scotsman to come to their house in order to copy works from his collection and sell them so as to raise money to rebuild an old church out in the Kent countryside. She had believed that it was a harmless way to support the church until one day she overheard the Scotsman and Miki talking, and realised that they had actually been selling the originals and replacing them in Julian's house with the copies. When she got that Russian email demanding money, she believed that Miki must have told his father what he was doing, and Semenov was now going to blackmail her for money to hide the truth. Julian was devastated by what she had told him, but he had to fly to New York, and he said that when he returned they would go through it all in detail and sort it out.

'To me it all made perfect sense; it was just as I had warned him. For the Scotsman, Julian's collection was the ideal set-up for such a scheme. He had free access to the artworks while Julian was away, to copy them without disturbance—not from photographs or brief visits, but for prolonged spells at close quarters, where he could get every shade, every hue, every brushstroke exactly right. And additionally he had access to the provenance documents, which he could also copy and steal.

'But while Julian was in America, Nadya died, apparently by her own hand, out of shame for what she had done. Julian was heartbroken, but he had to find out which works had been copied so that he could remove them from the catalogue of items he was trying to prepare for the Royal Academy. So, the morning after Nadya's memorial service, Julian went to see the Scotsman in Kent to demand answers. He found the man in a state of terror. He confessed that some time ago, through Egor, Miki had got in touch with his father in

Russia, who was very interested in their scheme and had come to England under a new name and taken over the business of looting Julian's collection. And he was there, with the Scotsman, when Nadya arrived after Julian had left for America and said that she was going to make the whole thing public. The Scotsman had watched, helpless, as the Russian had taken her away. When he returned, alone, he told the Scotsman to finish the works he had in progress and not say a word to anyone.

'The Scotsman was crying by this point. He said something about "screamers" and that it was all his fault and he would have to pay the price. When Julian asked him which paintings had been copied, he said he had a list, which he had deposited in a bank security box, and he would retrieve it and give it to Julian if he returned in a couple of days. Then Julian heard that the Scotsman had been found dead, hanged—like Nadya, an apparent suicide.

'Of course Julian should have gone to the police, but still the figure of his dead father loomed over him, telling him that the reputation of the collection must be protected at all costs; he couldn't make public the possibility that it had been corrupted with forgeries. So, sometime after the police declared the Scotsman's death a suicide, he broke into the man's studio in Kent and searched the place for the list. He found an underground cellar with equipment and papers, but no list. It occurred to him that the vicar of the church they were saving might have the list, and early one morning he went there and broke in to search for it. He was interrupted by the vicar and had to run off without any list.'

'Hang on,' Brock interrupted, 'you say *Julian* broke into the vicar's vestry? We found a flashlight with Miki's DNA on it.'

Rosa shrugged. 'Julian must have taken Miki's torch.'

If that was so, Brock reflected, then Miki hadn't been entirely lying when he'd been arrested at Fitzroy Road.

'Anyway,' Rosa went on, 'after that he was in despair. Without that list the whole collection was in doubt, scandalously corrupted. So he decided to set a trap. When Miki was released on bail to stay in his house, he told him that he had to go to New York over Christmas but that on his return he would be carrying out an inventory and transferring the whole collection to a secure store prior to handing it over to the Academy. He then flew back from New York unannounced in the hope of catching them in the act of pilfering what remained of the collection.

'And it worked brilliantly. He returned, quietly entered the house and saw the door down to the cellar open. He crept down and listened to Miki and Egor and Semenov discussing which items to steal. And then he heard Egor say that Miki should be very grateful to Egor for finding such a rich man for his mother to marry. Julian said it hit him like a lightning bolt, the realisation that Egor had set him up with Nadya, that he had taken her and Miki into his home where they had stolen, piece by piece, his father's collection.

'Filled with anger and shame, he went quietly to the garage at the back of the house, where he found a can of petrol and a bottle of turps and some paraffin, and he took them back to the cellar steps and removed their caps and threw the petrol can into the room where all the treasures were stored and where the intruders were, then backed up the stairs splashing the paraffin and turpentine and struck a match and locked the door. His arm was on fire—he had splashed paraffin on his coat—and while he tried to put it out he heard the muffled screams from the basement. Then he walked away and came to me.'

25

After three days it was apparent that things were not going well for Julian Babington. The smoke from the fire had sparked a major flare-up in his emphysema which the doctors were struggling to control. Each day Brock had attempted to visit him in hospital, and each day he had been turned away. On the fourth day he looked through the small window in the door to his room and saw Julian lying prone in his hospital bed, an oxygen mask over his face. Sitting alongside his bed were two women visitors. One was Sharon Sargent from Long Island, holding his hand, and the other Rosa Lipmann. Rosa glanced over and saw Brock's face at the door. She got to her feet and came out to speak to him. They sat together in the corridor and she told him that Julian was very ill. Three days ago he had asked her to phone Sharon, which she had done, telling her that Jack had been badly hurt in a fire. Sharon had arrived the previous day, and Rosa had met her at the airport.

'He knew that he was going to die,' Rosa said, 'and that while you may have two lives you can only have one death. Sharon was going to have to know the truth. But by then his voice was gone and he could barely speak, so he asked me to tell her.'

'Can you imagine someone telling you a truth like that?' Rosa went on. 'Like letting off a bomb beneath everything you thought was solid. But I told her. I told her everything.'

'How did she take it?' Brock asked.

'Disbelief, anger, sadness. But I think she'd already guessed that something wasn't right. She mentioned that a London detective had visited their home in Long Island and Jack had been strange afterwards, as if he'd seen a ghost.'

They looked back through the window. Julian was straining to tell Sharon something, and she was leaning down, their faces almost touching.

'The day before yesterday he asked for his lawyer,' Rosa said, 'to make a new will leaving all his remaining assets to Sharon. I was the witness. Now she has to decide what to tell her children, her relatives, her neighbours.'

~

Later Brock and Kathy attended a briefing for Commander Torrens. When they'd finished he shook his head. 'Five dead plus another on the way! Pity you couldn't have worked it out sooner.'

Kathy began to protest, but Torrens waved his hand. 'I know, I know. Major Russian mafia ring, breakdown in immigration security between us and the Americans over the identity of Gorshkov, mistaken suicide findings for the first two victims. But still . . .'

'Anyway, moving on, Kathy tells me we should have you back in Homicide, Brock. What do you think?'

Brock frowned to hide his surprise. 'Well . . . yes, I'd like that, sir.'

'You don't sound sure.'

'No, I am sure. I'd like it very much. My own team?'

'Not possible—all the team leader positions are filled. I'm thinking of a roaming appointment aimed at the cases that go cold and slow us down, bloat our statistics and make us look bad. We could put them in a separate category X and take the heat off the rest. So you would be our specialist homicide X case officer and could draw on support from the teams as appropriate. In the first instance, you might look to Kathy for support. Why don't you write a job description for me to look at?'

'Right, I'll do that. Thank you.'

Outside, Brock said to Kathy, 'This was your idea, was it?' He was beaming.

'Bren and I dreamed it up. Thought it was what you needed.'

'Well, thank you both.'

'Bren also phoned me this morning about the Babington case. His friends in the Home Office finally came up with something via their buddies in the Foreign Office, looking into the identity of Semenov alias Gorshkov. They've discovered that Nadya never actually divorced him either before or after she ran away to London with Miki. So her marriage to Babington was a sham. He was never actually a bigamist.'

Brock shook his head. 'It seems that everyone and everything in this mess has been a fake.'

'Well, at least the Royal Academy have ended up with a real *Sunflowers*.'

'Have they? We really don't know, do we? If Callum McAdam made a copy of it, how do we know he didn't switch it for the one in Babington's basement? And if it was as good a fake as his others, with a provenance to match, who's to say which *Still Life: Vase with Thirteen Sunflowers* is the real one: the one in Burlington House or the one in the mansion of a billionaire who acquired it from the Russians? Perhaps Callum made his point after all.'

~

Babington's funeral was held five days later at the crematorium at Kensal Green Cemetery. It was a small private gathering, with Rosa Lipmann among the mourners who made their way down the avenue of grand Victorian funerary monuments to the chapel in the wooded grounds.

Brock was there, and when the service was over Rosa retrieved a package from the boot of her car and gave it to him.

'This is for you,' she said. 'Open it later, when I've gone.'

Brock watched her car drive away, then opened the package. Inside was a framed watercolour he recognised only too well. With it were two envelopes, the first with a message inside.

Dear Brock,
If you are reading this then I am dead, and it is my wish that
you should have this work from my collection—John Singer
Sargent's Santa Maria della Salute. *I trust that it will find its*
place in your own unique collection.
   With best wishes,
   Julian Babington

The second envelope contained the provenance documents detailing the picture's history. Brock was stunned, his
eyes absorbing the deft brushwork, the subtle colours, and it
took a few moments for the question to occur to him—was
this a John Singer Sargent or a Callum McAdam? Either way,
it was indeed unique.

~

The following week Brock returned to the ancient church of
St Chad-on-the-Marsh. He had received an invitation from
the Reverend Alwyn Bramley-Scott to attend the service of
thanksgiving for the lives of Nadya Babington and Callum
McAdam and for the rebirth of the church. The service was
well attended and the church almost full when Brock arrived,
but when he made to sit in a pew at the back, Father Alwyn
appeared and took him to a reserved place at the front.

The service began, the old hymns—'Glorious Things of
Thee Are Spoken' and 'Christ the Lord Has Risen Today'—
accompanied by a young woman with a cello whose vibrato
reverberated achingly from the stonework. As he listened,
Brock felt a keen sense of regret. If only Nadya had never

received that email, now confirmed as a random scam with no connection to her Russian husband. If only Nadya's death had been investigated as a murder from the start, so the other deaths might have been avoided. If only people had been satisfied with straightforward lives without duplicity and deceit. Even the Reverend Bramley-Scott up there, beaming like a cherub at the fulfilment of his great mission, had had an indirect hand in those deaths.

Brock reflected that the past two months had shaken him up, left him struggling in a world in which he had no expertise. His situation had been the opposite of Julian's: Brock wanted to return to his previous role whereas Julian wanted to escape from his—the identity of each so firmly shaped by that role. He regretted now his approach to Suzanne about moving in with her. It had been a moment of weakness which now made him realise that their longstanding relationship—faithful to each other yet independent—was exactly what each desired. He was proud of her confident new move into the art market but he had no wish to follow her there. His field was murder, to which he had now returned. And, most importantly, the builder had started work on his roof.

~

On his way back from St Chad's, Brock decided to detour to Westmoreland Road, Barnes, something he'd been meaning to do ever since his visit to the Sprengel Museum. Number 39 was a typical brick and pebble-dash semi-detached house of the 1930s London suburbs, distinguished from its neighbours by the small blue plaque on its wall declaring, *Kurt Schwitters,*

1887–1948, Artist, lived here. He had called in at the local library to see if they had any references to Schwitters' stay in the borough, but found no information about the house or its owner. Now he was here, but there was nothing that the house could tell him, he told himself gloomily, and he restarted his car and signalled to pull out. Just then the front door opened and an elderly man stepped out, holding a broom. As Brock watched he began to sweep the crazy paving that covered the front garden of the house. Brock switched off his engine and went to the front gate.

'Hello, I'm interested in Kurt Schwitters,' he said, pointing to the plaque.

'Oh yes.' The man came over. 'We've had a few people call here since they put that up. Local historian, are you?'

'Art history,' Brock said. 'He was here in forty-three, I think.'

'That's right, with his son.'

'Do you have any records from that time, by any chance?'

The man shook his head. 'No, nothing about Schwitters.'

'What about the owner of the house?'

'No idea, I'm afraid.'

'What about the house deeds?'

'Yes, we've got those. I don't know what they'd tell you, though. Want to have a look?'

'If you wouldn't mind.'

The man frowned suddenly. 'You're not selling something, are you? Solar panels? Double glazing?'

Brock smiled. 'No, nothing like that.'

He waited while the man went indoors and then returned with a thick envelope containing the title deeds and plans, together with copies of title registers identifying the property's owners. One of these referred to the first purchasers of the house from the builder in 1934. They were Henry Rouse and Lily Crab (née Rouse).

The man, seeing Brock's face light up, said, 'Is this useful?'

'It is! It's exactly what I was looking for.'

'You know you can get copies of these online? Anyone can.'

'Really? I didn't know that. Mind if I take a picture of them?'

Back in his car, Brock felt a sense of relief and optimism. Lily Crab had lived at the house where Schwitters lodged, along with Henry Rouse, presumably her brother or father. The line of provenance of his Merz was secure. Perhaps the world wasn't entirely fraudulent after all.